THE BROKEN CHASE

Also by Cap Daniels

THE
BROKEN CHASE

CHASE FULTON NOVEL #2

CAP DANIELS

ANCHOR WATCH
PUBLISHING
** USA **

The Broken Chase, Chase Fulton Novel #2

Copyright © 2018 Cap Daniels

13 Digit ISBN: 978-1-7323024-3-3
Library of Congress Control Number: 2018946373
Cover Design: German Creative
Printed in the United States of America

ANCHOR WATCH
PUBLISHING
** USA **

This book is dedicated to . . .

Anna, the real life "Skipper," who has overcome challenges that would have left a lesser person in tears. You are a constant reminder of how determination, drive, and self-discipline can conquer all. You're inspirational, frustrating, brilliant, beautiful, and fearless. Never stop ignoring limits and stretching boundaries . . . those are for the people who accept mediocracy, not you.

Special thanks to . . .

My phenomenal editor:
Sarah Flores – Write Down the Line, LLC
www.WriteDowntheLine.com

Her dedication to this series and to making me a better writer is not only remarkable, but invaluable. Her heart-of-a-teacher and spirit-of-a-cheerleader drive me to push myself beyond what I ever imagined possible in the creation of intriguing story lines, fascinating characters, and dramatic action. She makes everything I write immeasurably better. I hope I never have to write without her.

Inspiration:
Everyone who crossed my path in my five decades on Earth and provided the inspiration for countless characters who have been set free on the pages of this and other works of fiction. I hope my readers feel and hear themselves in my writing. I lack the imagination to create characters so full of life, energy, and passion, as the people in my life who constantly demonstrate that normalcy is never acceptable.

Table of Contents

Prologue

It was Christmas 1981 when my missionary father told me we were going to Mar del Plata, Argentina, to help nuns care for children living in an orphanage. He told me it was important to make sacrifices to help people who weren't as fortunate as we were in the U.S.

I was terrified. I didn't want to go. It wasn't because we were going someplace I'd never heard of—Mar del Plata sounded like a very cool place to a bilingual, six-year-old boy from Georgia. And any place called Sea of Silver had to be magical. I wanted to see it, just not at Christmastime. How was Santa Claus going to find me? How would he know where to bring the bicycle I'd been begging for all year?

The sea wasn't silver. It was gray and I hated it. It wasn't even Christmastime there; it was the beginning of summer. How could it be winter in Georgia and summer in Mar del Plata? I was never getting that bike.

I don't think there was an orphanage either. If there was, I never saw it. I saw navy ships and a lot of soldiers with guns. My parents didn't seem surprised there was no orphanage. I guess the whole point of being missionaries is to help whoever needs help wherever you are.

My mom stayed with me most of the time. We practiced our Spanish with the locals, and many times they wanted to practice their English with us. I liked that part, but not everything was fun. Some of it was horrifying.

The last night we were in Mar del Plata, my dad said, "Chase, you need to go to bed early. Your mom and I need to talk to Santa Claus."

Of course I couldn't sleep. Like any excited, curious boy, I pretended to go to bed then snuck into a little closet beside the kitchen. I hid behind a mop and broom and some old boxes and watched through the gap in the door. Santa Claus never came. Instead, my parents argued with an angry group of men, specifically one named Admiral Anaya.

Dad told him it was *"un plan mortal,"* a deadly plan, to invade some place called the Falkland Islands.

Admiral Anaya drew his knife, held it to my father's throat, and growled in terrifying Spanish. "It would be a shame for your beautiful wife and little boy to wash up on the beach because you and your American masters were meddling in the affairs of Argentina. Now get out of my country before I am forced to feed you to the sharks."

Three months later, Argentina invaded the Falkland Islands, but we weren't there to see it. The morning after the meeting with Admiral Anaya, we were on the next plane out of Mar del Plata. I'd asked my dad if Santa Claus was an admiral in South America, but he never answered me.

We arrived home on Christmas day, and my new bike was waiting for me on our front porch. I'd never forget that Christmas, and looking back now, it should have been clear, even to a six-year-old, that my dad was no missionary.

1

What Now?

I watched Anya, the woman I loved, bury her knife into the chest of the man who'd cut her mother's heart out twenty years earlier. Anya stood over the body of Dmitri Barkov, billionaire Russian oligarch, and reveled in the knowledge that her face was the last one he'd see before stumbling through the gates of Hell, and her voice was the last voice he'd ever hear.

She collapsed to the deck of the yacht and sobbed as her fury and realized vengeance poured over her.

I knelt beside her and pulled her close, hoping to find the right words. "It's all over now, Anya. It's done, and now it's time for you to have the life and freedom you want. It's time for you to have everything you want."

Dr. Robert "Rocket" Richter, former fighter pilot turned American covert operative turned psychology professor—and Anya's father—scanned the horizon for approaching boats. "I hate to break this up, kids, but we've got company."

Anya wiped her tears and leapt to her feet. "What do you see, Papa?"

"It's some of Barkov's yacht crew, and they're in our dinghy. Here, Chase. Take the binoculars. Your eyes are younger than mine."

I trained the binoculars on the approaching boat. It was our dinghy all right, and they were pushing her as fast as she'd go and approaching our port stern quarter.

"There's five of them, and they appear to be unarmed. We shouldn't have much trouble repelling five unarmed men, but I have no idea what they're planning."

"They're planning to take back their boat," said Dr. Richter, "and we're not going to let them."

Anya had already retrieved her rifle and taken up a firing position across the stern rail. I heard the report of the massive rifle and watched her absorb the punishing recoil without taking her eye from the scope. Through the binoculars, I saw only four of the five men in the dinghy. The one who'd been on the bow was meeting his maker.

Dr. Richter headed for the interior of the yacht. "Keep holding them off. I'll get us headed somewhere deep so we can put a little distance between us and them and get rid of Barkov's body."

Anya cycled the bolt of her rifle to eject the fired shell casing and send another round into the chamber.

"*Der'mo! on zastryal!*" she grunted.

The rifle had jammed, failing to eject the fired shell casing.

"Give me pistol," she demanded, laying her rifle on the deck.

I handed her my pistol and went to work on the jammed rifle, but it was no use. The shell wasn't coming out.

The massive yacht slowly picked up speed as Rocket added power, but the dinghy was still closing in on us. Anya squeezed off two rounds from my pistol. I looked over the rail, hoping to see two more dead Russians, but shooting with a pistol and expecting to hit a target moving at twenty-five knots is a fool's faith.

"Save your ammo. You can pick them off as they try to board."

"Tell Papa to slow down. I will sink raft."

I ran to the bridge and told Dr. Richter her plan. He pulled the throttles back, slowing the yacht to just under twelve knots. When I made it back to the stern deck, Anya was squeezing off rounds toward the dinghy as it advanced ever closer. I saw a bright flash and a puff of white smoke.

What was that? Did Anya hit the engine?

"Flare!" I yelled. "Get down!"

The signal flare left the dinghy, winding and soaring toward us. The burning phosphorous flare struck the bulkhead just above the door to the main salon behind us and fell to the deck. It ricocheted like a pinball. The brilliant orange fire racing across the deck and the white smoke filling the air caused me and Anya to stumble and collide with each other in a desperate attempt to evade the flare. Finally, it came to rest against Barkov's body and continued to burn.

I was blind from staring at the burning flare. I called out, "Anya, are you okay?"

"I cannot see," she said, "and I cannot find pistol."

Almost nothing worse could've happened to us at that moment. We had no weapon to fend off the four remaining Russians advancing on us. Even if we had a weapon, neither of us could see to fire it. We were sitting ducks. Blind ducks.

"Can you get to Papa?"

"I don't know," I said. "I can try."

"We must go fast again. We are in serious trouble."

That may have been the understatement of the century. I fumbled and stumbled my way through the yacht, trying to remember and feel my way to the bridge. I found the stairs and crawled up them as fast as I could, yelling "Full speed, full speed," as I went.

The yacht picked up speed, but I feared it was too little too late. I found my way back toward Anya, hoping she'd regained at least some of her vision. When I reached the aft deck, I could barely make out her silhouette. From the sound and smell, I could tell she was emptying a fire extinguisher toward what was left of the burning flare. The fire died, and I could make out vague shapes and detect movement in front of me.

She put her hand on my arm. "Are you hurt?"

"I'm not burned, but I'm still blind. How about you?"

"I am same. I do not know what to do, Chase. This is very bad."

I thought about what I'd do if I were in a dinghy chasing a mega-yacht. "There's only one way aboard. They'll have to come across the swim deck, and only three of them can make the jump while the driver holds the dinghy as close as he can. We've got to get down there and try to hold them off."

We stumbled to the starboard side and found the ladder leading down one deck. We clumsily traversed the ladder and worked our way aft. Minute by minute, my vision was returning. I hoped the same was happening for Anya.

At the swim deck, we took up positions behind a pair of columns, hoping to ambush the Russians as they leapt aboard.

"How are your eyes?" I yelled.

"Is not good, but is getting better."

"Mine, too."

We appeared to be at top speed, and I could vaguely make out the outline of the approaching dinghy. It was going to be a challenging jump for the men, even if the driver could maneuver the dinghy through our wake and to the swim deck.

"They are almost here," Anya yelled.

Through my distorted vision, the dinghy appeared to be gaining on us at an alarming rate. They were plowing through the turbulent water and closing in quickly. The men were yelling orders at each other, but I couldn't make out what they were saying.

Anya shouted, "They are going to run raft up onto yacht."

Their plan was a good one, and it worked flawlessly. As my eyesight improved, I saw the dinghy's bow lunge over the edge of the swim deck and continue forward until three quarters of the dinghy was aboard the yacht. All four men leapt with practiced confidence, landing unbalanced on the deck.

Taking advantage of our ambush position and their lack of balance, I leapt forward and landed a front kick in the first man's chest, sending him tumbling backward into the turbid water. I heard Anya engage another of the men but couldn't see anything out of my peripheral vision. A fist I hadn't seen coming landed squarely on my left jaw and sent me staggering back toward the interior of the yacht. I was dazed and still only able to make out shapes directly in front of me. I turned my head wildly, trying to make the most of my limited vision. I caught a glimpse of a man racing toward me, so

I threw my best right jab at what I hoped was his face. He ducked the punch and plowed into my gut with his shoulder. Knowing there was a bulkhead behind me, I let his force propel me backward, hoping his head would hit something solid before mine did. It almost worked, but our heads crashed into the bulkhead simultaneously, sending both of us to the deck, dazed.

As I tried to gather my wits, I could see Anya in silhouette fighting desperately for her life. I had to finish off the man who'd driven me into the wall and get to Anya before the other two men overcame her. I scrambled to my feet and powered forward toward my opponent, throwing punches as I went. Some of them landed, but most were wasted effort. He grabbed my wrist and twisted away from me with such speed he ripped me off my feet, leaving me sprawled across the deck, vulnerable. His boot landed solidly in my left kidney, and I yelled in pain. By some miracle, I'd captured his foot immediately after his kick, so I jerked as hard as I could and felt him land on the deck beside me. He threw two more punches that landed perfectly in my ribs, knocking the breath from my lungs.

I was in the fight of my life, but Anya was battling two men while I only had to deal with one. I hoped she was doing better than me. My aggressor wasn't getting up very quickly, so I took advantage of my position and threw an elbow at his face, hoping to break his nose. I missed and landed my elbow in his throat, crushing his airway. Although he wasn't unconscious, I'd taken away his ability to continue. Not willing to risk the chance of him rejoining the fight, I threw a right cross to the side of his head, knocking him out cold.

I blinked, trying to focus on Anya's fight. My vision was better, but still not back to normal. I could see that one man had Anya in a vice-like grip from behind, while the other tried to advance on her from the front. She was kicking like a wild animal and thrashing violently. It didn't appear either of her attackers saw me dispatch their partner, so I had a momentary advantage. I capitalized on it and drove my left arm under the chin of the man holding Anya. I secured the choke hold while Anya kept kicking, holding the other attacker at bay. The headlock did its job and the man in my arm collapsed. Anya dropped to the deck, landing on her left hip, and thrust a thundering side kick to the remaining aggressor's groin. It doubled him over just feet in front of her. As the man bent forward, I forced my palm into the back of his head and sent him accelerating toward the deck. When the collision of face and deck occurred, the man's body turned to pudding, and he also collapsed in an unconscious heap.

"You are okay, yes?" she breathed.

"Yeah, I'm good. How about you?"

"I am not hurt, and eyesight is coming back. We must push bodies into water now."

Although I was uncertain about dropping three more Russians into the Florida Straits, I followed her directions, and we slid the bodies into the foaming water behind the yacht.

We felt our way into the interior of the yacht and headed for the bridge.

"It's about time you two showed up. Did you roll out the red carpet for our guests?"

"Oh yeah," I said. "We made them feel right at home, and now their new home is somewhere on the bottom of the ocean."

"Well done," he said. "Now we have to send Barkov to join them."

Anya and I returned to the stern deck where Barkov's flare-burnt corpse lay.

She found a pair of diving weight belts in a locker and held them up. "This will send him to bottom forever, yes?"

I loved Anya's Russian-accented English.

"Yeah, I think forty pounds should do it."

We strapped the weight belts to the body of the man who'd caused Anya so many years of pain. After learning that the man she'd known and worked for had been the animal who murdered her mother, Anya had finally avenged the woman whose death had haunted her for two decades.

We wrestled Barkov's bulk across the stern rail and watched him disappear into the turbid water in the yacht's wake.

Anya placed her hand atop mine on the rail. "*Zakonchennyy.*"

Indeed, it truly was finished.

Anya, born Anastasia Burinkova, had been a Russian SVR officer until her mission to capture, interrogate, and possibly kill the American assassin who'd killed the legendary Russian assassin, Anatoly Parchinkov, aka Suslik the gopher. Suslik had turned out to be three men—identical triplets who'd roamed the globe for a dozen years, killing at the behest of the Russian mafia. I was the American assassin Anya had been dispatched to find. She found me all right, but when she and I fell in love, instead of delivering me to her Russian master—Dmitri Barkov, who now lay dead at the bottom of the Atlantic Ocean—she joined forces with me to find and kill the remaining Parchinkov brothers.

After I'd killed the first Parchinkov brother in Havana Harbor, through serendipity, fate, or the hand of God, I'd introduced Anya to my mentor, Dr. Richter, and we discovered he was Anya's father. That revelation led to Anya learning that Dmitri Barkov had killed her mother, Katerina Burinkova, by cutting her heart out in a jealous rage over her relationship with Dr. Richter. Anya had killed one of the three Parchinkov brothers in Gibraltar. She, Dr. Richter, and I had killed the third and final brother minutes before we'd come aboard Barkov's yacht, where Anya had exacted her lethal revenge on her mother's murderer.

Will I ever know the feeling Anya's experiencing? Will I ever get to send my parents' killers to Hell?

We returned to the bridge to find Dr. Richter at the helm and holding his arm at his chest. He'd suffered a gunshot to his shoulder during the gunfight that seemed somewhere in the distant past, but had only happened less than an hour earlier.

"How is shoulder, Papa?" asked Anya.

"It's all right, but I'm going to need a doctor pretty soon. I'm not sure if the bullet's still in there or not."

"We'll get you to a doctor as soon as possible, Coach, but for now, why don't you go lie down? I can manage the boat."

Years before, I began calling him Coach accidentally, but it soon became a moniker he appreciated.

Dr. Richter scoffed. "It's just a gunshot wound, my boy. I've survived worse."

Anya wore a look of distress. I wondered how someone so deadly as her could feel bad for killing Barkov and defending us from the crew determined to kill us and retake their boat.

She caught me staring at her. "From moment Papa told me story of mother and Dmitri, I begin planning how to kill him. Now is done, and I do not feel, um . . . *otomshchennyy*. I do not know English word for this."

"Avenged," I said. "You thought you'd feel avenged, but you don't. Feeling guilty is okay."

"No," she demanded, "I do not feel guilty. I am happy he is dead and I am happy I killed him. I am sad it will not bring back my mother. You said to me is time for me to have everything I want, but I cannot have back my mother. What do we do now?"

"That's what I've been wondering. Here we are on Barkov's yacht. America's over there. Cuba's that way somewhere. And straight ahead are The Bahamas. I guess we need to decide where to get rid of this boat and get back into the States without getting arrested." I peered out over the endless blue expanse of the Florida Straits where I'd watched *Aegis*, my beloved home, burn and disappear into the depths. "Everything I had was aboard my boat, Anya. Everything was on *Aegis*. Now it's all gone."

"No, Chase. Not everything you have was on *Aegis* boat. You have me, and you have Papa. You can buy again everything else."

I sighed. "Of course, you're right . . . you're always right."

2

Found Money

"We've got a pretty big problem," I said. "Sooner or later, the Coast Guard is going to find what's left of *Aegis*."

"I've already taken care of that," said Dr. Richter. "I talked with the commander at the Coast Guard station. He's an old friend of mine, and he assures me there'll be nothing in tomorrow's paper about the fire and sinking of a sailing yacht off Key Largo."

"It's nice to have friends in high places," I said, relieved, "but you're still hurt, and we have to get you to a doctor."

"We have some options," he said, "but all of them have their own set of problems. If we head to a hospital in the States, they'll have to report a gunshot wound. There's almost no way around that. And that'll lead to police involvement and a whole lot of questions we don't want to answer."

"How about The Bahamas?" I asked. "Can't we duck into Freeport and pay a local doctor to patch you up? It can't be more than a hundred miles."

"That's an option, but there's a couple little problems with that plan, too. First, we don't have any cash, and second, we're on a big boat that somebody is going to recognize if we pull into Freeport. We don't need the locals talking about the two Americans and the Russian woman on the big, flashy yacht."

"There is money on boat," said Anya.

That caught our attention.

"How do you know?" asked Dr. Richter.

"I have been on Barkov's boats many times. He always has money. All we must do is open safe."

I locked eyes with Dr. Richter, then he turned to program the navigation system. "I'll get us headed to Freeport. You two find the safe and get it open."

Anya and I ran down the stairs.

"You start on the lower deck and work up. I'll start up here and work down toward you," I said. "Finding the safe can't be too hard."

"No, Chase. I know where is safe. Come with me."

She led me through a doorway and into the luxurious master stateroom.

I couldn't believe my eyes. "This looks like something that should be in a five-star resort, not a stateroom on a boat."

"Dmitri is"—Anya paused—"Dmitri was very wealthy man. He lived like king, even on boat."

"You know, Anya, we have to work on your English now that you're going to be an American girl. You'll have to start using articles like *the*, *an*, and *a*. Dmitri lived like *a* king, even on *the* boat."

Anya frowned and placed her hands on her hips. "I will make deal with you. First, you put my toe back on foot, then I use English articles. Is deal?"

During our first face-to-face confrontation, I'd shot off Anya's little toe on her right foot to stop her from drowning me off the beach in Charlotte Amalie. The wound healed, but she'd never stop teasing me about it.

Anya opened a locker beneath the portside dressing table. "Safe is in here."

Inside the locker was a solid steel door with a digital keypad and short chrome handle. Anya drew her knife from its sheath and stared at the drying blood that coated the blade before prying the digital panel from the front of the safe. When the panel finally fell into her hand, she went to work on the circuitry. I leaned in to watch her work. She probed carefully with the point of her knife, shorting almost microscopic circuits on the complex circuit board until a green light illuminated, and she turned the chrome handle. The door swung open.

"You'll have to teach me that little skill."

"I will teach many things for you," she said coyly.

Inside the safe were stacks of banded cash from all over the world. Anya pulled twenty thousand dollars from the shelf and tossed it to me.

"This will pay for *a* doctor in *The* Bahamas for Papa, yes?"

I kissed the top of her head and walked back to the bridge. "She's got skills, Coach. She cracked a digital safe in less than two minutes. How's it possible she knows so much? She's no older than I am."

Dr. Richter cocked his head. "Can she catch a ninety-mile-per-hour breaking ball and gun down a runner sliding into second?"

"Come on, Coach. You know what I mean."

"Yes, Chase, I know exactly what you mean, but you're not hearing what I mean. While you were learning to catch breaking balls and gun down runners, she was learning tradecraft. She was a gymnast or a ballerina or a swimmer or a who-knows-what—maybe all three. But while she was learning to flip or dance or do the breaststroke, she was also being taught a staggering assortment of ways to kill a man, and how to pick any lock ever made. If you'd started training when she did, you'd have the same skill set. She had a few years' head start. That's all. Learn from her, my boy. Let her teach you things, and you teach her the things you learned here in America while she was being programmed in the Rodina—good ol' Mother Russia."

I wrinkled my brow. "What could I possibly teach her? She's a much better operator than I am. She has skills I've never dreamed of having, and she already knows everything I know."

"I'm not talking about teaching her tradecraft, son. Take her to a ball game, and teach her how to eat a chili dog and drink warm beer from a plastic cup. Teach her to surf and sail and scuba dive. Teach her how to be alive, Chase. Life isn't always about the cloak-and-dagger bullshit. Sometimes it's about dancing in the rain and counting the stars together. I'll bet no one ever taught her how to do that behind the Iron Curtain."

Before I could reply, Anya came bounding up the stairs and onto the bridge. She pointed to the stack of money lying on the console. "That is enough to pay for a doctor, yes?"

Dr. Richter patted the bills. "Yes, of course, my dear. It's more than enough, but the problem of this recognizable boat still remains. We need to come up with a plan to jump that hurdle."

"I know what to do," I said. "I know exactly what to do. Coach, can you make it through the night without a doctor?"

Dr. Richter placed his hand over his wounded shoulder. "Yes, it'll be fine as long as it doesn't get infected. What are you thinking?"

"Trust me. Head for Miami, Coach. I need a phone."

"There is phone in main salon," Anya said.

I leapt down the stairs, three at a time. I made my phone call and rushed back up the stairs, but I stopped near the top when I heard Dr. Richter and Anya talking about me.

"What do you think he is doing, Papa?"

"I have no idea, but I trust him. Don't you?"

"*Da*," she said. "I trust him, and I will like for him to teach me to eat chili dog and go to ball game."

Dr. Richter laughed. "Do you know your boyfriend there was one of the greatest collegiate baseball players to ever play the game?"

"Papa," she said, "I do not know this game, American baseball."

"Ha! You don't need to know the game to understand that Chase Fulton was one of the best. The game defined him once. He would've been a professional player if he hadn't suffered that damned injury in the final game of his life while winning the College World Series. I wish you could've seen him play. He was fearless."

Anya turned to see me topping the stairs onto the bridge.

"Head for Fowey Rocks Light," I said. "It's just southeast of Key Biscayne."

He frowned. "Yeah, I know where it is, but why? There's nothing up there except rocks and shallow water. That's no place for a boat like this."

"You're right, Coach, but trust me on this one. I've got it all figured out."

Dr. Richter turned to the console and programmed the chart plotter for the Fowey Rocks Lighthouse. The autopilot brought the yacht around and she settled on her new course.

* * *

"Okay, Chase. It's time you let us in on your plan," said Dr. Richter as the Fowey Rocks Light came into sight.

"We're trading down," I said. "I called Dominic Fontana in Miami, and he's coming out to meet us. He's bringing us a less conspicuous boat, and he'll be taking this one back to Miami where it won't draw as much attention. It'll still be a big yacht, but in Miami, it won't be the biggest."

"Chase, you can't start calling in favors like that. Involving more people in this only makes our situation worse."

"I know, but it's Dominic. He's one of us, and he's the best boat guy I know. Getting him involved isn't like bringing in an outsider."

"You're right, but you have to let the rest of us in on these decisions. They affect all of us. Not just you."

"I understand. I'm sorry, but I knew Dominic could help."

"Who is Dominic Fontana?" asked Anya. "His name does not sound like name of real person."

"He's an old friend who helped build *Aegis*. Remember *Aegis*, Anya? *Aegis* was my home, my boat. The boat you sank with a very nice shot with an incendiary grenade a few hours ago."

"Yes," said Anya. "I remember *Aegis*. That is where I tied you up and cut your tongue in half because you would not answer questions."

Anya had snuck aboard my boat in Charlotte Amalie, tranquilized me, and tied me to my bunk with piano wire. The interrogation that followed left me with a nasty tongue wound from her knife.

"Yeah," I said, "you got lucky that time. But as I was saying, Dominic's meeting us at the lighthouse. Let's get outside and get some fenders overboard."

Anya and I went to work hanging fabric-covered rubber fenders over the starboard rail so Dominic could lay alongside without damaging either boat. When the fenders were in place, I found four sections of line and prepositioned them for tying the boats together. A gorgeous, fifty-foot sailing catamaran came alongside. I tossed the lines to the deckhand standing on the bow of the cat, and soon the two boats were secured together.

Dominic Fontana strolled from beneath the hardtop of the catamaran and looked up at the much larger yacht as I leaned over the rail.

"Well, Chase Fulton, as I live and breathe. Where have you been, sailor?"

I smiled at my old friend. "It's good to see you, Dominic. Come aboard. We've got a lot to do."

Dominic disappeared beneath the hardtop, then returned with a bag thrown over his shoulder and three other men in tow. The four of them leapt aboard the yacht and headed for the main salon.

Dr. Richter welcomed the group aboard but cautiously surveyed the three men he didn't know.

Dominic introduced the trio. "These are captains Egan and Bellamy. They're here for the boat, and this is Doctor Cribb. He's here for you, old man."

Dr. Richter surveyed the group, but didn't speak. He and Doctor Cribb left the main salon and headed for the galley where the light was much better. The two captains set about surveying the yacht, familiarizing themselves with the layout and controls. Anya, Dominic, and I stayed in our seats.

"So, Chase, who's this beautiful young lady?"

"Dominic, meet Anya. She's one of us now, and she's the reason I need a new boat. I'll tell you all about it sometime soon over a bottle of scotch, but for now, suffice it to say we're extremely happy to see you."

Dominic kissed Anya's hand. "It's truly a pleasure to meet you, Anya. If you're running about with this bloke, I may have my doubts about your sanity, but it's still a pleasure."

Anya smiled, obviously taken by the charming older man. "Is pleasure to meet you, Dominic, but I'm not running about with Chase. I'm looking after him because he keeps getting himself in trouble."

Anya and Dominic laughed at my expense.

"Okay, enough picking on me for one day. We've got a lot to do. First, Dominic, you need to know a little about this boat. Until a few hours ago, she belonged to Dmitri Barkov of the former KGB, and most recently of Russian mafia fame. Currently, if the sharks haven't made a buffet of him yet, he's a couple thousand feet beneath the Florida Straits with a nice little knife wound in his chest, courtesy of the lovely Anya here. She's pretty handy with sharp objects, and she isn't a bad shot either."

Dominic gazed admiringly at Anya, expressing his newfound respect.

"So," I went on, "what you do with the boat is up to you. I suspect there will be a few people looking for her, so a paint job and some exterior remodeling might be in order. We'll get your catamaran back to you as soon as possible. As I told you on the phone, *Aegis* suffered a similar fate to Barkov, so I'm a little homeless at the moment."

"No," he said, "the catamaran is yours, Chase. We can't have you living under a bridge, now can we? She's well-equipped, but purely non-tactical. She was a hurricane salvage, but we put her back together, polished her up a bit, and set her back afloat. You'll want some upgrades if you decide to keep her, but she'll make a fine honeymoon suite for the two of you."

"What is honeymoon suite?" asked Anya.

"I'll explain later," I said.

Dr. Richter came back into the main salon with his shoulder bandaged and his arm supported by a sling. He wore a grim look.

Anya ran to him. "Papa, what did doctor say? You are okay, yes?"

He kissed Anya's cheek. "No, my dear. Unfortunately, I'm not okay. It doesn't appear the bullet's still in there, but there's damage that needs to be repaired. I'm an old man and not as bulletproof as I was thirty years ago. I'm going back to Miami with Dominic and the good doctor here. Our friends there can get me fixed up without involving anymore unnecessary folks in our little adventure."

"Oh, Papa, I will go with you."

Dr. Richter took her hands in his. "No, Anastasia. You belong with Chase. I'll be fine, and we'll be together again soon. We still have a lot of paperwork before we officially make you an American, but it won't take long. I'll be in touch in a few days, and we'll go from there. In the meantime, you go with Chase. Somebody has to keep him out of trouble."

Anya didn't protest. She hugged her father and kissed his cheeks. "*YA lyublyu tebya, Papa.*"

"I love you, too, my child." He brushed Anya's long blonde hair out of her face and tucked it behind her ear. "Now, go. You two make your way toward where you first met *Aegis*, and I'll make sure someone meets you there with what you'll need. Go on. We don't have time for long goodbyes."

I rose from the settee, shook Dominic's hand, and thanked him for everything.

Dominic looked at Dr. Richter, then at Anya, and finally back at me. "He's her father?"

"It's a long story, but I'm sure Dr. Richter will fill you in on the trip back to Miami. Take good care of him, okay? He's one of the last remaining good guys left on Earth." I turned to Dr. Richter. "We'll see you soon, Coach. You do what the doctors say. And no flirting with the nurses."

"I'd rather die than live by those ridiculous rules. Now get out of here."

I chuckled, knowing Dr. "Rocket" Richter would be the star of the orthopedic ward in a day or two.

I reached for Anya's hand and walked away from my mentor. Once again, I'd set out on the ocean with the woman who both terrified and thrilled me beyond my wildest imagination.

3

Honeymoon

I stepped from the deck of the luxurious yacht onto the portside hull of the smaller catamaran and offered my hand to Anya. Not surprisingly, she ignored my offer and leapt gracefully aboard, landing soundlessly on the deck, and then she went into the cabin.

I started both diesel engines and watched the gauges come to life. I then went to work casting off the lines that held my new boat to Barkov's former yacht. Once clear of the yacht, I turned the cat into the southerly wind and set about getting some sails in the air. There was a bit of a learning curve as I mentally labeled each halyard, reefing line, and sheet. With the sails aloft, I let the cat bear away from the wind onto a northeasterly course, and watched the enormous white sails fill with the fifteen-knot breeze. I trimmed the sails and shut down the engines, then reveled in the near silence of the majestic sailing cat as she accelerated and settled on ten knots.

After savoring the first setting of the sails on my new boat, I set about learning how my new chart plotter and autopilot worked. Soon, I could plot a course and have the boat steer herself in the direction I wanted. With the boat sailing true and my sails trimmed to perfection, I headed for the interior to find Anya, but I didn't have to go far. She came bouncing through the doorway from the main salon and onto the aft deck wearing the smile of a child on Christmas morning.

"Oh, Chasechka, it is beautiful and so big. I love it. I love it so much and we are not flipping over."

She threw her arms around me and made a sound that would perhaps be a normal woman's squeal of delight, but I'd never known Anya to squeal.

"Yes, these are beautiful boats, and they don't flip over, as you put it."

Anya climbed onto the captain's chair behind the wheel and peered over the controls. It was nice to see her relaxing and finding joy in being alive. Her life had been constant work for people who demanded her constant perfection. Those days were gone, and it pleased me to be the reason she could start living, rather than merely existing to serve her domineering masters.

"Come. Come." Anya grabbed my hand and pulled me to the trampoline that made up the foredeck of the cat. She jumped and giggled like a schoolgirl before lying facedown and staring at the water through the mesh.

I watched the rise and fall of her shoulders as she breathed. I remembered the first time I'd watched her breathe. I was peering through my binoculars from a half mile away, and she was poised behind a rifle on top of a water tower in Elmont, New York. I knew so much more about her than I had back then, but I was still just as fascinated and smitten. I admired the curve of her back and the toned, long muscles of her legs. I sat in awe of her until her shrill scream pierced the air.

"Chase, look! Look!"

I peered through the trampoline to see a pair of bottlenose dolphins swimming millimeters beneath the surface of the water, perfectly matching the speed of the boat.

Anya wouldn't look away. "Is this really our boat now?"

I gazed across the deck of the beautiful sailing cat. "I think it is."

Anya rolled onto her side and pulled me toward her until we were wrapped in each other's arms and kissing passionately.

The emotions the two of us had experienced over the previous twelve hours were more than any normal person could've endured, but the minds and bodies of two well-trained assassins are far from normal.

I wanted to surrender and make love with her right there on the trampoline, but I couldn't. Not yet. I was consumed by a tsunami of thoughts that wouldn't let me give myself to her.

If Dr. Richter doesn't survive, can we still keep Anya in America and grant her citizenship? What will become of Barkov's yacht? How will I replace everything I lost aboard Aegis? *Oh shit, it'll be dark soon.*

"Anya, listen." I took her perfect face in my hands. "There's nothing I'd rather do than make love with you, but we have to get ready for nightfall."

"Yes, Chase, I know. Time for this will come later."

We rose from the trampoline and made our way back to the cockpit where I went to work on the chart plotter.

"Tell me what you are doing," Anya said.

"I'm looking for a place to anchor. It'll be dark soon, and we're going to collapse from exhaustion. Neither of us has the stamina to sail through the night."

"I do," she said confidently, "but I do not know how to sail this boat. You will teach me, yes?"

"Yes," I said, "I'll teach you, but now is not the time for a sailing lesson."

I scanned the chart for several minutes. "Here it is. We'll run across to Bimini. Honeymoon Harbor is a great anchorage. We'll run in there for the night and head north again tomorrow after we get some sleep."

Anya wrinkled her brow. "There is that word again, *honeymoon*. Tell me what this means."

"It's just the name of the harbor. It doesn't mean anything."

Anya made a disapproving face. She wasn't going to let me get away with that answer.

"Okay, okay. A honeymoon is a vacation people take right after they get married, but really, in this case, it's just the name of the harbor . . . really."

"We will have honeymoon someday, yes?"

I tried to ignore the question. "It's about thirty miles to the Great Bahama Bank. We'll make that in less than three hours, and we'll be sound asleep a few minutes after that."

Anya was still grinning at me, waiting for an answer, but I wasn't going to play her game—at least not yet.

"Let's check the lights to make sure they all work. We don't want to have to deal with the Coast Guard if we don't have to. We don't have any identification."

Apparently, she wasn't interested in checking lights because she walked off and left me alone on deck. I flipped the switches for all of the navigation lights and found them to be working perfectly. The anchor light, deck lights, and spotlights were also in working order. Satisfied with the light check, I programmed the destination into the chart plotter and let the autopilot bring the big cat around on her new course. I retrimmed the sails and settled into one of the large, cushioned seats in the cockpit.

Anya emerged from the main salon, carrying a tray, and wearing a Miami Dolphins t-shirt and a pair of shorts drawn tightly around her waist.

"Where'd you get that outfit?" I tried not to laugh at how the baggy clothes hung from her thin frame.

"They were inside boat, and I like dolphins, so I take. You like?"

I laughed, "Yes, I like."

Anya placed the tray beside me on the cushion. It held two sandwiches, an apple, and two Diet Cokes.

"Where'd you get the food?" I asked.

"It was also inside boat. Now eat."

I did as I was told and devoured the sandwich and one of the drinks. I watched Anya open the Diet Coke, sniff at it, and then take a reluctant sip.

She wrinkled her nose. "I do not like. Is terrible."

"It's better with rum." I pointed off to the west. "Look at that gorgeous sunset."

She sighed. "It is. I never look at sun going away until you show me this on first *Aegis* boat."

I remembered the first sunset she and I watched together before we knew we could trust each other, before we knew our lives would become perfectly entangled with each other's. As we approached the Great Bahama Bank, I motioned for her to join me in front of the chart plotter. She hovered over my shoulder to get a view of the screen.

"Now watch the depth sounder. It's the big number in the lower left corner," I said.

"Three hundred twenty meters?"

"No, it's feet, but watch."

Her eyes widened as she watched the depth fall from over three hundred feet to eleven feet in less than a minute.

"Chase! The bottom is going to hit us."

I chuckled. "It's deep enough for us. This is the Great Bahama Bank. I wanted you to see how quickly the depth changes here."

"Is mountain in ocean. No. Is *a* mountain in *the* ocean," she said.

I squeezed her. "My American girl."

"This is honeymoon place?"

"No. Honeymoon Harbor is right over there. We'll be there in a few minutes."

"Okay," she said. "I will make for you honeymoon drink. Inside boat is alcohol, too."

I furled the sails, turned on the lights, and motored into Honeymoon Harbor. There were only three other boats in the anchorage, so I easily found a spot to anchor for the night.

For the first time, I left the exterior of my new home and ventured into the main salon, which also contained a kitchen, or a galley, and a navigation station. The interior was as beautiful as the exterior, if not more. The countertops looked like marble, but were no doubt a manmade solid surface material to keep the weight down. The plumbing fixtures were brushed nickel, and the electronics were more impressive than the equipment in the cockpit. There was a well-stocked bar and pantry full of provisions sufficient for several weeks. Dominic had taken very good care of us.

I heard the whine of the pump come to rest and wondered why it was running. Moments later, Anya appeared on the stairs with wet hair. There was no sign of the Miami Dolphins t-shirt or baggy shorts.

"After your shower," she said in Russian, "your drink and I will be waiting for you in your bed, my stinky captain."

Exhausted from the last several hours of my life, my body and mind needed sleep, but neither my body nor my mind could resist Anya. We made love, trying to forget what we'd endured. Then, merciful sleep overtook us. We found ourselves lost and entangled with each other, and we slept as if we hadn't in weeks.

* * *

I awoke with the sunrise and watched Anya sleeping peacefully in my arms. When I tried to sneak from the bed without waking her, she stirred.

I kissed the top of her head. "You sleep. I'm going to make breakfast."

I found some clothes provided by Dominic that almost fit, and I headed for the galley. In minutes, I had coffee brewing, eggs frying, and I'd cut a pineapple into bite-sized chunks. I couldn't understand how Dominic had stocked the boat so well in such a short amount of time, but I was thankful he had.

With plates and mugs balanced on a tray, I negotiated the stairs and tiptoed into the master stateroom. I rested on the edge of the bed and watched Anya sleeping peacefully with her arms wrapped around my pillow. I traced my fingertips across her hip. Her skin was still pale, but the sun would soon turn her flawless Eastern European skin to a golden brown.

"What took so long?" She stretched her arms and yawned.

"I'm sorry to have kept you waiting, my *czarina*."

"No! I am now American girl. Never *czarina*."

"My apologies. I'm sorry to have kept you waiting, my American princess."

"Even I know you do not have princess in America."

"Maybe not, but I have one on this boat. Now eat up, princess. We have a big day ahead of us."

She stuck out her bottom lip. "But why must we leave honeymoon place? I like it here, and I think you like also."

I was surprised by her affection for the anchorage. "Oh, I love being here with you, but we have to get to Jekyll Island. Perhaps we'll have a real honeymoon here someday."

"Someday?" She raised her eyebrows.

We drank our coffee and fed each other pieces of pineapple. "I'm going to check the weather. Would you like more coffee?"

"No," she said. "I will come with you to see weather. I must learn to be American sailor girl."

Remembering what Dr. Richter had said about teaching her to sail and dive and eat chili dogs at a ball game, I complied. If she wanted to learn to sail, I'd gladly be her teacher.

I showed her how to pull up the weather forecast and how to use the chart plotter. "This is where we are now. We're going to Jekyll Island, which is up here," I said, pointing to the barrier islands of Georgia.

"Why are we going there?" she asked.

"Do you remember when your father told us to head for the place I first met *Aegis*?"

"Yes."

"Well, that's where I saw *Aegis* for the first time. That's where your father and some of his old friends recruited me into this life—this life that led me to you. It's a beautiful island, and you'll love it. It's off the coast of Georgia."

I had taken Anya to meet Dr. Richter in Athens, Georgia before we'd embarked on the mission that sent *Aegis* to the bottom of the ocean. That's where she learned Dr. Richter was her father and where her decision to defect had been solidified.

"I will never forget your Georgia, Chase, and now is my Georgia also."

I continued the lessons. "We'll be sailing north with the Gulf Stream, so we'll probably make fourteen knots along the route."

She blurted out, "Three hundred fifty miles at fourteen knots means twenty-five hours to get there. Is simple mathematics, yes?"

"Yes." I was impressed. "But I don't want to sail for a solid twenty-five hours. That would mean we'd have to take turns sleeping while the other stood watch. Until you're comfortable handling the boat alone, we'll stick to daytime sailing and anchoring at night."

"Chase, is only twenty-five hours. Any person can stay awake twenty-four hours."

"Yes, you're right, but it's not that simple. The wind will not be as strong at night, and the further north we go, the slower the Gulf Stream will be, so we can't make fourteen knots all the way."

"Okay," she admitted. "I have much to learn."

"So do I."

She refilled our coffee mugs and waited for me to decide where we would anchor next. Instead of making the decision myself, I pulled her chair toward the navigation station and showed her how to find anchorages and measure distances on the chart plotter.

"Let's see if you can find us a good place to anchor tonight."

She scrolled through the chart plotter up the east coast of Florida. "I see Cape of Canaveral. That is where your NASA space-ships are."

I smiled. "Yes, you found it. That's where we launch the space shuttle and other rockets carrying satellites and all sorts of other things into space."

"We will see this place, and your spaceships, yes?"

"We'll see the island, but I don't think there'll be any spaceships."

"And we will see also Disney World and White House and Liberty Statue and Great Canyon?"

I was amused by her excitement of experiencing America. "Well, we'll see all of those places together, but not on this trip."

"On honeymoon we will see them."

Desperate to get the navigation lesson back on track, I said, "So, where are we going today?"

She busied herself with scanning the chart again. "I think we will go to Fort Pierce, but if cannot, we will go to Saint Lucie Inlet."

"That's a great plan," I told her.

We left the main salon and ventured into the cockpit where I was going to start the engines, but she stopped me. "No, let me do it."

I loved her eagerness to learn, so I tried to stay out of her way, giving only small suggestions. She started the engines, raised the anchor, and motored out of the anchorage. With very little help from me, she unfurled the headsail and shut down the engines.

I showed her how to trim the sail for maximum efficiency, and then how to program the chart plotter and set the autopilot.

"That's it," I said. "Now, all we have to do is watch for other boats for seven or eight hours and keep her pointed toward Fort Pierce."

"I am sailor now," she proclaimed proudly.

"Well, you're a downwind sailor now. We'll sail into the wind at some point, and that's a little different, but we'll get to that in time."

She repeated, "I am sailor now."

I realized my mistake. "Yes, you are a sailor now."

The day turned out to be a sailor's dream. The waves were less than three feet, the wind was strong and consistent, and the boat performed flawlessly. We saw two cruise ships outbound from Fort Lauderdale, headed for The Bahamas, and Anya feared we might collide. I assured her we'd stay well away from the cruise ships, even though, technically, the larger ships were supposed to give way to a sailboat.

"That is silly rule. We are tiny bug, and ships are big and powerful. Rule should be we stay away from them."

"I agree, but there are reasons for the rules. We're less maneuverable than powerboats, so that's what the rule is based on."

"Is still silly rule," she insisted.

I conceded. I wasn't going to win that one.

"I have read about cruising ships. They are luxurious, yes? Is that right word, *luxurious*?"

"Yes, that's exactly the right word. I've never been on a cruise ship," I admitted, "but I'd like to go. How about you?"

"Yes. We can do that on honeymoon also with Liberty Statue and Great Canyon."

Again, with the honeymoon talk.

"Hey, American girl. It's called the Statue of Liberty and the Grand Canyon."

"Yes," she said, "but is still called honeymoon."

The wind and current were a little better than forecast, so we made Fort Pierce Inlet well before sunset. Anya proved as competent at anchoring the big cat as she had been at weighing the anchor earlier that morning. I led her through the procedure of allowing plenty of room for the boat to swing around on the anchor chain when the wind or tide changed directions. Then I taught her to back down on the anchor with both engines at full power, in reverse, to seat the anchor solidly in the bottom. She mastered the skills in no time.

"Is nothing hard for you?" I asked.

She gave me a blank look. "What do you mean?"

"Everything seems so easy for you to learn. Isn't anything difficult?"

She bit at her bottom lip then motioned for me to sit down. She sat on my lap, ran her fingers through my hair, and curled her long legs beneath her.

I could see there was something troubling her, and I wanted her to tell me everything so I could help.

"What is chili dog?"

"What?"

"I want to eat chili dog at ball game with you, but I do not know what it is."

I laughed. "Words can't do a chili dog justice. You have to experience one for yourself. I promise you'll love it."

"I will love everything with you, my Chase."

4

Passing Storm

For the first time, Anya and I tried cooking together, and it was an unmitigated disaster. Every time she'd reach for anything, I was in her way. Every time I started to add a spice, she'd veto the addition. Frustration built until I finally put my psychology degree to work.

"You know," I said, "I'm a terrible cook, but I'm a great bartender. Why don't you finish up with this? I'll make us a couple drinks, and I have a few things to do on deck as well. There's a storm coming tonight, and we don't want to lose anything when the wind picks up."

"Is best idea you have, Chase. Besides, is for woman to cook in America, yes?"

"No, Anya. Maybe some people believe that, but certainly not me. I want us to do things together. Nothing is your job or my job. There will be things each of us does better than the other, but we're still a team . . . always."

"I am better at more things, I think. Now make drink for me, sailing teacher."

I stuck one finger behind the waistband of her shorts and pulled her to me. "As you wish, my princess."

I left the galley and set about securing everything on deck and stowing anything I couldn't secure. As an additional precaution, I let out a few more feet of anchor chain in case the storm was worse than forecast. I'd learned it's always better to be prepared for the worst.

As agreed, I made drinks and she finished making dinner.

"What is this?" I asked. "It's delicious."

She poked at a small cube of braised beef on her plate. "I do not know. I cook what we have, and it taste good, yes? You will buy for me American cooking book."

I liked how her questions often sounded like statements.

"I will buy for you whatever you want."

"I do not want *things*, Chase. I never have childhood. I only know working, and now maybe you will give to me fun and not work . . . and maybe American cooking book."

"Definitely an American cooking book," I said.

* * *

I cleaned the galley and double-checked that the boat was ready for the coming storm. Satisfied we could weather anything short of a hurricane, I decided to have a more thorough tour of my new boat. My first foray into the portside hull surprised and pleased me. The aft cabin had been converted into a well-equipped workshop, while the forward cabin and head remained a comfortable living space. I couldn't have been happier with my new home.

As I started down the starboard side stairs, I found Anya standing in front of a full-length mirror, turning her hips to look at herself. She was tracing a faint, newly formed tan line where the hem of her shorts had been. I sat on the stairs, admiring her.

She caught me watching and grinned. "Sun is making my skin brown, but only where I do not have clothes. I think I will not wear clothes in sun so I will be same color everywhere."

"I think that's a wonderful idea. Now I'm going to shower. I'd like to get an early start after the storm passes so we can make St. Augustine before dark. I want to make Jekyll Island in forty-eight hours."

She tilted her head. "I will be in bed when you finish shower." As we slid past each other in the narrow walkway, she purposely pressed her body into mine.

* * *

I climbed onto the bed after my shower, and she sat between my legs as I brushed her long hair.

"I remember when I was child and mother would brush my hair. I am sad for her. Papa loved her like you love me, Chase. You are kind man, and I think Papa is same. If bastard not kill her . . . I so hate him . . . if he not kill my mother, Papa would love her and brush her hair like this."

I laid the brush beside the bed and pulled her backward against my body. "I'm sorry, Anya. I know you miss your mother, and I wish I could bring her back for you and Dr. Richter. I think you're right. I'm sure he loved her very much and misses her like you do, but maybe having you in his life will ease some of his sorrow. No one can replace your mother, but I promise to give you the best life I can, and we'll spend as much time as you want with your father."

"I love you, Chase."

"I love you, too, Anya."

* * *

The storm rolled in and the wind howled. The rain poured down in sheets, making it impossible to sleep. I climbed the stairs into the main salon and turned on the deck lights. From there, I could see every inch of the boat through the windows. Everything was in place, and the rain was washing the decks. I checked the radar to find heavy rain in all directions, but it was moving quickly to the northeast and would be over in a few hours.

A sleepy Anya peered up the stairs. "Everything is okay?"

"Yes, everything's fine. The storm should be over in a few hours. I'll be back down in a minute."

Anya lay on the stairs and crossed her arms on the top step. She rested her chin on her hands, barely able to keep her eyes open. "I will wait with you."

I finished my work and lifted Anya from the stairs. She sighed as she draped her arms around my neck, and I carried her to the bed. I slid in behind her, joining her in sleep.

When the rain stopped, I woke and checked my watch to see that it was a few minutes past three a.m. I turned to make sure Anya was still sleeping, but she wasn't there. I rolled over and peeked through the hatch, thinking she may have made a late-night trek to the head. She wasn't there either.

I crawled from the bed and called to her. "Anya? Where are you?"

"I am in kitchen, and I have idea. Come, come."

"A kitchen on a boat is called a galley. And why are you up so early?" I put one foot in front of the other, struggling to find my way out of deep sleep and up the stairs.

"Look. I have plan."

I rubbed my eyes and stared at the navigation station and chart plotter. There were calculations and notes written everywhere. Some were in English, some were in Russian, and some were in a crazy combination of the two.

"What's all this?" I asked.

"Is plan, Chase. I do figures, and is two hundred fifty miles to your Jekyll Island, and wind is strong behind storm. If we go now, I think we can do average eight knots. Even in darkness, yes?"

"Yeah, I guess so. Maybe a little better than eight knots, but that's probably pretty close."

"Okay, if eight knots, we arrive at your Jekyll Island in thirty-one hours. I can now sail while you sleep. Thirty-one hours is short time for not sleeping for me, but I know you need sleep." She winked at me. "You are weaker."

"It's your plan," I said, "so you make it happen. I'm only here to keep you from sinking another one of my boats."

Anya gave me a stern Russian glare. "You demand I use English articles when I speak, so I demand you use correct pronoun when you speak. Is *our* boat, not *your* boat."

"Forgive me, my princess. I shall not make the same mistake again."

"Good," she huffed.

She started the engines, brought up the lights, and weighed the anchor. Just as I'd taught her, she carefully maneuvered the boat from the anchorage as if she'd been behind the wheel of a boat for years.

I leaned over her left shoulder and turned the radar on so she could see the other boats in the anchorage, as well as the buoys leading us through the channel. Entering or leaving an unfamiliar harbor or anchorage in the dark is a terrible idea, but Anya's timeline made sense, so the risk of running aground would've been worth the benefit of getting underway.

"You're doing great," I said, "but there's something you have to consider when we leave the inlet."

Anya listened closely.

"When we leave the inlet, the current will be flowing from the south and the wind is out of the north. The current will turn us to the north and the sea is going to be choppy. Do you understand?"

"Yes. Boat will try to go to left, and I must keep in channel between rocks and buoys."

"Exactly," I said. "All you have to do is stay to the right and be ready for the boat to pull left. When she does, use all the control inputs you need to keep her in the channel. We don't want to be aground in a falling tide. We'd be stuck for a long time until the tide came back in."

As we exited the inlet, clear of the jetties, the bow of the boat pulled violently to port.

Anya responded quickly, keeping us centered in the channel. "Is stronger than I expected, but I did it, yes?"

"You certainly did. Now keep her between the red and green buoys for another couple of miles, and we'll be in deep water with plenty of wind."

In a show of confidence, I left the cockpit and returned to the galley to make more coffee. I occasionally peeked through the windows to make sure she was still in the channel. At every peek, she was doing exactly what I would've done at the helm.

We passed the buoy marking the end of the Fort Pierce Inlet, and she turned the boat to the northeast. Leaving the engines running, she unfurled the genoa and let it fill with the crisp wind. Once the sail was correctly trimmed, she idled the engines and shut them down.

"Look at you, sailor girl," I said, coming through the door into the cockpit. "Here's a fresh cup of coffee for you, Captain Burinkova. You did a fine job, but you forgot one little detail."

She took the mug and nonchalantly flipped off the spotlights and steaming light.

I pulled out a pair of water-activated life jackets from a locker and handed one to her. "I've always thought it was a good idea to wear a life jacket at night. If one of us goes overboard, we'd be hard to find in the dark."

"You are good teacher, Chase."

"You're a good student," I said as I clinked my coffee cup with hers.

"What will we do at your Jekyll Island?"

"We're going to meet some friends who'll have some things we're going to need. I called the bank in Grand Cayman and had them overnight a pair of credit cards and wire some cash. We're going to need a little money. You have some shopping to do. I can't be seen running around with a woman in a dirty old t-shirt and pants that don't fit."

She pulled at her oversized attire. "I will be wearing nothing when sun comes up."

* * *

We arrived at the sea buoy in the mouth of the Brunswick Harbor–St. Simon Range as the sun was coming up the second day. Anya's calculations proved to be spot-on. We entered the busy channel, and there were cargo ships, shrimp boats, and fishing vessels of every shape and size. With that amount of ship traffic, she chose to relinquish the controls to me.

We motored up the channel, dodging other boats until we arrived at the wooden dock near the Jekyll Island Club. The dock was exactly as I remembered it from the first time I'd seen it. That was the day I stepped off the deck of *Aegis*, before she was my boat, and into another life—a life that turned me into a weapon, gave me a window into a world I never knew existed, and led me to Anya, the gorgeous former Russian spy who had trouble keeping her clothes on each time the sun came up.

With fenders deployed, Anya leapt onto the dock and tied us securely in place. I shut down the engines and slipped the keys into my pocket. I stepped from the boat and found Anya talking with a young man in a golf shirt. Once he saw me, he abandoned his conversation with Anya and reached for my hand.

"Mr. Fulton," he said, "I'm Clark Johnson. We've been expecting you. It's nice to finally meet you."

I shook his hand. "Who's *we?*"

"Sir?" The man was obviously confused.

Having learned to be cautious about how much I revealed, I thought it might be a good idea to keep the guy on his toes. "You said, 'We've been expecting you.' Who's *we?*"

"Well," he said, seeming somewhat flustered, "I actually meant the royal *we*. Dr. Richter sends his best."

I was still skeptical, but Anya leapt at the sound of her father's name.

"You know Papa? He is okay, yes?"

Clark gauged my reaction and then turned back to Anya. "He's going to be fine. He's in good hands with Dr. Cribb."

"Okay, Clark," I said. "What do you have for us?"

"I have no idea. I've got two locked cases and a golf cart. That's all I know. I'm just the courier."

That sounded more believable, so I let down my guard a little. "Now we're getting somewhere, Clark. Let's see this golf cart of yours and take a look at those cases."

He nodded toward the end of the dock and led us to the waiting golf cart. We climbed in and headed for the Jekyll Island Club.

"So, Clark, what room are you in?"

"I'm in one-oh-four."

"Great." I patted him on the shoulder. "We'll drop you off on the back side near the bar. One-oh-four is a couple doors down from there. I'll have a bellman come by and grab those cases and bring them up to our room."

"Perfect. I'll be waiting."

I dropped him where I'd promised and watched him walk through the old wooden door. I kept my eyes on him as I saw him turn to the left and toward the room he'd named.

Clark never looked back, which is exactly what I would've done if I believed I was being watched.

5
Cloak and Dagger

Anya and I drove around to the front of the club and walked into the massive, ornate lobby.

"Good morning. I'm Chase Fulton. I think you have a couple packages for me," I told the young woman behind the desk.

"Oh, hello, Mr. Fulton. I do have some things for you."

She placed a sealed manila envelope, bearing overnight postage from Georgetown, Grand Cayman, on the counter, and produced a small slip of paper for me to sign. "I'll need your signature for this one," she said.

I signed the paper and slid it back across the desk.

"Thank you, sir, but I also need to see your ID before I can release the package and the remainder of what I have for you."

"Of course." I patted my pants as if I were looking for my wallet, which was with my boat, several hundred feet under water. "I think I must've left my wallet in our friend's room. Would you mind ringing Mr. Clark Johnson's room and letting him know I'll be coming by to grab my things?"

I watched as she made a few keystrokes on her keyboard and then dialed one-zero-four on her telephone.

"Mr. Johnson, this is Stephanie at the front desk. I'm here with your friend, Mr. Fulton. He says he'll be on his way to pick up his things from your room."

"Thank you," she said, and hung up.

Convinced Clark was who and where he claimed to be, I strolled down the hallway to room one-oh-four and knocked twice. I saw a shadow pass over the peephole before hearing the locks click. The door swung inward, and a cautious peek around the doorframe allowed me to see Clark, hands visible, stepping back from the door to give me room to come inside.

"Thanks again, Clark. I'm sorry for all the cloak-and-dagger, but I needed to know you are who you claim to be."

"No problem," he said. "I did my time at The Ranch, too, so I know the game."

"Oh, you did? Is that little round guy they called Gunny still in charge of the tactical training?"

He cocked his head, squinted his right eye, and had a moment of obvious recognition. "Nice try, Chase. Gunny is six feet tall with one percent body fat, and he'll be in charge of tactical training until he dies. Maybe longer."

I reached out to shake his hand. "Okay, Clark. No more tests."

We relaxed for the first time since we'd met.

I said, "On my first day at The Ranch, that guy kicked the shit out of me and knocked me out cold against the concrete wall of the cave he calls an office." I remembered how my body ached for days after that encounter.

"He's quite the people person, isn't he?" Clark pointed into the room. "Your cases are on the dresser beside the TV. I hope it's everything you need."

The cases were stainless steel with six-digit combination locks. I dialed in the first and last three digits of the serial number of my Walther PPK, and the locks popped open, just as I knew they would.

Clark laughed. "I'm glad to see you knew the combo. No one told me, so I wasn't going to be any help."

I ignored him as I pilfered through the cases until I found what I'd been looking for—a leather wallet that looked like it could've been in my hip pocket for years. "Good ol' Rocket never lets me down."

Clark looked at me as if I were speaking Mandarin, clearly unaware that Rocket was Dr. Richter.

"Thanks, Clark," I said, pocketing the wallet and closing the cases. "Are you all set? Is there anything you need from me? A lift somewhere?"

"No, but thanks, Chase. I'm in the King Air out at the airport. I'll be heading back to Virginia in a day or two. I need a couple days off, and Jekyll Island is as good a place as any to get some rest."

I made my way back to the lobby and handed my newly minted, but purposely worn driver's license to Stephanie. She promptly handed it back and slid over the envelope with my name printed across the seal. She held up one finger, indicating that I should wait a minute, then picked up the phone and dialed some numbers. I wasn't quick enough to see what they were.

"Jack, Mr. Fulton is here," she said into the phone. "Would you please come open the safe?"

Jack, who I assumed to be the shift manager, came through a two-hundred-year-old door, pulling on his suit coat and sticking out his hand.

"Mr. Fulton. I'm Jack Ford, the operations manager here at the Jekyll Island Club. It's a pleasure to meet you."

I shook his hand, returning the courtesy.

He walked back around the counter. "I'll have your package for you in just a moment." He knelt, spun the dial on the aged iron safe, and pulled the door open. He extracted five stacks of bank-banded hundred-dollar bills and placed them on the counter. "There you are, Mr. Fulton. Fifty thousand dollars wired from your bank yesterday morning."

Until then, Anya hadn't made a sound, but when she saw the stacks of bills piling up on the counter, she let out a little squeal.

Jack asked, "Is there anything else we can do for you, Mr. Fulton?"

"We could use a bed and a shower. Oh, and a rental car if you could arrange one for us. Something sporty would be nice."

"Of course. Stephanie will take care of everything you need, and if I can be of service to you, please don't hesitate to call on me, day or night."

He handed me his card after writing his private number on the back. I thanked him and saw Stephanie printing our paperwork.

She slid a pair of keys with decorative green chains across the desk. "How long will you be staying with us?"

Anya squeezed my arm.

"You wouldn't happen to have a honeymoon suite available, would you?" I asked.

Anya's eyes lit up.

"Absolutely," said Stephanie.

She snatched the keys from the counter and replaced them with an even more decorative set.

I signed for the room. "We'll be here a few days if you have room for us. Maybe three or four nights, if that's okay."

"Of course," she said. "I'll show you as here for four nights. Let us know if you'll be staying longer."

"By the way," I said, "we need to keep our boat at the dock while we're here. It's the fifty-foot sailing catamaran tied up at the end."

"No problem. Your boat will be fine right where it is."

I picked up the keys, the cash, and the remaining envelope from the counter. "When can we expect the car?"

"I'm sure it'll be here by lunchtime. Enjoy the honeymoon suite, and congratulations."

* * *

The honeymoon suite was exquisite.

"Oh, Chase. It is beautiful. I love this place. I will never want to leave." Anya danced around the enormous room.

"You never want to leave anyplace we go," I said.

She leapt onto the bed and rolled over onto her stomach, her chin perched on top of her hands. "I want to have honeymoon forever with you, my Chase."

I kissed her forehead. "I'm going to take a shower and a nap. We'll play honeymoon later."

She stuck out her bottom lip, pretending to pout, but I could see in her eyes she needed sleep as much as I did.

* * *

When we awoke, we discovered an envelope someone had slid under our door. Inside it was a futuristic-looking key on a Porsche key ring. I tossed it onto the dressing table and carried the two stainless steel cases and the sealed envelope back to the bed. I sorted through the items inside the cases, lifted a small purse from the first case, and tossed it to Anya.

"I'm pretty sure this one is yours. It's not my color."

She opened the purse and pulled out a driver's license and social security card. "Chase, what is this?"

"I have no idea. I didn't pack it. This is all your father's doing."

"It is Florida driving license with my picture, but name is Ana R. Fulton."

I laughed. "Well then, maybe this is our honeymoon after all."

As I continued to dig through the cases, I found a pair of passports for Chase and Ana Fulton that were dated eighteen months earlier. I also found a pair of matching Walther PPK pistols and an assortment of holsters. Along with the pistols were two boxes of Plus-P, Talon, hollow-point ammunition, so I loaded each magazine and handed one of the weapons to Anya. She took it from my hand, racked the slide, and watched a round smoothly seat into the chamber. She then re-holstered the pistol and placed it on the nightstand.

There were a few papers pertaining to the boat as well as a satellite phone and a pair of cell phones. I supposed it was time I had my first cell phone. After all, it was 2001, and I was already behind the technological power curve.

I opened the envelope from the bank in the Caymans and found two black credit cards with my name embossed on the bottom of each. I tossed one to Anya. "You might need this. It's a card linked to one of the accounts in the Cayman Islands that you insisted I open."

"You do listen to me sometimes," she said with a wry smile.

"Yes, sometimes I do." I slid the case and remaining contents aside and grabbed her around her waist. "So far, you've never steered me wrong."

"It is now time you take me for shopping. I need new dolphin shirt."

"Okay, we'll go shopping and get you a Braves hat and a Bull-dogs shirt. No more Miami Dolphins for you."

"Aww, Chasechka, you not love me now? What is Braves and Bulldogs?"

I scoffed. "You've got a lot of work to do if we're going to pass you off as an American girl anytime soon. The Braves is the baseball team from Atlanta, and the bulldog is the mascot of the University of Georgia. It's where I played ball."

"And they have chili dogs there, yes?"

"They have the best chili dogs in the world. In fact, I need a phone."

Anya or Ana, as the state of Florida seemed to think, pointed toward the phone beside her Walther on the nightstand. From memory, I punched in the numbers.

"Georgia Bulldogs ticket office," came a lady's slow Southern drawl.

I cleared my throat. "When's the next baseball game?"

"Just a moment, sir. Let me take a look."

I heard her typing and humming.

"We're playing Alabama tomorrow afternoon at one o'clock here in Athens," she said.

"Thank you, ma'am," I said in my best Southernese. I rolled back over to face Anya. "Looks like you'll be getting that chili dog before you know it. We're going to Athens tomorrow to see my Bulldogs kick the stuffing out of Alabama."

"What does this mean, kick the stuffing? I do not know baseball much, but I do not think kicking is part of game."

I chuckled. "Let's go find you something to wear."

* * *

We picked up a pair of sandwiches from the dining room of the Jekyll Island Club and headed out in search of our rental car. We didn't have any trouble finding it. Parked near the curb in front of the lobby was a gorgeous red Porsche 911 convertible. I pushed the unlock button on the key fob to make sure it was ours. The lights flashed and the door locks popped open.

I opened Anya's door and she slid into the leather seat. She snatched the key from my hand and leapt across the center console into the driver's seat. Knowing I'd never win that argument, I slid into the passenger side and buckled my seat belt.

"Do you even know how to drive?" I asked.

She smiled mischievously. "I have Florida driving license. Would you like to see?"

"No, you don't," I said. "Some chick named Ana Fulton has a Florida driver's license."

"Yes, this is me."

Arguing with a woman is exhausting, and arguing with a Russian woman is little more than an exercise in masochism.

We left the parking lot as if we'd robbed a bank. She was a maniac behind the wheel, but a maniac in control. Her command of the powerful sports car was astonishing. She took ninety-degree curves at eighty miles per hour and never strayed an inch from the center of the lane. The speed limit on most of the island is thirty-five, but limits didn't seem to be a concept she understood.

We arrived at a stop sign beneath the shade of a two-hundred-year-old oak tree dripping with Spanish moss, and I finally relaxed my grip on the door handle.

"Is nice car, but needs more power," Anya said.

"You're a maniac. Now slow down and pull into that parking lot on the left."

She pulled into a parking space at approximately the speed of sound and brought the car to a stop perfectly centered in the space, six inches from the curb. I didn't know who taught her to do it, but Ana Fulton could drive.

"Where did you learn to drive like that?" I asked with obvious admiration.

"What do you mean? This is first time for me driving."

* * *

Shopping with a woman can be one of the most frustrating endeavors imaginable for a man, but Anya was no ordinary woman. We spent a total of twenty-seven minutes shopping, during which time she picked out four dresses, six pairs of shorts, two pairs of blue jeans, fourteen shirts, a windbreaker, and three pairs of shoes. I bought a few things for myself and two University of Georgia Bulldogs baseball hats. Our shopping was complete, and I wondered if Anya was ever going to let me drive the Porsche.

We spent the afternoon at the beach on the Atlantic Ocean side of the island. It was nice to pretend we were just normal people out for an afternoon where no one knew we were a pair of deadly assassins. We met several other couples, most of them forty years our seniors, walking hand in hand. Anya seemed to pay particular attention to the older couples who were doing what we were doing—digging their toes in the sand, picking up shells, and holding hands.

She smiled at me. "We will be like them someday, yes?"

"No! We're never going to be old."

We watched the waves crash on the beach, and we savored our quiet afternoon together.

Dinner was in the Grand Dining Room at the Jekyll Island Club after another hair-raising ride back with the Russian Mario Andretti. Her appetizer of crab cakes and mine of fried green tomatoes came, and Anya stared, mystified by the contents on my plate.

"They're delicious. Try a bite," I said. I cut a small piece from one of the tomatoes and offered it across the table.

She tentatively took the fork from my hand, smelled the tomato, and placed it in her mouth. Her eyes lit up with delight, and she made a sultry, seductive sound.

"I told you they were delicious."

Without a word, she slid her plate of crab cakes to me and took the rest of the fried green tomatoes for herself.

With a mouthful of food, she said, "This will be in American cooking book you will buy for me, yes?"

"Absolutely. Maybe you'll make them for me since I'm obviously not getting any of those."

The entrees came, and once again, she eyed my plate. It was fun watching her discover Southern American food.

"Have you ever tried grits?"

She shook her head no, so I offered her my fork loaded with grits and a beautifully grilled shrimp. She took it, surveyed it closely, and touched her tongue to the grits. Soon, my plate was in front of her, and I was having the short ribs.

Before she could ask, I said, "Yes, that will be in the cookbook, too."

It occurred to me that in my life I'd eaten two meals in the Grand Dining Room at the Jekyll Island Club, and both meals were with people who would dramatically change my life forever.

The first was with Dr. Richter, Ace, Beater, and Tuner, the four men who recruited me into the service of my country . . . or, if not my country, at least some group claiming to represent my country.

This time, across the table from me, sat a former Russian SVR officer turned defector, carrying several pieces of identification bearing my last name.

Who would've believed a baseball playing psychologist and son of missionaries would end up an American assassin in love with a Russian spy?

6
Southern Hospitality

I couldn't believe she let me drive. I agreed with her assessment of the car except for the need for more power. We left on the Jekyll Island Causeway, the only road onto and off the island. We wound through eastern Georgia and a couple dozen quaint, southern towns.

Anya was fascinated by the town squares and picturesque court-houses. "Is all of America like this?"

"No, not all of it," I said. "Only the good parts."

An old man riding by on a bicycle waved at us and showed a toothless grin.

"Everybody knows you and waves. You are very popular here, yes?"

"No, none of these people know me. They're just friendly and wave to everyone."

"That is silly, but I like," she said. "I think I will also wave to these people."

That became her game for the remainder of the drive to Athens. She waved to everyone, and most of them waved back. It's not every day people get to see a gorgeous Russian in a Porsche 911 convertible waving at them on the town square.

It was after noon when we arrived at Foley Field, the University of Georgia's baseball stadium. I wasn't prepared for the emotional experience of seeing the stadium again. I'd become a champion in that stadium. I'd caught uncountable pitches crouched behind home plate. I'd sweat, cried, bled, cheered, mourned, and most of all, I'd found my home on that field. I'd never felt more at home than when I was there, hot and sweaty, and playing in the dirt. I'd dreamed of someday wearing the uniform of the Atlanta Braves and catching at Turner Field. I remembered the elation and agony of my last game when we beat Oklahoma State to win the nineteen-ninety-six College World Series; the game in which I broke my right hand so badly that my dreams of becoming a major leaguer went up in smoke. I couldn't help but tear up.

"What is wrong, my Chase?"

"This place just brings back a lot of old memories. You know, I used to be pretty good at this game. But that feels like a lifetime ago."

Perhaps she didn't know what else to say, so she tugged at the bill of her cap. "I like our matching Bulldog hats."

"Me too, but what I really like is your ponytail hanging out the back. That's way sexy."

She grabbed my hand, and we started for the ticket window.

"Do you have two seats behind home plate, ma'am?" I asked the lady behind the heavy glass.

"Let me see." She went to work searching for available seats, then she stopped and stared at me. "You're Chase Fulton, aren't you?"

I was a little embarrassed, so I didn't answer.

"I knew it! You are Chase Fulton. You wait right here. I'll be right back."

"I think she is going to get chili dog for me," Anya said.

I laughed and appreciated her unique way of making everything all right.

Still behind the window, the ticket lady returned with Bucky Buchanan in tow. Bucky was the longtime pitching coach and one of my mentors when I was a player.

"Well, I'll be darned if it ain't Chase Fulton. It sure is good to see you. Come around to the side door, and I'll let you in," said Bucky.

I led Anya back out of the stadium and toward an inconspicuous door around the corner. It swung open and Bucky hugged me as if I were his long-lost brother.

"Damn, it sure is good to see you, Chase. Where in the hell did you run off to? Ain't nobody heard a word from you in nearly three years. How's that hand?"

Bucky always talked faster than I could listen and never failed to ask more than one question at a time.

Before I could begin answering him, he caught sight of Anya. "Well, who might this be? She surely ain't with you. She's way too pretty to be an ugly old catcher's girl."

He stuck out his hand. "Hey, ma'am, I'm Bucky Buchanan. How you doin'?"

Anya appeared dumfounded. Bucky wasn't easy to take at first. It took a few minutes to get used to his energy, but I was proud to see Anya stick out her hand and smile.

"Hello, Bucky. I am Ana, Chase's driver."

"Driver? Ha! That's a good one. That accent of yours sure ain't South Georgia. You ain't from around here, are you?"

"No, I am from east of here," she said. "About ten thousand kilometers east."

Bucky grinned and slapped me on the shoulder. "You done got you one of them mail-order brides from Russia, ain't you, boy? Good for you, Chase. Good for you. Now come on with me. Bobby ain't never gonna believe you're here."

Bucky galloped down the hallway the way he always did, expecting us to keep up, but keeping up with Bucky was never easy. We wound our way through the maze of the stadium and ended up in the dugout where I saw Coach Bobby Woodley, the man who turned me from a decent high school catcher into a champion.

Coach Woodley lifted his head to see who'd wandered into his dugout and locked eyes with me. "Where the hell have you been, Chase?"

"Hello, Coach. It's been a long time."

Coach Woodley was the verbal opposite of Bucky Buchanan. He never said much, but what he did say was powerful. In an uncharacteristic show of affection, he hugged me as if I were his own son.

The embrace lasted a few seconds before he stepped back and saw Anya, who still appeared overwhelmed with the whole scene.

Unlike Bucky, he didn't ask, but I introduced her anyway.

"Coach Bobby Woodley, this is Ana Fulton," I said proudly.

Coach Woodley smiled at Anya. There was a sadness in his eyes that I had never seen in the years I'd played for him. His trademark smirk, quiet confidence, and game-day intensity I'd come to know and love were missing. Something was wrong.

"Are you okay, Coach?"

He cast his eyes down at his cleats and spit a long stream of tobacco juice onto the floor of the dugout. "It's good to see you, Chase. You two can sit down here with us and watch the game from the dugout if you want."

"Thank you, but we'll sit up there behind home plate. You know that's the only place where I understand what's going on out there on the field. Besides, I promised Ana I'd buy her a chili dog. If you don't have plans this evening, I'd like to talk with you after you show Bama how the Bulldogs play baseball."

He forced a smile. It hurt me to see him like that, and I had to know what was going on.

He said, "How 'bout we meet at Milly's when we wrap this up?" He turned and walked up the steps of the dugout and onto the field where the team was warming up.

Former catchers always like to watch games from behind the plate, so Anya and I hiked our way into the stands and found seats directly behind the plate, about six rows up. I noticed a sign at the top of the stairs that read, "Chase Fulton Section, 1996 College World Series MVP." I didn't know they named a section of the stadium after me. I was honored. And I was thankful Anya didn't notice the sign.

The field was perfectly manicured, the grass was a vivid green, and the bright white of the bases and home plate shone like beacons against the red-brown sand and clay of the field.

"These people are very strange," she said when we settled into our seats.

"They're just different," I said. "There's something going on with Coach Woodley, though. I wish I knew what's bothering him."

"Maybe we can help him," she said.

I considered that. "Maybe we can."

7
The Game

I held up two fingers and yelled to the vendor. "Two chili dogs and two beers!"

The vendor stood in the empty row behind us with his enormous tray suspended from the padded strap around his neck. He handed us the chili dogs then motioned for the drink guy to bring us our beers.

I watched Anya tear open the foil wrapper of the chili dog. The anticipation on her face was more exciting for me than watching the game. When she saw the contents in the wrapper, her excitement turned to trepidation. In spite of her obvious uncertainty, she lifted the dog to her nose and inhaled the aroma.

I wanted her experience to be unforgettable. She opened wide and took her first bite of a chili dog at her first baseball game. At the same instant she bit into the bun, the leadoff batter for Alabama fouled a high fastball off the top of his bat, sending the ball straight back into the net, twenty feet in front of us. Anya saw the ball coming at her and leapt backward as if she were about to be hit by a train. The chili dog and beer exploded into the air at the same time her scream left her throat. The ball stopped within milliseconds of hitting the net, but the dog and beer did not. It all came crashing down onto her brand-new clothes.

I bit the inside of my jaw, trying not to laugh. She was soaking wet and covered in chili and mustard. The chili dog was on the ground at her feet, one bite missing from the end.

I was terrified she was going to be furious, but with a protruding cheek full of chili dog, she burst into laughter. Relieved, I joined her in the absurdity of the situation.

I heard the telltale sound of an aluminum bat hitting a baseball exactly the way it was designed to do. A high fly ball trailed away toward the left field fence, and it climbed, ready to leave the stadium. The left fielder ran toward the fence with the speed of an Olympic sprinter, but there was no use. Everyone in the stadium knew the leadoff batter for Alabama had crushed a hanging curveball into the cheap seats.

Disappointed by the opening play, I turned to help Anya get cleaned up from her debacle, only to find her with my chili dog in her hands—at least two bites already missing. Not only had she swiped my dog, but my beer was also nestled on the seat between her legs.

Through chili-covered lips, she said, "You were right, Chase. Chili dog is wonderful."

All I could do was laugh. "Come on," I said. "Let's go get you some clean clothes. I can't be seen with a woman wearing chili and beer."

We headed for the vendors who were selling everything from Bulldogs toys to t-shirts. We opted for the t-shirt guy.

"We had a little accident with a chili dog and a foul ball," I said, pointing to Anya.

"I see that," said the vendor. He took a long look at me just as the ticket lady had done. "Dude! You're Chase Fulton." He took a look at my right hand.

"It's fine," I said. "Almost as good as new. But my baseball days are long behind me now."

"Dude, you're like a legend around here. Wait. Check this out!"

He sized up Anya and then slipped through a curtain in the back of his booth. In seconds, he came back with a red Bulldogs jersey. It had my old number twenty-one on the back and Fulton printed across the top.

He handed it to Anya. "I'm sure you've got a ton of these at home, but this one's on me. It's like, really cool to meet you, man."

Anya took the jersey, held it up in front of her, then handed it to me. She pulled off her ruined shirt and yanked the jersey from my hand. The vendor's eyes turned to saucers as Anya stood there in her bra and shorts. I pulled the vendor's cap down over his eyes and gave him a playful shove as Anya buttoned the jersey.

* * *

Most of the fans had left the stadium long before the end of the game, but we stayed and watched every pitch. Anya asked a lot of questions about the first baseball game she'd ever seen, and I answered them the best I could. She didn't seem to care that we'd lost; she was just excited to be doing something new.

In the car on the way to Milly's, she finally asked the question I'd been expecting all afternoon. "Why do all these people know you?"

Humility ran in my family. My mother and father spent their adult lives as terrifying deadly assassins, but from all outside appearances, they were simple, lowly missionaries caring for children throughout the Caribbean and South America. I hadn't learned what my parents truly were until four years after their death. That tradition of humility continued in me, and I never would've bragged about the caliber of ballplayer I'd once been.

"You know I played ball here in college. In my junior year, I was lucky to be on a team with some really good players. They were so good, in fact, we won the College World Series in ninety-six. I was seriously hurt in the last game of the series. I was the catcher, the guy who squats down behind home plate and catches the ball when the pitcher throws it. There was a close play at home, and the runner and I collided. I broke my right hand and wrist bad enough that I couldn't play ball anymore. But because I held on to the ball during the collision, the runner was out, and we won the game. I didn't really do anything special. The team won the game. I just did my job. But they named me the most valuable player of the game. It was a great honor, but I believe everyone else on the team deserved the award as much, if not more than me."

Her response surprised me. "I think this is very American thing to say."

"What does that mean?" I asked.

"In Russia, if man win award, he tells everybody how great he is, but he is average athlete. You were great athlete and won award, but you tell no one. I think that is American thing."

I shrugged and smiled at my Anya Ana Burinkova Fulton.

* * *

We pulled into the parking lot at Milly's, an old log cabin perched on the banks of one of the most beautiful creeks in Georgia. It was the kind of place only locals knew about and tourists could never find. There were always seven or eight lazy dogs wandering around the property or sleeping under the bushes out front.

Coach Woodley and his wife Laura pulled up beside us and stepped out of their car. Introductions were made, and Laura's hug appeared to freak Anya out a little. It was going to take some time to turn my Eastern Bloc beauty into a Southern belle.

Coach Woodley wasn't the only one out of sorts. Laura wasn't her usual cheerful self either. Something was amiss. I hoped they'd be willing to tell me what it was.

The dinner conversation was relatively light and full of lies for the first several minutes. I didn't like lying to my old coach, but when he asked what I'd been doing for the past two years, and how Ana and I met, I couldn't exactly say, "Well, Coach, I went to spy school and learned how to kill people, and then I met a Russian SVR officer who was also a trained assassin while I was chasing a Russian hit man all over the world."

My story came out a little more benign. I told him I'd been working overseas as a consultant for the government and had met

Ana on one of my trips. It wasn't entirely a lie, but it was far from the whole truth. By the look on her face, I could tell Laura wasn't buying my story.

She took a long swallow of water and asked Anya, "So, dear, what is it that you do?"

Oh, boy. This should be interesting.

"I also worked for government in Russia, but now I am learning all about Chase's life, and I'm eating things, but I cannot remember the names."

I hoped everyone's laughter might change the subject, but it only resulted in uncomfortable silence.

Our dinner arrived before the awkwardness became unbearable. Anya kept eyeing my shrimp and grits, so I offered her a bite. She eagerly accepted and declared them to be as good as the Jekyll Island Club.

Laura finally smiled her trademark Southern debutante smile. "Oh, Ana, so you've been to Jekyll Island. Isn't it just gorgeous out there?"

I sat back and watched the show. I should've known it would turn into more than I wanted to explain.

"It is paradise, and we are staying in honeymoon suite."

"Oh, Chase Fulton!" Laura squealed. "Congratulations! I'm so happy for you both."

I noticed Coach checking both of our left hands for wedding rings, but I didn't flinch. In a desperate attempt to change the subject, I asked, "How's Skipper? I didn't see her at the game today. I don't ever remember her missing a game."

Laura's face paled and she dropped her head. Coach Woodley put his hand on her back in an obvious effort to comfort her. When Laura raised her head, her eyes were filled with tears and she was biting her lip.

"You've got to tell him, Bobby," Laura said. "Skipper and Chase were like brother and sister when he was playing ball for you. You've just gotta tell him."

"Tell me what?" I insisted.

Coach nervously scanned the dozen people sitting nearby. "Let's go for a walk, Chase. I'd rather not talk in here."

I kissed Anya. "I'll be back in a few minutes. Are you okay here with Laura?"

With a faint nod, she gave her wordless answer. Coach Woodley and I stood and excused ourselves from the table. We walked in silence for a few hundred yards until we reached a small bench overlooking a bend in the creek. I wasn't going to push. I waited patiently for him to start talking.

"Chase, it's good to see you again. Everyone wondered what happened to you when you vanished. Most of us assumed you needed to get away from Georgia baseball, and you'd come back when you'd whipped those old demons."

I couldn't look into his eyes, but I said, "That's not exactly what happened, but it's a pretty good assumption, I guess. Now let's talk about what's going on with you and Laura. What's happened to Skipper?"

He cleared his throat and wiped a tear from the corner of his eye. "She's gone, Chase."

My heart sank and my stomach churned. "What?"

"Her senior year in high school she started running around with a bunch of kids who were no good for anybody. They were into drugs and alcohol and God knows what else." He paused to catch his breath.

I sat in terror of hearing what he would say next.

He gathered his composure. "She ran off with these pieces of shit, Chase. They went to Florida . . . down in the Keys, we think. But we can't be sure. We went to the police, but they wouldn't help."

"Why not?"

"They say because she's over eighteen, she can run off anywhere she wants with whoever she wants, and there ain't shit we can do about it. That's my little girl. Hell, you know her as well as anybody. She loved you like a brother, and I know you always thought of her as . . . well, forgive me, but I always believed that maybe you thought of her as the sister you wished was still alive."

My sister and parents had been murdered by militants in Panama almost a decade before, leaving me with no family at all. Coach Woodley, Laura, and Skipper had become the closest thing I had to take the place of my murdered family. Skipper was two years younger than my sister, but every time I'd looked at her, I saw my murdered sister's curly hair and bright, happy eyes. Skipper was the person who made me believe I could do anything. She made me believe I could keep living even though my family was gone forever.

I swallowed hard. "Have you thought about hiring someone to find her?"

"Yeah, we did that. We hired a big-time private investigation firm out of Atlanta. It cost me two hundred grand, and all they did was sell the story to the Atlanta Journal-Constitution. Big headlines, Chase. 'Georgia Baseball Head Coach's Daughter on Wild Ride,' or some bullshit like that. I tried hiring some guys out of Miami, but all I got from them was a drawerful of bills and a donkey cart full of excuses. I've been down there myself a dozen times, but I don't know how to find her. The truth is . . . I wouldn't know what to do if I did find her, short of killing every son-of-a-bitch I could get my hands on."

I stilled myself. "Coach, I wasn't entirely honest with you back at the restaurant. I'm not an overseas government consultant. I don't even know what that is. I do work for the government, though. I find people who don't want to be found, but it's not usually teenaged girls. I hunt for killers and hit men and that kind of scum. I'm good at what I do . . . but that's not all. Ana is Anya Burinkova, a former Russian intelligence officer who could track a butterfly in a hurricane." I put my hand on his shoulder. "Coach, we'll find your daughter, and we'll bring her back. You have my word." I looked him squarely in his sunken, desperate eyes. "And Coach, we'll drill holes through any son-of-a-bitch who gets in our way."

His shoulders dropped and he sniffled. "I can't pay you, Chase. I've already spent every dime we have and then some trying to find her."

"Don't worry about that. I don't need your money, and I wouldn't take it even if I did. Now let's get back and check on our girls."

We walked back to the restaurant to find Laura and Anya leaning against the back of our Porsche. Laura was crying, and Anya, in a rare display of compassion, was hugging her.

Laura pulled back and took Anya by the hands. "Thank you, Ana. Thank you so much." She fell into Coach Woodley's arms. "Oh, Bobby, you're never going to believe it. You're never going to believe who she and Chase really are. They're gonna find Skipper, Bobby. They're gonna find our baby girl, and they're gonna bring her home."

"I know, sugar. Chase told me everything. It's gonna be all right."

He reached out for my hand, and I took his. He pulled me in close. "When you find the bastards, if they've hurt my baby girl—"

"I know, Coach. Don't worry. We'll take care of everything. You get Laura home and worry about winning a few ball games, huh?"

We climbed into the Porsche. The hunt was on, but this time our prey wasn't some shadowy, mysterious hit man. We were out to find a bright-eyed, beautiful, nineteen-year-old girl, and we weren't doing it for money or because it was our duty. This time, for me, it was personal. And no one was going to stop us.

8
Lies

With Anya at the wheel and driving way too fast, I called the Jekyll Island Club on my new cell phone. It turned out to be much easier to use than the satellite phones that required clunky folding antennas and clear lines of sights to satellites to make the things work.

"Thank you for calling the Jekyll Island Club. This is Stephanie. How may I help you?"

It was nice to hear her familiar voice.

"Stephanie, this is Chase Fulton. Has our friend Clark Johnson checked out of one-oh-four yet?"

"Oh, hi, Mr. Fulton. Give me a second and I'll check."

I could hear her fingers clicking on the keyboard.

"Mr. Johnson is still here. Would you like for me to ring his room for you?"

"Yes," I almost yelled into the phone. "Thank you, Stephanie."

The phone rang three times before Clark picked it up. "Yeah?"

"Clark, Chase Fulton here. I'm glad I caught you. Listen, I need a ride to Key West, and you have a King Air. We'll be back on Jekyll Island in about four hours. Can you have the plane fueled and ready to go?"

The line was silent for several seconds, so I checked the screen of my phone to make sure we were still connected. I lifted the phone back to my ear.

"Uh, Chase," Clark said, "I can't just take the King Air to Key West anytime I want. It's not my plane. I'll have to get authorization."

I wasn't interested in playing ask-daddy-for-the-keys with him. "Here's your authorization, Clark. Either have the plane ready to go when we get there, or leave the keys with Stephanie at the front desk and we'll take the airplane without you. It's your choice, but if that plane isn't on Jekyll Island and full of gas when I get there, you can explain to a very important man that his daughter is dead because you weren't authorized to take Daddy's plane to Key West."

I wanted to slam the phone, but as I learned, a cell phone doesn't have a slam function. Pushing the little red button isn't remotely as satisfying.

Thanks to Anya's skills on wheels, we made the five-hour drive in just over three. When we arrived back on the island, I told her to drive by the airport before heading back to the club. I wanted to make sure Clark hadn't taken off in the King Air. Thankfully, he hadn't. It was still sitting on the ramp, and the fuel truck was pulling away when we drove by.

We whipped into the drive at the Jekyll Island Club and Anya parked with practiced precision, exactly where we'd picked it up the previous day.

Hustling through the lobby, I asked to see Stephanie, but the clerk on duty told me her shift had ended two hours before.

"How about Jack Ford?" I asked.

"Mr. Ford doesn't typically work on weekends. Can I help you with anything?"

I fumbled through my pockets and found the card Jack had given me, so I asked the clerk to call the number. She was hesitant, but finally relented and dialed.

As soon as I heard her speaking to Jack, I snatched the receiver from her hand and stuck it to my ear. "Jack, this is Chase Fulton. I'm leaving the Porsche keys with the desk clerk. We're flying back to Key West tonight, but I need to leave my boat with you until I can have someone pick it up. An emergency has come up and it's unavoidable. I'll be happy to pay for the use of your dock until I can have it moved in a few days."

There was no time to wait for his reply. I handed the receiver back to the clerk and thanked her. I tossed the Porsche keys onto the counter and headed off toward our room. While I'd been talking with Jack, Anya had hurried to our suite and packed everything. We headed for room one-oh-four where we found the door propped open and Clark sitting on the edge of the bed waiting for us.

He stood when we came through the door. "Let's go," he said, "but you're paying for the gas."

"Fair enough," I said.

* * *

The four-hundred-mile flight was uneventful and took less than two hours. Clark turned out to be a competent, if a little overly cautious, pilot.

On the ramp at Key West International Airport, I asked the lineman to top off the King Air with fuel and find a place to park it overnight. I slid my credit card across the counter to the young lady at the FBO and told her what I had asked the lineman to do. Pointing toward Clark, I said, "This is Clark. He's the pilot, but charge everything to my card and find him a place to stay for the night. He and the airplane have to be back in Virginia tomorrow."

I thanked Clark for the ride and turned to leave.

"Hey, wait a minute," he said. "Whatever you're doing down here, I can probably help."

I thought it was kind and ambitious of him to offer, but I refused. "I appreciate the offer, Clark, but this one's personal. It's not company business."

"Okay," he said, "but if you change your mind, I can be back down here in three hours."

* * *

Anya and I had changed clothes on the plane. She wore a new summer dress, and I wore a tropical print shirt.

Anya eyed me questioningly. "You look like tourist."

"That's the idea," I said.

We hailed a cab and climbed into the back seat.

"Hey, welcome to Bone Key, folks. Where we headed tonight?" the cabbie asked.

"We are looking for girl," said Anya.

The cabbie grinned. "Oh, so that's how you guys get down. Party on. It's cool. I know just the guy. He can get you any kind of girl you want . . . redhead, blonde, Brazilian, whatever. I mean, this guy's the real deal."

When Anya realized what the cabbie was saying, she blushed, and the angry Russian started to emerge. I put my hand on her leg to stop her from lashing out.

"Cool," I said. "We partied with a girl from somewhere up in Georgia once last time we were here. I think her name was Skippy or Skipper or something like that. She was tall and skinny, maybe six feet, long brown hair, Southern accent. It'd be hot to hook up with her again."

The cabbie squinted at me in the rearview mirror. "Hey, man, I don't know nothin' about that. I just know the guy. That's it, man. It ain't my gig, you know."

"I didn't mean to imply you had anything to do with it," I said. "I was just saying we liked the girl. So, where does this guy of yours hang out?"

The cabbie's voice was getting shaky. "Hey, man. He ain't my guy. I just know who he is. That's it. He's always at the Green Parrot. He goes by the name Micky. I don't know if that's his real name or what. Like I said, it ain't my gig, and he ain't my guy. Cool?"

We pulled up in front of the Green Parrot Bar at the corner of Whitehead and Southard, and I paid the cabbie with a fifty-dollar bill.

"Man, I ain't got change for this," he said.

"It's cool," I said. "Keep it. Thanks for the ride and the hookup with your man, Micky."

"He ain't my man. I done told you that. He ain't my man," he said as we walked away.

Anya was already getting looks from the drunken frat boys and middle-aged fat guys on the street. She laced her arm through mine so everyone would know she wasn't looking for a boy toy that night.

"Damn it," I said. "I should've gotten a picture of Skipper from Coach."

Before I could finish beating myself up for such a ridiculous mistake, Anya pulled a wallet-sized picture from her clutch. It was Skipper's senior picture.

"I asked Laura, and she gave to me."

What would I do without her?

I took the picture, slid it into my shirt pocket, and we pushed our way through the crowd and into the bar. It was loud and hot inside and took a great deal of effort to make it to the actual bar.

An overworked bartender came over to us. "What can I get you?"

"We're looking for Micky," I yelled over the noise.

The bartender reflexively eyed a man in a Panama hat and a linen shirt unbuttoned halfway down the front. He wore a gaudy golden eagle pendant on a thick chain around his neck.

"Sorry, man, I don't know no Micky. What can I get you to drink?"

"Maybe you didn't hear me right." I slid a hundred-dollar bill onto the bar. "I said . . . me and my friend Benjamin here are looking for Micky."

He peered at the hundred. "Oh, you said Micky. Sure, I know Micky. That's him in the hat at the end of the bar."

"I thought you might know who I was talking about. It wouldn't have hurt so bad if you'd answered my question the first time," I said.

"What wouldn't have hurt so bad?"

With my left arm, I trapped his hand over the hundred on the bar and held it firmly in place while I delivered a sharp blow to the back of his elbow with my right hand. I didn't hit him hard enough to break the elbow, but it was definitely hyperextended and would cause a lot of pain. He lashed out, swinging wildly with his remaining good arm. The punch came in slow motion, and I blocked it with my left forearm. When I was certain I'd stopped the punch, I shoved my hand behind his head and grasped the back of his neck. I pulled his head forward and down in one swift motion, driving his nose and chin into the top of the bar hard enough to leave him seeing stars. To his credit, he didn't go down, but with blood pouring from his nose, he staggered backward and into a wall of glasses.

I lifted my hundred from the bar and nudged Anya toward Micky, who had watched the whole episode. He started for the door, but Anya wasn't going to let him get away. She shoved her way through the crowd, crouching low as she set a course to intercept Micky before he could make it to the door. A bouncer, who had watched the scene unfold, stepped in front of Anya and grabbed her by the right shoulder. I cringed, thinking how dearly he was going to pay for that mistake.

Anya stood erect while extending her right arm up and behind the bouncer's shoulder. She stuck her left foot in front of his right shin and turned in a violent one-hundred-eighty-degree arc while capturing his arm with her right hand and driving him to the floor with her left. His forehead hit the floor first, and his lights went out. She stepped on the back of his hand and continued her rotation. I could almost hear the bones in his hand breaking.

The bouncer hadn't stopped us, but he had slowed us down enough for Micky to disappear. Anya scanned the room and then pointed toward the front door. I shoved my way to the door and out onto the street. She did the same and came out the other side onto Whitehead Street. I ran around the corner just in time to see her sprinting into the alley a few hundred feet down the block. I followed her and saw a pair of bright headlights coming toward us and picking up speed. The alley was just wide enough for the car, leaving Anya no place to escape being run over.

I saw her look quickly left then right as she realized her predicament. With nowhere else to go, she leapt straight up a millisecond before the front bumper of the car would've plowed her over. She tucked her arms in against her chest and rolled onto her side, landing on top of the car. With the headlights in my eyes, I could barely see what was happening, but it looked like the roof had caved in from the force of her impact. I lost sight of her as she rolled off the back of the car, but I was confident she'd survived, probably unscathed.

Running out of ideas and time, I pulled out my suppressed Walther and pointed it at the driver's side windshield. I stood defiantly in front of the car, but the driver kept accelerating. I lowered my pistol and put three rounds through the radiator and into the engine block. The next two rounds busted the headlights as the car coasted to a stop inches in front of me. My eyes adjusted to the darkness, and I saw why the roof seemed to collapse under Anya's weight—it was a ragtop Cadillac.

Anya was pulling her knife through the heavy fabric of the convertible top, opening an enormous hole in the roof. Micky leaned across the front seat in an obvious panic and reached for the glove compartment. I was sure he was going for a gun, but Anya was too quick. She slid through the hole she'd cut in the top of the car and landed on her feet behind Micky's seat. She grabbed the thick gold chain around his neck and pulled with all of her strength, burying the wings of the eagle pendant into his meaty throat. His hands flew to his neck then he grasped at Anya behind his head. She dodged his grasp while continuing to pull the chain like a garrote. His flailing persisted until his face turned blood red and his eyes bulged. His arms collapsed limply to his sides, and his tongue fell out over his bottom lip.

I squeezed alongside the Cadillac until I was standing beside the driver's door. Anya released the chain and pulled his head back over the seat to ensure his airway remained open. I pulled the laces out of his shoes and tied his hands through the steering wheel. His chest rose and fell, and then the coughing came. He sputtered, gagged, and gasped as he returned to the land of the living.

When he opened his eyes, I jammed the muzzle of my suppressor against his left cheekbone. Anya simultaneously placed the tip of her knife beneath his right ear and applied just enough pressure to make him feel the razor-sharp tip piercing his flesh.

"Welcome back," I said. "How are we supposed to have a conversation with you running away and passing out?"

"Who the fuck are you people?" he growled.

"We are nightmare," Anya said calmly.

He turned his head to the right to see her, but she stopped him by slicing off a half inch of earlobe from his head. He bellowed in pain as the blood streaked down his neck and through the hair of his exposed chest.

"What do you want from me?"

I pulled Skipper's picture from my shirt pocket and held it in front of his face. Anya pulled out a flashlight she'd lifted from the bouncer and shined the beam on the picture.

As soon as he started to speak, I stuck my muzzle into his mouth, past his teeth, and pressed it solidly against the roof of his mouth. Instinctively, Anya moved a few inches to the right to avoid the high velocity brain matter that could've been seconds away from spraying through the top of his head.

"Listen very closely," I said. "There's only one thing you can say that will keep you alive. You're going to tell me exactly where she is. If you don't know *who* she is, you are useless to me, and you die right here, right now. If you don't know *where* she is, you die right here, right now. If you tell me a lie, I will find you—and you know I can—and I will kill you wherever you are." I pulled the pistol from his mouth. "Now that we've established the ground rules, tell me where she is."

The beads of sweat on his forehead and the twitching of his eyes showed the torment of his decision.

Anya was a little impatient. "Let me kill him and play in his blood."

Panic filled his eyes. "Okay, okay. I've seen her around, but she don't work for me. She's a dancer at Three Sheets, a strip club over on Truman. Now call off your crazy bitch before she cuts my head off."

Anya grinned. "I will not kill you yet, but you are right. I am crazy bitch, and you will learn how crazy if you lied to us."

She tossed the bouncer's flashlight into the air, caught the small end in her palm, then clubbed Micky in the temple, causing him to slump forward over the steering wheel. Anya slithered into the front seat and opened the glove compartment. Inside she found a .38 revolver and a pint of Jim Beam.

Using her knife, she removed the revolver's spring that held the cylinder closed. She placed the revolver back in the glove compartment and poured the bourbon over the unconscious man.

We pushed Micky and his destroyed Cadillac down the alley and out of sight, and then we headed toward Duval Street.

9

Duval Street

Every night, the theme on Duval Street is Mardi Gras meets *Animal House*. From drag queens to the crazy cat man in Mallory Square, if it's debauchery you're looking for, you'll find it.

When we turned the corner from Angela onto Duval, we came face-to-face with Darth Vader on a unicycle playing a banjo.

Anya froze in disbelief and then exploded into laughter. "What is this place, Chase?"

"This, my dear, is Duval Street at its finest."

"It is carnival?" she asked.

"No, it's just Saturday night in Key West."

The banjo-playing, unicycle-riding Darth Vader was far from the craziest thing to see on Duval after the sun went down.

I hailed a bicycle cab and he pulled to the curb in front of us. Anya stared, perplexed by the strange, three-wheeled contraption with a bench seat only wide enough for two people. Reluctantly, she climbed aboard.

A fit young man was at the pedals. "Where to, guys?" he asked.

"Three Sheets on Truman."

He peeked over his shoulder at me. "All right, man. Right on."

He lifted his fist to offer me a fist bump, but Anya surprised him when she tapped his fist with hers, and said, "Right on."

"That'll be seven bucks if you're in a hurry, and it'll take about seven or eight minutes, but if you want the scenic route, it'll be twenty bucks for about a thirty-minute ride and I'll show you the sights."

"We're in a hurry," I said, "And it'll be an extra hundred for every minute you get us there under six."

He stood on the pedals and started pumping like his life depended on it. We rolled up in front of the Three Sheets strip club less than five minutes later with our pedaler sweating and panting like a dog. He yanked a squeeze bottle from a pouch beneath his seat and shot a long stream of water into his throat.

I checked my watch. "Well done, my man," I said as I handed him two hundred dollars.

"Cool, man. Thanks," he said breathlessly as he stuffed the bills into his shorts pocket. "I can pick you up later if you want."

"No thanks. We're meeting a friend here, so we'll catch a ride with her."

We walked through the front door and paid the cover charge. Anya got in free since it was ladies' night . . . whatever that meant. I had a feeling every night was ladies' night at Three Sheets. As we made our way through the second set of doors, it took a couple minutes for our eyes to adjust to the near darkness of the room in contrast with the bright stage lights where the girls were dancing, most of them devoid of clothing, and the others soon on their way to the same degree of undress.

We found an empty table in a corner where we could sit with our backs to the wall and watch not only the people coming and going through the front door, but where we could also see down the dimly lit hallway into what appeared to be back offices on one side, and the dancers' dressing room on the other.

We hadn't been at the table thirty seconds when a young, raven-haired waitress materialized. In an unmistakably Eastern European accent, she asked, "What you will have?"

"Jack and Coke," I said.

The waitress turned to Anya.

In her natural accent, Anya said, "For me, same."

"You are working?" the waitress said, implying Anya was a prostitute.

Anya laughed and grabbed my hand. "No, we are on honeymoon."

"Congratulation," she said, and turned away into the darkness of the dingy club.

"She is Kazakhstani, I think," Anya said.

"Do you speak Kazakh?" I asked.

She shook her head and tried to yell over the blaring music. "No, but she will speak Russian. All Kazakhs speak Russian. It is official language of Kazakhstan."

"I learn something new every day with you."

"Today, I learn from you about Duval Street."

Dr. Richter was right. She could teach me tradecraft, and I could teach her how to enjoy being alive.

"Do you think she'll talk to us?" I asked.

Anya peered at the bar. "No, she will not talk to us, but she will talk to me."

When the waitress returned, she placed my drink in front of me, then slowly slid Anya's across the small table to her.

Anya reached out, gently touching the back of the waitress's hand, and said, "*Spasibo, krasivaya.*"

The girl kissed Anya's cheek, leaving a lipstick smear, and said, "*Spasibo,*" before she walked away again.

"Yes, I think she is Kazakh, and I think she is not old enough to be working in this club."

"I don't know about the Kazakh part, but I agree with you about her age. Do you think you can get her to tell you about Skipper?"

"No," said Anya. "I do not think so. She is young and only waitress, not dancer. If she knows anything, she would be afraid to tell anyone, even a Russian like me."

"Maybe we can just wait and see if Skipper's here. It's Saturday night. Surely most of their girls will be working."

Anya frowned. "You are on honeymoon. You are not to be looking at dancing naked girls . . . only looking at me."

I thought she was kidding, but I wasn't certain. We nursed our drinks and watched a dozen girls come and go down the hallway. None of them were Skipper.

"I don't think she's here. I think we've seen all the dancers. We need to find someone who'll talk to us, one way or another. Do you have any ideas?"

Anya surveyed the room. "I think you are right. If I try to talk with Kazakh girl, she will tell bouncer, and we will have to fight again. I think I have idea, but I think you will not like."

"Let's hear it," I said. "I'm willing to try almost anything at this point."

"Okay. But do not interfere. It will not work if you interfere." Anya stood as if she were headed for the ladies' room, but she instead strode confidently down the hallway and into the dressing room.

I made sure no one suspicious followed her. Minutes later, the dressing room door opened, and Anya walked out wearing six-inch stiletto heels, lacy pink panties, and a pink feather boa draped around her neck. Without looking my way, she walked across the hall and pushed against one of the office doors. It was locked, and she moved farther down the hall to the next door. It opened as soon as she turned the knob, and she stepped inside the room.

I tried telling myself she was the deadliest person in the club— and probably on the whole island—and that I shouldn't be worried about her, but I couldn't quash the sickening feeling in the pit of my stomach. I needed to know what was happening on the other side of that door.

The Kazakh waitress returned to the table, but her playful smile was gone. "Where is wife?" she asked.

"She's gone to the bathroom," I said over the beat of the music.

"She is not in bathroom," she said. "Both of you are in very big trouble. You should leave now."

I grabbed her wrist. "What do you mean we're in trouble?"

She twisted her high heel into the top of my right foot and yanked her wrist from my grasp. She knew exactly how to break free of a man's grip. With a stern look similar to Anya's, she scowled at me and walked away.

I tried not to overreact. I drew in a deep breath and surveyed the room. I'd counted five bouncers, and I was sure they hadn't seen the waitress try to warn me. I knew they hadn't seen me grab her wrist because if they had, they'd have been on me instantly.

I felt for my pistol, making sure it was still tucked beneath my shirt, then I set off toward the offices. I made it about five steps when the beefy hand of one of the bouncers landed on my shoulder.

"Hey, buddy, where do you think you're going? No one's allowed back here except the ladies."

I turned around to size him up, and in my best drunken voice, I said, "Hey, I'm sorry, man. I was looking for the . . ." I bent over as if I were going to hurl on the bouncer's feet.

He jumped backward, giving me the opportunity I needed. I stood up and kicked him in the crotch. After he collapsed, I pounded a fist sharply into the side of his neck, leaving him soundly unconscious.

I reached for the first door Anya had tried a few minutes before, but it was still locked. I stepped to the opposite side of the hall and delivered a kick beneath the knob. The door swung open, sending splinters of the jamb into the air. I drew my pistol and cleared the room. It was empty except for a dingy twin bed and a couple chairs. I grabbed the bouncer's collar and pulled his limp body into the room. Then, from where I stood outside the room, and while still holding his collar, I pulled him backward and let his weight fall against the door, holding it closed against the busted jamb.

The next room to the right was the one Anya had disappeared into. I pressed my ear against the door, listening for voices from inside, but the music was too loud. With my pistol drawn, I tried to twist the knob. It didn't turn. Scenarios of why the door would've been locked behind her ran through my head, and I didn't like any of them.

A small sliver of light shone from beneath the door, so I watched for shadows or any sign of movement before I delivered another powerful kick, hoping to breach the door as easily as the previous one. My kick slammed the door open, and I powered through with my pistol leading the way. I caught a glimpse of Anya tied to a straight wooden chair with a gag in her mouth and blood dripping down her face. Two goons were standing in front of her. I couldn't imagine what series of events led to Anya being tied to a chair, but my senses came alive knowing we weren't dealing with small-time thugs. It would've taken someone with remarkable skill to put Anya in that chair.

The instant I realized I hadn't adequately scanned the room for threats, I felt the thud of a wooden club against the base of my skull.

* * *

When I came to, I was shirtless, tied to a chair, and my head felt like it'd been crushed in a vice. I wasn't sure what we'd gotten ourselves into, but it wasn't playing out the way I'd hoped. Thankfully, Anya was still there and conscious. The look on her face told me that if she survived, she would kill everyone in that room. A pissed off Russian intelligence officer is like a cornered cobra—you may kill her before it's over, but you won't evade her bite, and you'll never survive her venom.

Whoever our captors were, they'd gotten the drop on both of us. Based on that fact, they deserved some measure of respect for their aggression and violence of action.

"Oh, look," came an echoing voice from behind my head. "The big man with the pistol and silencer is awake."

The voice was familiar, but my head was ringing, and I couldn't put the voice with a face.

"How does it feel, pretty boy? How does it feel to be the one tied up and bleeding? Did you really think you and your little slut over there could get away with shooting up my car and leaving me in that alley?"

Micky. Why did I let him live?

"You should've killed me when you had the chance," he snarled.

I caught a glimpse of brass knuckles as his fist collided with my cheekbone. It was a good punch, but I didn't go out. I swallowed a mouthful of blood and tried not to show my agony. Through my blurred vision, I could see he was holding an object in front of my face. I blinked, trying to clear my sight, but it wasn't happening. I closed my left eye, and the whole room dissolved into a pink fog. When I opened my left and closed my right eye, I could almost see clearly.

Micky was holding Skipper's picture. "Who sent you to look for this girl?"

I didn't answer. He hit me again, but this time I rolled with the punch and took it as a glancing blow that did little additional damage. He held up the picture again and slapped it against my face several times. Each time, the picture came away with more smeared blood. With that much blood loss, I didn't know how much longer I'd remain conscious. I needed a plan. I turned to Anya again, and saw she was blinking in a deliberate pattern.

Long-long-short, short-short-long, long-short.

I turned back to Micky, and when I saw his right hand, I realized what Anya had been trying to tell me. She'd been blinking the word *gun* in Morse code. Brilliant.

Micky was holding his Saturday night special .38 revolver. He forcefully struck my nose, sending my head back and my mouth open. He forced the short barrel of his revolver into my mouth just as I had done to him two hours earlier. I tried to remain calm, but staying calm with a pistol barrel in my mouth wasn't easy.

Anya was not calm. She started yelling through the gag and flailing around to the limits of her restraints. She jerked and twisted so violently she managed to work the gag from her mouth. "Please do not kill him! I am having baby!"

She's pregnant? Holy shit!

Micky grinned. "Oh, really?" Seizing the opportunity, he stepped back, pulled his gun from my mouth, and slowly approached Anya. He knelt at her feet and snapped his fingers at me several times. "Look at me, boy! Watch me put a bullet in your pretty little girl's gut."

"You won't do it," I said.

"What's that? You think I won't do it?"

"You don't have the balls to do it," I said. "You know I'll rip your head off if you hurt her."

He cackled. "You're in no position to be making threats, little boy. Tell me who sent you to find that girl, or your little Russian girlfriend here gets gut shot, and you get to watch her and your baby bleed out."

"You won't do it. You're too weak. You'll slap us around, but you don't have the stones to pull the trigger."

His face burned blood red, and I watched the muscles in his jaws strain. I was getting under his skin. The plan was working.

"Shut up, or I'll do it!" he yelled. "I'll pull the fucking trigger if you don't tell me who sent you right now. I'll do it. I'll do it right fucking now!"

"You won't!" I was trying to push him over the edge.

The muscles in his jaw twitched, and he squeezed the trigger. I watched the hammer of the revolver rise until it reached its zenith at the end of the trigger pull. Anya squeezed her eyes shut and turned her head away as the hammer started to fall. The explosion came in a deafening crack as the cylinder of the revolver fell open a fraction of an inch. Anya's spring trick worked. The explosion blew the revolver apart in Micky's hand and expelled super-heated gas and flames up his arm and into his face.

Before the echo of the explosion ended, Anya lunged forward and twisted to crush her wooden chair into Micky's recoiling body. The collision demolished the chair and left Anya with two chair legs tied to her ankles and a broken chair leg in her right hand.

Micky stumbled backward, grabbing his face and screaming, while the two other men reached for their pistols. Anya kicked Micky in the center of his chest, sending him colliding into one man, knocking the gun from his hand, and sending them both tumbling to the floor.

The second man leveled his pistol at her the same instant the broken chair leg left her hand. The spear-like point of the leg struck the would-be gunman at the inside bend of his elbow, burying itself into the joint, and sending the gun crashing to the floor at his feet. He grabbed the wood with his left hand and yanked it out of his gun arm. Blood poured from the wound, and the man dived for his pistol as it slid across the floor.

As soon as the man's hand reached his gun, Anya discovered her favorite knife, still on the desk, and wrapped in the feather boa she wore into the room. She grabbed the knife and planted her right foot on the man's hand as he gripped the gun. She spun around, tearing the flesh from his hand, and knelt on his shoulder as blood gushed from his arm.

The first man who had tumbled to the ground with Micky was scrambling to pick up the pistol he'd lost during the collision of bodies. Micky was still screaming, adding confusion to the already grisly and chaotic scene. Anya stood up and stepped toward the second gunman as he brought his pistol to bear on her chest. She positioned the knife in her hand in a perfect throwing grasp, but it was too late.

Two rapid pistol shots split the air and drowned out Micky's screams. Terror overtook me as I waited to see the exit wounds in Anya's naked back and watch her fall to the floor. To my surprise, the exit wounds didn't appear, but the gunman was blown backward as a spray of blood covered the wall behind him.

Not understanding what I was seeing, and trying to make sense of the last few seconds, I blinked repeatedly in a desperate attempt to clear my vision. Smoke streamed from the barrel of a Colt Government .45 in the hands of our pilot, Clark Johnson, who was standing in the doorway of the room.

Anya surveyed the scene and cut me free. She pulled the gag from around her neck and shoved it in Micky's mouth. "Stop screaming like little girl," she told him.

She cut the remaining ropes from her ankles and ran back across the hall to get her dress and purse. I collected my gun from the corner of the room and Skipper's bloody picture from the floor.

We made our escape through the back door, dragging the whimpering Micky behind us. We piled into Clark's rental car, and Anya sat in the back seat with Micky, already interrogating him again.

10
Drownproofing

"How bad are you hurt?" asked Clark as we tore out of the parking lot and headed east on Truman Avenue.

"Slow down," I said. "We don't want to get stopped by the cops and have to explain why two bloody assassins and a blown-up pimp are hauling ass down Truman in a rented whatever this is."

Anya said, "I am not hurt, but I think Chase has maybe broken bones in face. Micky is not hurt, but soon will be."

Micky wouldn't survive the night if he didn't start talking soon. Anya would drag the information she wanted out of him and then do what she did best.

"Where are we going?" I asked as we turned left onto White Street.

Clark didn't answer. He fumbled in his pocket for his cell phone and punched in a number. "Billy, Clark Johnson. Can you get me in the gate? I've got one hostile and two friendlies in a blue rented Town Car. I'm on White Street, ETA two minutes. If you've got a doctor, we sure could use him. And a couple of guys to help the hostile answer some questions would be nice, too." He hung up and tossed the phone onto the seat beside him.

Anya was still questioning Micky and breaking his fingers one by one each time he chose not to answer her.

"What was that call about?" I asked Clark as I divided my attention between him and the back seat.

"I've got some friends on the navy base. They're going to help us out a little."

We pulled up to the gate at the Naval Air Station Key West Trumbo Point Annex to find two navy shore patrol vehicles blocking the intersecting road with their blue lights flashing. Clark didn't slow down as he roared past the gate guard who was waving his flashlight and signaling us in. He flawlessly navigated the narrow streets of the navy base, and we were soon crossing over the bridge to Fleming Key.

I'd never been on the base, so I didn't know where we were heading or who'd be at the end of the road, but Clark had saved our butts back at the strip club, so I thought I should probably trust him, at least for a few more minutes.

We accelerated, heading northwest on a desolate road that seemed to be headed for nowhere, but we soon approached a fenced compound with warning signs everywhere and well-armed guards at the access gate. One of the guards saw us coming and pushed the gate open far enough for our car to narrowly fit through. We slid to a stop outside an innocuous looking building as three men poured out of a dark doorway and approached our car. The men were wearing combat boots, tight khaki shorts, and black t-shirts that showed each of their powerful physiques. These were not common navy sailors, but they did appear to be on our side.

One of the men jerked open the rear door of our car, grabbed Micky by one foot, and yanked him out onto the gravel-covered parking lot. Micky kicked and tried fighting off the man, but it was no use. The man skillfully dodged each of Micky's kicks, then rolled him over until he was facedown on the gravel, and planted a heavy combat boot at the base of his skull.

"Now you calm down while we figure out what's going on here, okay?" the man said.

Micky squirmed and tried to cuss while his face was grinding into the gravel, so the man pressed a little harder with his boot and slid Micky's face about a foot across the rocks. That shut him up.

We got out of the car and Clark approached the man with his foot on Micky's neck. "How've you been, Billy?"

"Well if it ain't Baby Face Johnson. You always did know how to make an entrance," the man said, sticking out his hand.

He and Clark did some kind of secret handshake that looked more like a thumb war.

Clark turned toward Anya and me. "Guys, meet Sergeant First Class Billy Porter. Billy, meet Chase and Ana Fulton. We sort of work together."

Billy nodded at us. "It's Master Sergeant Porter now. The army finally got around to remembering they owed me a stripe. Welcome to the Special Forces Under Water Operations School. It's nice to meet you folks. Why don't we get your guest inside and see if we can't get him to tell us whatever it is you want to know?"

The two other Special Forces divers yanked Micky to his feet and frog-marched him into the building. The facility was spotless and smelled of swimming pool chlorine.

Porter said, "It looks like you two got roughed up a little. We're looking for a real doctor, but in the meantime, we've got a navy medical corpsman on the way. To tell you the truth, I'd rather have the corpsman put me back together than any navy doc. They're either waking him up or sobering him up. Either way, he'll be here in a few minutes."

Micky had become quiet and was beginning to tremble. I'd say he had every right to be afraid. We kept moving deeper into the building until we came to an enormous indoor swimming pool with dive gear stowed all around it. The men dropped Micky to the concrete deck beside the pool and awaited further instructions.

Porter asked Clark, "So, what is it you want this piece of shit to tell you?"

Clark pointed at me. "This ain't my gig. I'm just the driver and hired gun. This is their show."

I pulled Skipper's bloody picture from my shirt pocket and handed it to Porter. He wiped off most of the blood and stared at the picture.

"We're looking for that girl. She's my little sister, and he knows where she is."

Porter bent down, grabbed a handful of Micky's hair, and lifted his head off the concrete deck. He held the picture in front of Micky's face. "Are you going to tell me where I can find this girl?"

Micky turned his head and defiantly spat bloody saliva in Porter's face. Porter calmly wiped the blood and spit and looked back at me. "He said he's not going to tell us, so let's get him cleaned up and send him home." He paused. "On second thought, maybe he wants to tell us but needs a little confidence builder first. Let's drownproof him, boys."

Drownproofing is a military training technique that involves tying a diver's ankles together and his hands behind his back, and then tossing him in a pool where he must slowly exhale and sink to the bottom. The diver then kicks off the bottom, pushing himself to the surface where he can briefly get his mouth and nose above water and take a breath before starting the process over again. With practice, this can be effectively done until Kingdom come. It builds remarkable water confidence and helps the diver learn to stay calm in stressful situations. Something told me Micky wasn't going to do well at the exercise.

The two other men tied Micky's feet and hands and tossed him into the pool. He flailed about like a panicked, wounded fish. Finally, exhaustion overtook panic and he sank. Porter checked his watch and let a minute pass. "Okay, go get him," he said.

The two divers dived headfirst into the water, promptly came up with Micky between them, and they deposited him on the deck.

Porter knelt beside him and again held Skipper's picture for him to see. "Now that you've had a chance to think about it, tell me where this girl is. Her folks miss her, and I'm an old softy when it comes to family."

Micky was still spitting pool water from his lungs and trying to catch his breath. Through gasps and gags, he said, "Fuck you. You're going to kill me anyway, so you can shove that picture up your—"

Porter didn't let him finish. He jammed the toe of his boot in Micky's mouth, breaking at least two teeth. "I think you were about to say something nasty, and there's a lady present. I can't let you talk nasty in front of a lady. That'd be plain rude, and we don't take kindly to rudeness around here."

Micky spat out several pieces of bloody, broken teeth.

Porter turned to his men. "Let's give this gentleman a lesson in manners and a good core workout, shall we?"

The two men grabbed Micky by the shoulders and dragged him forward until the upper half of his body was hanging over the edge of the pool deck. Each man then placed a knee under Micky's butt to keep him from falling into the pool. The exercise was designed to make a man hold his upper body erect to keep his head out of the pool, building a strong core.

I followed Porter's gaze through the glass door to see a man in his late twenties jogging down the hallway toward the pool. He had a black medical bag hanging over his shoulder.

"Here's our corpsman," Porter said. "He'll get the two of you fixed up, and then he'll stick around just in case . . . well, you never know what accidents your friend here might have in the next couple of hours."

We left the pool deck and met the corpsman in the hallway.

"I'm Chase, and this is Ana. We stumbled into a little trouble tonight."

"Nice to meet you both. I'm Doc. Let's step into the office over here and I'll take a look at the two of you. Then we'll decide if you need a real doctor. Sit down, please, sir."

I pointed at Anya. "Look at her first. I'm okay for now."

The corpsman looked at Anya, but she shook her head and pointed back at me. "No, him first. I am fine."

The corpsman was smart enough to listen to her instead of me, so he went to work poking around on my face. "Brass knuckles?"

"Yeah. How'd you know?"

He huffed. "I've been a navy corpsman for sixteen years, assigned to a SEAL team for five of those, and now I'm attached to these

Green Berets. Folks like SEALs and Green Berets tend to get in more fights than the average grunt, so I've seen about everything that can happen to a man in a fight."

I winced as he pressed his fingertips against my cheekbone. He turned to his bag and pulled out a portable ultrasound machine and fired it up. He pressed the wand against my face and stared intently at the small screen.

"I don't think it's broken," he said, "but you'll have a nasty shiner, and you'll need a few stitches to close these cuts. Do you want me to do it, or would you prefer a real doctor?"

"I hate doctors," I said coldly.

Before I knew it, he was injecting me with a local anesthetic and stitching my face. Sitting silently wasn't easy. The anesthetic wasn't doing its job.

When he finished sewing, he said, "Now stand up and let's see about those ribs."

"My ribs are fine," I said. "They liked hitting me in the face, but they stayed away from my ribs. I have no idea why."

The corpsman lifted my shirt. "Well, your ribs are already bruising, so something happened to them." He ran his hand down my left side, and I drew back when he touched the last two ribs.

"I don't remember them hitting me in the ribs."

"No," he said, "it doesn't look like you've been hit down here. This is from something else. Were you tied up?"

"Yeah, they tied us to chairs."

"Ah! That's it. You broke this bottom rib while you were strug-gling against the restraints. All we can do is tape them up and give you some pain meds, but it's going to hurt for a while."

Great. I got my ass kicked and did most of the damage to myself. Just my luck.

"Thanks, but I'll tough it out. I appreciate you sewing me up, Doc."

He chuckled as if he knew something I didn't. He changed his gloves and knelt in front of Anya. "Hey. My name's Jimmy, but everybody calls me Doc. Here's a bottle of pain pills for Mr. Tough Guy over there when he starts crying like a little girl tomorrow."

Anya took the bottle from his gloved hand. "I am Anya . . . I mean Ana, and I am not hurt."

"You may be more stubborn than him. How about I take a look just to make sure? I don't want Porter trying to drown me because I didn't check you out."

Anya relented and let him examine her face. He cleaned a few scrapes, but she wasn't cut bad enough to require any stitches. Her hands were another story altogether.

When Doc saw her bloody knuckles, he made a guttural sound. "What did they do to your hands?"

"They did nothing to my hands. Is . . . ah, *nastupatel'nyye rany.*"

"Offensive wounds?" said Doc.

"Yes," Anya said. "You speak Russian?"

"A little," he said, humbly.

He cleaned her hands and continued the exam but didn't say another word in English. His Russian was far better than mine. Seeing that she was in capable hands, I left the two of them alone to speak their rapid-fire Russian.

Porter's men were pulling Micky out of the pool again. They threw him to the pool deck and he coughed up more water and blood for several minutes.

I lay down beside him. "You don't look like you're enjoying this, Micky, but we certainly are. In fact, I'm pretty sure we could do this all night. I think it's time for you to tell me everything you know about the girl and exactly where I can find her. After that, we'll stop, and you can go home."

Micky cried. Sooner or later, all detainees cry. It's the Holy Grail of interrogation. Once they start, they're minutes away from spilling their guts.

Through coughing, gagging, and spitting, Micky said, "If I tell you, they'll kill me."

Sometimes during an interrogation, it's best to remain silent and let the detainee talk himself into confessing. I stared into his eyes. I didn't speak, and I didn't blink. He was imploding—as they all do sooner or later. His mind and body had reached their limits.

"Okay, Micky. Tell me about these people you're afraid of. Who are they?"

He shook his head. To help me push his talk button, Porter's men grabbed Micky by the feet and dragged him back toward the pool. It worked.

"Okay! Okay! It's the Russians. They're Russian mafia, and they'll fucking kill me."

Porter's men looked at me for direction. I held up one finger, signaling them to stop.

I leaned down to within a few inches of Micky's face. "So, it's the Russians you're afraid of. That makes a lot of sense, actually. Wait right here. Don't go anywhere. I have someone you might like to meet."

Clark was standing with Porter as I walked past and whispered, "Blindfold him and hang him upside down from whatever you can find. I'll be right back."

I left the pool deck and found Doc finishing Anya's exam.

"Doc, come with me," I said. "I'll explain later, but right now, I need your voice. Grab somebody's cell phone and yell into it in your angriest Russian. It doesn't matter what you say. Just sound pissed off. You're going to see a very unhappy guy in there blindfolded and hanging upside down. When I give you the signal, tell that man that we're holding your father hostage, and that we're going to kill the old man if he doesn't tell us what we want to know. I need you to do it in English with a nasty Russian accent."

Doc agreed. His time spent with SEALS and Special Forces had evidently made it impossible for him to be shocked by any crazy plan.

"That's not all," I said. "After you tell him, a couple of pretty big guys are going to drag you out of there. Are you okay with that?"

"Sounds like fun," he said. "Let's do this."

We went through the door and onto the pool deck with Doc yelling into his phone. Micky was hanging from a rack with his head covered by a black cloth bag. He was squirming and begging for us to get him down. When he heard Doc yelling in Russian, he became silent. I pointed to Doc and then at Micky, and the gambit was on.

I grabbed Porter. "As soon as I tell you, I want you to grab Doc and drag him out of here like you're ready to kill him. He's in on the game."

Porter nodded. I was really beginning to like those Special Forces guys.

Doc grabbed Micky and yanked the bag from his face. I didn't want him to take the bag off, but if Micky was scared and disoriented enough, my plan might still work. Doc put on an Oscar-worthy performance.

He yelled, "Tell these people whatever the fuck they want to know. If you do not, they will kill father, and if you let that happen, I swear you will follow him into grave."

Micky's eyes went wide, and panic overtook his face. Porter bolted into action and yanked Doc off his feet, dragging him violently out the door.

I reached above Micky's feet, cut the rope, and he fell to the deck like a sack of lead.

"So, now you tell me where the girl is, and I'll make sure the Russians don't touch you. If you don't want to tell me, the old man gets it, and I'll deliver you right to their door where the Russians can have a field day with you. What's it going to be?"

"Yes! Yes! I'll tell you. Just don't kill the old man. The girl's in Miami. We sold her to a porn producer named Giovani. I swear that's all I know. Please let the old man go. They'll cut me to pieces if you kill him on my account."

I yelled for Porter to bring Doc back in. When they returned, Micky's face showed the realization that he'd been played.

"What old man?" I asked. I pointed to the corpsman. "This is Doc. He's here to patch you up and make sure you're okay."

I grabbed Micky's hand and gave it a nasty yank, pulling him to his feet. The three broken fingers from his back seat interrogation with Anya were already swollen to at least double their original size.

I marched him outside and said, "I seem to remember making you a promise. Do you remember that promise?"

"Yeah," he said, wiping the blood and sweat from his face. "You promised you'd keep me safe from the Russians if I told you where the girl was."

"No, not that promise," I said. "That promise was a lie. I don't even know the Russians. I'm talking about the promise I made you in the front seat of your Cadillac. I remember promising you I'd come back and kill you if you lied to me about where the girl was. You told me she was at Three Sheets, and that was a lie. Now, Micky, I'm a man of my word. This is for Bobby and Laura Woodley, you piece of shit."

I put two pistol rounds into his forehead and watched him wilt to the ground where a pool of blood formed around his tortured, lifeless body.

11
Brothers-in-Arms

"Chase, you and Ana take the car to the Sheraton. I'll take care of this mess and meet you back at the hotel in a couple hours. Your bags from the plane are in the trunk." Clark handed me his room key and patted my shoulder.

I didn't know that he, Anya, and Porter were standing behind me when I'd pulled the trigger on Micky seconds earlier.

I took his key and walked silently toward the car with Anya at my side. We drove to the hotel without saying a word. After a shower and a fresh change of clothes, I paid for a room two doors down from Clark and left him a note with our room number.

Anya and I sat on the edge of the bed staring out the window across Smathers Beach toward Havana. She placed her hand on my leg and laid her head on my shoulder.

"I didn't have to kill him," I whispered.

As if she didn't hear me, she said, "How did Clark know where to find us?"

"I don't know. But I'm glad he showed up."

She hugged me in silent support of the battle raging inside me. I winced and let out a childish whimper when she squeezed my ribs. I was hurting more than I'd realized in both my body and my mind.

A rap on our door jolted us, and Anya pulled her pistol from the nightstand.

"Relax," I said. "It's probably Clark."

Telling her to relax was like telling the wind not to blow. Through the peephole I saw Clark standing in the hallway. I opened the door and motioned him inside.

"Are you guys okay?" he asked.

"We're fine," I said. "How about you?"

"I'm good. So, are you going to tell me what tonight was all about?"

Anya forced her lips into a thin horizontal line and kept quiet.

I poured each of us a drink from the mini bar. "First," I said, "we need to know how you found us tonight."

He'd either practiced his answer or he was being honest when he confidently said, "Believe it or not, it was dumb luck. I was closing up the plane and noticed your bags still in the back, so I grabbed them and set out, hoping to find you on Duval Street. I'd given up and decided to head back to the hotel when I saw one of those bicycle cab guys pedaling like a maniac with the two of you in the back. By the time I made it around the block and tried to catch up to you on Truman, the cab was empty and headed back toward Duval. I chased him down and bribed him to tell me where he'd dropped you. When he told me, I knew something was up, so I pulled into the parking lot and checked out the exits from that, uh . . . place."

Anya set his mind at ease. "It was strip club."

"Yes, it was. Thank you, Ana. Is it Ana or Anya?"

I started to answer, but she beat me to it.

"I was Anya, but now Ana."

She had a beautiful way of simplifying things without over explaining.

"Okay, then," he said. "I scoped out the exits from the strip club, and I heard an explosion that sounded almost like a gunshot, but not exactly. That's when I converted one of the exits into an entrance and heard the commotion coming from the room where you were. I burst in and decided it was a pretty good time to start shooting. I'm glad you're all right, but I've got a lot of questions."

I considered his story and wanted to believe him, but I was still a little skeptical. "Okay, Clark," I said. "Since you saved our lives, I guess we at least owe you the truth."

"My old baseball coach at Georgia has a daughter who's a few years younger than me, but she was more like a little sister when I was playing ball up there. She got mixed up with the wrong crowd and ended up in some serious trouble down here in the Keys. My old coach and his wife are like family, so when I heard their story, I had to get involved."

Anya interjected, "*We*, Chase. Not only you."

"Yes. *We* had to get involved. I promised them we'd find her and bring her home. When we left you at the airport, we got lucky with a cabbie who pointed us toward Micky, the guy from tonight . . . the one I shot." I paused, trying to digest the words. Thinking about what I'd done was bad enough, but saying it out loud plunged daggers into my gut.

I finished my drink and continued the story. "Anyway, the guy Micky turned out to be some kind of pimp, and after some persuasion from us, he sent us to the strip club and told us Skipper was working there as a dancer. It didn't take long for us to realize we'd been set up. Fortunately, Anya—I mean, Ana—had jimmied Micky's gun. It blew up in his face when he pulled the trigger, and that gave her an opportunity to fight her way out of the chair she'd been tied to. That's when you showed up and killed the guy before he could kill us. We owe you one, Clark."

He shook his head. "That's quite a story."

"Yeah, but your involvement makes the story even more unbelievable. What's your connection with the Special Forces guys at the navy base?"

"Let's have another drink," he said. "We're probably going to need it."

I poured another round and noticed that Anya's glass was untouched, and she was still holding her pistol loosely in her right hand against her thigh.

She's not drinking. Is she really pregnant?

Clark said, "So, unlike you, I didn't go to college and play ball. I went to the army right out of high school. I was pretty good at being a soldier, so Ranger school and then Special Forces were the next logical steps for me. Finally, I wound up down here teaching at the Special Forces Under Water Operations School. That's where we were tonight. I made a lot of great friends and got to see a lot of places most people have never heard of. I thought it might be cool to try out for Delta Force, so I trained up and finally got picked for Delta selection in Virginia. It was the most grueling thing I'd ever done. They made us do some of the craziest stuff you could dream up, but the most bizarre thing about it all was this psychologist. They had this weird little guy there who dressed like a royal jackass and always smelled like French fries. He snatched me and another SF guy from the selection and put us to work for the same people you work for."

I was amazed by his story and knew exactly who the French fry guy was. It had to be the psychologist I called Fred from my days at The Ranch. His assessment of Fred was dead on. The story sounded plausible, but he looked way too young to have done everything he described.

"How old are you?" I asked.

He chuckled. "I get that a lot. You probably heard Porter call me Baby Face tonight. That's a moniker I picked up back in Ranger battalion, and it stuck. I'm thirty-four, but I've always looked younger. It's a curse, but I still do pretty well with the college girls."

I heard Anya moving behind me, and I turned to see what she was doing. She had slipped her pistol back into its holster and placed it on the nightstand. She was buying his story.

Clark smiled at her. "I wondered if you were ever going to put that thing away."

Instead of responding to Clark, she asked me, "Now we go to Miami and find Giovani, yes?"

Anya didn't yet understand how our little organization worked. I gave her a glimpse by laying it out for Clark.

"This isn't your fight, Clark. This isn't a company gig. We're doing this one freelance and for free. Nobody's getting paid. It's a favor for people I consider to be my family. I'd never ask you to get involved in this any deeper than you already have. It would probably be best if you walked away before you get any of this on you."

He finished his glass of whiskey. "So, this is a family thing for you, right?"

"Yeah," I said. "That's exactly what it is."

"If that's the case, understand that you're my family now. You and I are soldiers in the same army. We're brothers-in-arms. And even though I can't figure out how Ms. Ana fits into all of this, apparently, she's one of us, too. You saw tonight how SF soldiers stick together. Porter and his guys never once questioned what we were doing or why we were doing it. I needed their help, and they helped. It's that simple. That's what you get from me, Chase. If you need or want my help, you've got it. If you want me to drop you off in Miami and disappear, that's up to you, but I'm not walking out on you now. Here's my skillset: I can fight, kick in doors, shoot, fly, and dive. I can be a diminutive courier delivering packages to Jekyll Island, or I can kick down a door and start spraying bullets. I think I've demonstrated both of those recently. If you need any of that done, I'm your guy. If not, I can probably find somebody to do pretty much anything you need."

Anya surprised both of us by quoting part of the U.S. Army Ranger Creed . . . almost verbatim. "I will never leave fallen comrade to fall into hands of enemy, and under no circumstances will I ever embarrass my country."

"Exactly," said Clark.

I appreciated his willingness to crawl around in the trenches with me. "Have you got any friends in Miami who might know this Giovani character?" I asked.

"I know a guy who works Dade County vice, but I'll bet that pretty little Russian girl behind you could ask around and find Giovani before my vice cop can."

"I have skillset, too," Anya said.

Clark stood and placed his empty glass on the dresser. "I'm sure you do. I guess I'd better go sleep off this whiskey. It sounds like we'll be flying to Miami in the morning to find your little sister."

He pulled me into a hug I hadn't expected. "You've had a tough night, man. Try to get some sleep."

I grimaced and let out that little girl sound again.

Clark laughed and patted my ribs. "Rub a little dirt on it and embrace the suck, my friend. Goodnight."

I locked the door behind him and asked Anya, "What do you think? Should we keep him?"

"We should. And you should take medicine for pain and sleep."

I swallowed the two pain pills she placed in my hand, then we turned out the lights and crawled into bed. I was careful to avoid lying on my broken ribs, but they still hurt like I'd wrestled a bear. I found a position that didn't leaving me gasping in pain, and Anya placed her hand on my ribs.

How could a woman who was such a warrior be so gentle? The dichotomy of Anya Burinkova was almost beyond comprehension.

I brushed a few strands of hair from her forehead and found myself wanting to know everything that lay behind those beautiful eyes. "You're not really pregnant, are you?"

"Goodnight, my Chase," is all she said.

12

Have Faith

I don't know from which continent the continental breakfast originated, but the inhabitants of said continent have no understanding of a good morning meal. Cold muffins, cereal from a huge plastic tub, and a paper shot glass full of watered-down orange juice doesn't qualify as breakfast.

The pain meds did nothing to help me sleep or ease my pain. All they did was make me itch and left me incapable of thinking clearly for several hours through the night. Anya slept like a kitten. She curled up and never moved. I envied her ability to sleep in almost any environment. My inability to sleep was fueled primarily by my struggle to deal with the fact that I'd unnecessarily killed a man in cold blood. I could've justified it with a dozen excuses, but ultimately, there was no reason for me to kill him. We had extracted the information we'd needed. He'd been tortured mentally and physically beyond what anyone deserves, and after all, he was a human and may have had a family who depended on him. I could never take back what I'd done no matter how much anguish I suffered over the deed, but that didn't stop it from haunting me.

While I was pushing my bagel around on my Styrofoam plate, I overheard Clark ask Anya, "Is he all right?"

She just shrugged.

* * *

We left the hotel and crossed A1A, the four-lane highway running along the south side of the island, and began walking the mile to the airport instead of waiting for the shuttle. I watched morning runners and early-bird seashell collectors sharing Smathers Beach as the sun pierced the eastern sky and bathed the island with its orange light. The darkness consuming my psyche from ending Micky's life without necessity was not going to be so easily overtaken as the darkness that enveloped the island every night. It was going to take far more than an inferno-consumed star some ninety-three-million miles distant to burn away the darkness looming inside me.

The burning star I needed was walking beside me and crying inside because she couldn't bear seeing me torture myself over what I'd done.

Anya said, "We will meet you at airplane, Clark."

She took my hand and led me from the sidewalk, onto the white sand, and down to the water's edge.

We sat and watched the sun's light play across the gently breaking waves while pelicans dived on baitfish in the shallow water. It was a postcard scene come to life, but I was in no mood for postcards. I was focused on three things: finding Skipper and getting her home safely, finding out if Anya was really pregnant, and figuring out how long it would take to get over my guilt for ruthlessly killing Micky.

The relentless wind made Anya's hair float on the morning breeze. She pulled her hair into a ponytail then turned so her back was to the rising sun.

A smile came across her lips. "Chase," she said, "I love you, and I love how you care for your friends. Do not worry. I am not pregnant. Maybe someday for us I will bring you baby, but not now. It was only what I said to make horrible little man shoot me and not you. I knew his gun would fail, but I couldn't let him shoot you in case I was wrong."

She seemed to know my every thought, and her look of sorrow was breaking my heart.

She held my face in her hands. "Listen to me, Chase. You killed that man for hurting Skipper and for other girls. This is true, but not all of reason. You saw him point gun at me and pull trigger. He tried to kill me, and you made him pay for this. I cry when I think of this—when I think of how much anger you have for someone who tries to hurt me. You are protector of me and for all girls that man would hurt for rest of his life."

"How do you always know exactly what to say?" I asked.

She pressed her finger to my lips. "Quiet. I am not finished. Inside, you are also hurting and afraid for daughter of your friends. We will find her and take home to Laura. Do not doubt, Chasechka . . . believe. I do not know your God, but I see faith in you when you talk to Him. Have same faith we will find her."

Had she really been watching and listening when I prayed? Did my questions and doubts appear to be faith to her? How can this woman see so easily into my soul and understand the depths of my pain?

"You're supposed to be an assassin, Anya Burinkova, not a psychologist."

"I am many things. Assassin is only small part."

The truth of her statement was powerful, just like the woman herself.

"If we don't get moving, Clark is going to leave without us," I said.

"He will not leave us here. He will wait for us. We must first finish talk. I need to ask you question and you will not like to answer, but you must."

I stared into her hypnotic eyes and tried to imagine what was about to come out of her mouth.

Still cupping my face in the palm of her hand, she peered into my soul. "What is it you truly want, my Chase?"

"What do you mean?"

"I want to know what you want more than anything in whole world. Everyone wants something. What do you want?"

Without hesitation, I said, "I want to find Skipper and take her home to her folks."

"No, Chase. That is not what you want. That is mission for you. That is duty, and we will do that together, but after that, above all else"—she touched my chest with the tips of her fingers—"what is it that you want inside heart?"

I stared at her, dumbfounded. "I want to know about my father and my mother. I want to know who they really were and what really happened to them and my sister."

Anya bit at her bottom lip.

"I spent my childhood believing they were missionaries," I said. "Do you know what a missionary is?"

She nodded but didn't make eye contact.

"We traveled all over the Caribbean, my parents, my sister and me, and I thought we were building schools and caring for those people, but that's just what they wanted me and everyone else to believe. According to some of the people I, and now you work with, my parents were just like you and me. They were assassins and spies."

Anya licked her lips. "I know, Chase. I know about your parents and sister."

A sickening chill exploded through my body. Hearing her say those words made every hair on my skin stand on end. "What do you mean you know about my family? How could you know anything about them?"

"I told you, Chase. I am many things—assassin is only one."

I pulled away from her. She reached for my hands, but I wouldn't let her touch me.

"Tell me what you know," I demanded.

She gazed toward the airport and then back at me, still not making eye contact. "I promise I will tell you everything after we find Skipper. I cannot tell you now. You must understand."

"No! I must not understand. You know about my family and you think I'm just going to agree that you'll tell me later? No! That's not how this works, Anya. You'll tell me everything you think you know about my family, and you'll tell me now. That's how this works."

"No, Chase, not now." She reached for my hands again.

I stood up and dusted the sand from my pants, trying not boil over. I could see the frustration and pain on her face.

"Why, Anya? Why can't you tell me now?"

She stood, and I let her take my hands as my breath came in shallow gasps.

"My Chase. I love you with all of me, and I will tell you everything I know, but now you must focus on Skipper. She needs us, and we made promise to Laura and Coach. When we have made promise complete, I swear it. You will know everything we know."

"We?" I choked. "Who is we?"

"SVR, Chase. I will tell you everything SVR knows about your family."

I lifted her chin, forcing her to look into my eyes. "You will tell me everything the second Skipper is safe, and not a minute after. And you are not SVR. That's behind you."

"Yes, Chase, I promise."

We brushed the remaining sand from each other and headed for the airport. I signed for the fuel and overnight parking for the plane and found Clark finishing up his preflight inspection.

"Do you want me to file for Miami Executive?" he asked.

"No, let's go to the Ocean Reef Club. The airport identifier is zero seven Fox Alpha. We can pick up my car there. It'll be less than an hour's drive to Miami Beach, and we'll need wheels when we get there."

He agreed and filed the flight plan. We climbed aboard, Clark in the left seat, and me in the right with Anya in the first passenger seat. We went through the startup flow with me calling checklist items and Clark doing the work. The King Air was a magnificent airplane with a well-appointed cockpit and cabin.

"Key West clearance delivery, this is King Air one zero Uniform Charlie on the general aviation ramp with information Bravo, request IFR clearance to 07FA."

I made the radio calls while Clark set up the navigation radios and GPS. It was less than a hundred miles to the Ocean Reef Club airport on Key Largo, so it would only take about twenty-five minutes to get there.

The controller said, "King Air one zero Uniform Charlie is cleared to the 07FA airport direct. On departure, climb and maintain two thousand, expect one one thousand ten minutes after departure. Departure frequency is one-two-four-point-zero-two-five and squawk four-two-seven-four."

I read back the clearance and we taxied out to runway two-seven.

"Do you want to fly this leg?" Clark asked.

I rarely passed up a chance to fly anything, especially an airplane as sexy as the King Air. I needed to focus on the flight to keep my mind from guessing what Anya would have to say about my family.

"Sure," I said. "I have the controls. You have the radios."

Clark responded, "You have the controls."

His discipline in the cockpit was impressive. Everything was by the book. I wasn't always such a stickler for the rules, but in an airplane as sophisticated as that one was, being all business was a good thing.

He pushed the button on the yoke. "Key West Tower, this is King-Air one zero Uniform Charlie, holding short of two-seven, ready to go."

The crisp sounding tower controller said, "King Air ten UC, turn right on course, wind two-four-zero at niner, runway two-seven, cleared for takeoff."

"Right on course, cleared for takeoff, one zero Uniform Charlie," replied Clark.

I pushed the throttles forward and felt the airplane pick up speed.

Clark called out, "Airspeed alive and building, cross-check . . . V-one . . . rotate."

At the command of "rotate," I pulled the nosewheel off the ground and the plane leapt off the runway as if it yearned to fly. I gave the command, "Positive rate of climb, gear up."

He lifted the landing gear as I turned right, direct to Key Largo.

The departure controller cleared us up to eleven thousand feet, and we leveled off in less than seven minutes. I pulled the power back, set the props for cruise, and settled in for the thirteen minutes of cruise flight. Clark reported the airport in sight from thirty miles away and the controller cleared us down to three thousand feet.

About ten miles from the airport, Clark canceled our IFR clearance, and we made a visual approach to runway two-three.

Taxiing to the parking ramp, I noticed Hank strolling out of the FBO. He was the airport manager who'd flown with Dr. Richter in the service and had become a good friend to me. He shielded his eyes from the morning sun, certainly wondering who'd landed at his private airport.

I brought the plane to a stop on the parking ramp and shut down the engines. Anya had the cabin door open and the stairs deployed before Clark and I finished the shutdown checklist. I glanced out the small window to see her hugging Hank. He'd spent more than his share of time overseas doing some less-than-official dirty deeds for the good guys. Even though he was far from young anymore, he still loved having a beautiful young Russian greet him on an island airport.

"Get your hands off my girl, you old scoundrel," I said, stepping from the plane.

Hank grabbed my shoulders. "It's good to see you, Chase. Whose airplane have you stolen now?" he asked, looking up at the gleaming King Air.

"It's a company plane," I said, "and this is Clark Johnson. Clark, meet Hank. He flew with Dr. Richter, but now he sweeps up around here and flirts with girls who are fifty years his junior."

"It's nice to meet you, Hank."

"Nice to meet you too, Clark, and don't pay any attention to this lying dog. He don't know nothing about sweeping up or how to treat a woman like her." Hank ushered us into the office. "Where's your boat, Chase?"

Anya didn't give me a chance to answer. She said, "We have new boat now."

"Yeah," I said. "We had a little accident with ours and had to pick up a new one. We'll probably bring her back down here for the summer, but she's up at Jekyll Island for now. It's a long story, Hank, but I'll tell you about that when we have time to talk. For now, we need to leave the King Air with you and take my car. Do you have room for the plane for a couple days?"

"I've always got room for you, Chase. I'll tuck her away nice and safe 'til you get back. Leave her here as long as you need."

Even though home was wherever I happened to fall asleep, there was something comfortable about being back in Key Largo. That island was the place I missed most when I was gone, so maybe that's where home really was.

13
It's Just Business

Anya insisted on driving and I didn't argue. Even with the traffic, her skill behind the wheel put us in South Beach in less than an hour. Being there was one thing, but finding Skipper and convincing her to come with us was quite another. I was still trying to piece together a plan to make all that happen.

"I have been thinking," Anya said, "and I have plan to find girl."

Thankful someone had a plan, I listened intently.

She said, "First, we find Giovani person and make him understand he will give girl to us."

"How are we going to do that?" I asked.

"I'll call my buddy on vice." Clark dialed his phone, talked for two minutes, then hung up. "Okay, he gave me a list of likely spots where we might find this Giovani character. I say we start at the top of the list and keep trying 'til we find him. Oh, and guys, he says to be careful. These guys aren't amateurs. They're well connected and usually keep plenty of muscle around."

"We can deal with the muscle," I said. "We have to find this guy."

* * *

We quickly discovered the sleazy side of Miami. After striking out three times, we were starting to get discouraged, but a feeling in my gut told me we were in the right place when we walked into

Paradise Productions, a porn company specializing in girls who looked sixteen. I wanted to burn the place to the ground.

We barged through the front office like we owned the place, and a pimple-faced girl tried to stop us from walking into Giovani Minelli's office unannounced.

Anya grabbed the girl by the throat, forced her back into her chair, and said, "You are fired. Get out now and you will not get hurt."

The terrified girl ran from the office.

We burst through the door to find Giovani snorting a line of coke from the corner of his desk. Clark and I took positions left and right of the door with our pistols drawn and clearly visible. Giovani reached into his desk drawer for what I'm sure was a pistol, but Anya slammed the drawer on the back of his hand. He probably thought he could shoot his way out of the hell unleashed in his office, but he was sorely mistaken.

Anya jerked his hand from the drawer, twisted it sharply over his shoulder, and forced the man back into his chair. Full of cocaine-strength and fear, he took a swing at her as he landed in the seat, but she struck like a cobra inside his elbow with a blocking punch. The strike sounded like thunder in the small office and got his attention.

He wailed in pain until Anya punched him in the throat, shutting him up and leaving him gasping for air.

She held Skipper's picture in front of his face. "Where is this girl? You will tell me now and maybe I let you live, or maybe they kill you quickly. If you do not tell me, I will take my time killing you. Is up to you."

Giovani's terrified eyes darted in a cocaine-induced dance from the two of us standing by his office door, to Anya's stern gaze, and back to the picture of Skipper. His mind must've been exploding as he tried to process everything seconds after the drugs hit his brain.

Anya must have thought he hesitated a moment too long. "Come put bullet in knee to show we are serious."

"Okay!" he screamed. "I'll give you the girl. Everybody needs to chill out and put the guns away. I'm a businessman. It's just business. It's not personal."

I walked around his desk and smelled his cheap cologne mixed with sweat. I forced his hand onto the desk and pressed the muzzle of my pistol into the flesh of his wrist.

"Listen to my voice," I said. "Don't I sound calm to you? I could put a bullet through your hand or through your head, and my pulse rate would never get above sixty. You don't get to tell us when to calm down, and you most certainly don't get to decide what's personal."

I could feel his body trembling, but I didn't know if it was the cocaine or the fear. It was probably a combination of the two.

"Look, I'll give you the girl. Just don't shoot me, man. I'll give you the girl, all right?"

"She's not yours to give," I growled. "What you'll do is tell me where she is right now. The next time you open your miserable mouth, it better be to give me an address. Anything else gets you a brand-new bullet-sized hole somewhere in your body. Now speak."

"Okay, look. It's like this," he said. "We send the girls out to do shoots all over the place, so it's impossible for me to know where all of them are, so—"

I pulled the trigger of my suppressed Walther and watched the shock of the bullet pass through his wrist and travel up his arm. Blood sprayed his pressed white shirt. He screamed and grabbed his bloody wrist and his face turned pale.

"Here's what's going to happen next," I said. "You're going to get light-headed, and then you're going to pass out. If that happens before you tell me where the girl is, I promise you'll never wake up. I'll put two more rounds straight through the top of your head. I'm guessing you have somewhere between thirty and forty-five seconds before the pain is too much and you close your eyes—possibly forever—so let's hear it. Tick-tock . . . tick-tock."

Clark pulled a necktie from a hall tree in the corner of the office and fashioned a loose tourniquet around Giovani's forearm, just below the elbow.

"Give me the address, and we'll stop the bleeding, and you can get some help. Your only other option is far less appealing. It's important you understand that I want to put two in your brain. Scum like you doesn't deserve to live. I'm going to find the girl, with or without you. What you have to decide in the next ten seconds is whether or not she's worth dying for."

"She's on Fourteenth," he grunted through the pain, "seven blocks off the beach at a rented house on a film shoot. I swear. Now get me some help."

Clark turned the tourniquet two full twists and the bleeding slowed to a trickle. Giovani leaned back in his chair, moaning while sweat poured from every inch of his body.

I slapped him across his grimy face. "I knew you'd see it our way. Oh, by the way, Giovani, I lied to you."

"I knew you weren't going to shoot me again!" he blurted.

"No," I said. "That part was true. I was going to shoot you in the head. In fact, I was looking forward to that. I lied about you passing out. That's probably not going to happen. Lucky you. You're going to stay awake and look at what used to be your wrist until we verify you're telling the truth about where the girl is. Then, and only then, will you be free to call an ambulance or do another line of coke. Whatever you want."

I turned to Clark and Anya. "We have to either take him with us, or one of us has to stay with him until we know he's telling the truth."

"It's too messy to take him with us. There's too much chance of seeing a cop and him screaming like a little bitch," Clark said. "I'll babysit him while you and Ana go get the girl."

"Okay," I said, "we'll call you as soon as we have her. If you don't hear from us in one hour, kill him, and we'll pick you up at the rally point."

There was no rally point, but Giovani had no way of knowing that. I had no reason to believe anything Giovani Minelli told me, but if he lied about Skipper's location, it would be the last lie he'd ever tell.

14

That's My Girl

As we left the office, we were pleased to see the girl from the front desk gone. She didn't need to be involved in any of this.

The streets of South Beach weren't overly crowded, so we took Ocean Drive to Fourteenth and started counting blocks. When we made it to the seventh block, it was obvious which house was our target. The driveway was littered with vans and production equipment.

We drove by the house once to recon for exits and guards. They had one fat guy at the front door who they probably thought could keep out any intruders, but we weren't just any intruders. There was a garage entrance and back door into a small courtyard behind the house. If we could get inside undetected, we'd have a much better chance of getting Skipper out of the house without hurting or killing anyone. I'd done enough killing on this trip. I was hoping for a quiet resolution, but in my world, such a thing rarely exists.

"Let me out behind the house," I said. "I'll go around the east side toward the front door. I want you to get the fat guy off the front porch so I can get in without him seeing me. I'll find Skipper and get her out of there. You be ready to go when you see us coming out the front door."

Anya frowned. "This is terrible plan. You are walking into place and do not know how many men or where is girl."

"It's a porn set," I said. "They've got one guard on the front door and a bunch of cameramen and light guys inside. They're not expecting me to show up to snatch one of their girls."

"You heard Clark say these people are well connected and keep plenty of muscle around."

"Look, Anya. They have one fat guy on the front door. That's it. Do what I say, and we'll be out of here in five minutes."

I stepped out of the car. Before I closed the door behind me, I heard her say, "You are making big mistake."

She pulled away, and I headed for the side of the house. I took up a position at the front corner of the house just in time to see Anya bringing the car to a shuddering stop beside the driveway. She stepped from the car and slammed the door, then she yanked open the hood. Positioning herself perfectly for the door guard to see, she bent over the fender and pretended to inspect the engine problem.

I don't know any man who wouldn't leave his post to help Anya in that pose. I silently applauded her performance.

Human nature dictates that when a man walks toward temptation and away from his responsibilities, he often has the briefest moment of indecision and turns back to look at what he's walking away from. I wondered if the guy was human enough to have that moment. About ten steps from the front door, the walrus of a man checked his watch then glanced back at the front door. It took less than a second for him to decide that Anya would be more fun than playing guard. I quietly strolled through the front door.

Subtlety wasn't in Anya's nature, and I was impressed with her little charade to lure the guy away from his post. Before I closed the door behind me, I took one last look outside.

Anya was pointing at the engine and giving the guy her pouty face. The man fell right into her trap. He bent over to look at the engine of my car. Anya reached up, grabbed the hood with both hands and slammed it down onto the man's head. I watched his knees buckle and his big body fall limp across the fender. She raised the hood and slammed it twice more before rolling his body under a clump of shrubs and palms.

That's my girl.

I listened for sounds in the house. The marble floor created an echo chamber that carried the slightest sound throughout the first floor. I heard the ice machine in the kitchen and somebody snoring. Snoring on a porn set didn't seem normal, so I tucked that tidbit away with a plan to investigate it later if I needed to.

I crept into a huge open room in the center of the house, determined not to make a sound. There was a curved staircase against the wall to my right, and in the center of the room was a haphazard arrangement of sofas, bean bags, and overstuffed chairs. That's where I found the source of the snoring. It was a massive German Shepherd, drooling and snoring and coiled up like a kitten on one of the bean bags.

The dog was a problem, but not a problem I couldn't handle. I just had to keep him in the back of my mind and be prepared for when he woke up—and he would wake up.

I memorized the layout of the first floor of the house, and the position of the animal. Dividing my attention between the dog and the top of the stairs, I drew my pistol and began my slow, silent ascent. I reached the top of the marble staircase and I glanced back, relieved to see the German Shepherd still sawing logs.

I stepped around a corner and saw a spiderweb of extension cords taped to the floor and leading down a hallway. I paused to listen for movement, but I heard nothing, so I followed the cords. Through a set of closed French doors, I could hear the overacted moans and screams of a woman pretending to be in the throes of passion. I listened closely, trying to determine if the voice was Skipper's. It had been over two years since I'd seen her, so I wasn't certain, but it sounded like someone much older.

I drew in a slow, full breath as I prepared to burst through the door and grab Skipper. That's when someone yelled, "Cut! Nice job, everybody. Now clean this up and get the kid in here."

A middle-aged, tattooed woman wearing a headset, came through the bedroom door with a clipboard in one hand and a cigarette in the other. I was exposed with nowhere to hide and no chance of getting back to the stairs without the woman seeing me. I raised my pistol close to my chest and waited for her to catch a glimpse of me and start screaming. This whole operation was about to turn into a dumpster fire, and all I could do was pour gas on it.

The woman never glanced my way. She turned right after leaving the bedroom and grabbed a doorknob a few feet down the hall. The knob didn't turn, so she violently beat on the door and shouted, "Open this fucking door right now or I swear I'll beat you to death when I get in there."

She held the knob and threw her body against the door twice. It didn't budge, but on the third try, the cheap knob and lock surrendered and the door swung open.

I glanced through the partially open bedroom door to make sure no one else was coming out. There were perhaps ten people standing around while two actors, a man and a woman, stood naked beside a raised table smoking cigarettes and ignoring everyone else. I stepped across the cables taped to the floor and followed the tattooed woman into what turned out to be a huge bathroom. Before I made it through the doorway, I heard Skipper's voice.

"No, please don't make me go in there. I don't want to do that. Please! No!"

My pulse raced. I powered through the door with my pistol in one hand and my other hand raised to block the door should the woman decide to slam it in my face. I was too quick, and she never saw me coming. With my free hand firmly on her neck, I forced the woman's skinny frame through the glass shower enclosure. As she fell through the pane of glass, it exploded around her. She landed in a bloody heap inside the shower, unconscious and surrounded by shards of shattered glass.

Skipper was sitting on the toilet with a bathrobe wrapped around her shoulders. I grabbed her with my left hand and shoved her behind me as I raised my pistol and pointed through the doorway. The sound of the breaking glass still echoed, and I expected to see someone coming to investigate. I could hear Skipper breathing hard behind me, and she was clinging to my waist.

Two gargantuan men stepped through the door, filling the space and blocking any view I had into the hallway. Each of the men was holding a pistol and pointing it straight at me. Skipper gasped, and I could feel her body trembling in fear.

I was in the worst possible position, cornered, with an innocent victim behind me and two armed giants blocking the only exit. I'd been trained for countless scenarios, but this called for some creativity. I could get a bullet into either of the men, but probably not both before they opened fire, killing both Skipper and me. That left me with two options. One, I could take my chances of getting two shots off before taking a round to my chest, or two, surrender and let them take me. I could fight my way out later when my odds were better, but I didn't want to risk losing Skipper again.

Suddenly, a pink mist exploded from the giant's face on my left, and the big man melted to the ground. I put two rounds into the second man's chest and one into his face, and I watched him fall.

Skipper screamed and I spun around, covering her mouth with my hand. Her eyes were wide and full of terror. It took several seconds for recognition to overtake her.

I removed my hand from her mouth.

"Chase? What are you doing here? What—"

I didn't have time to explain. "Stay behind me and do exactly as I say. I'll get you out of here."

She wasn't moving, obviously terrified.

"Listen to me, Skipper! Stay behind me and do what I say! Do you understand?"

Regaining her senses, she said, "Yeah, okay."

I held her hand and led her across the two bodies and into the hallway. Anya was standing there with her pistol raised, and smoke was wafting from the muzzle.

I shoved Skipper toward Anya. "Get her to the car! If I'm not out in one minute, leave without me!"

Skipper hesitated and turned back toward me.

"Go with Anya! She'll get you out of here. You can trust her!"

Skipper ran to Anya and they raced for the stairs. The instant they reached the stairs, another giant of a man came pouncing from the bedroom with his gun raised, focusing on the two fleeing women. He didn't see me. That was a fatal mistake on his part, but I wasn't as quick as I needed to be.

My world turned deathly silent and time slowed to a crawl. I watched the muscles in the man's forearm tighten and the flesh of the back of his hand turn white. I saw the hammer of his pistol rise from the frame of the heavy black weapon. When it fell, an orange flame exploded from the muzzle and the spent shell casing leapt out of the ejector port. I brought my pistol to bear on the gunman's head and squeezed the trigger twice. The spent shells from my pistol flew out of the slide in immediate succession of his and collided in the air between us. In silence, I watched the sequence play out frame-by-frame.

I turned my head, hoping to see Anya and Skipper descending the stairs, but what I saw sent spears through my soul. Anya's right shoulder blade had taken the bullet. Her blood sprayed through the air and across the banister. The pistol she'd been holding had fallen to the stairs when she was blown forward by the concussion of the shot.

Skipper reached out for her as Anya's body tumbled across the banister and began the fall to the marble floor below.

15

Breadcrumbs

I subconsciously put two more rounds into the corpse in front of me as I heard the sickening thud of Anya's body strike the floor. I made an unthinkable number of mistakes in the coming seconds as some force drew me to Anya. I didn't think about anything else happening around me.

I had no plan, and no backup if things got worse, but how could things possibly get worse?

I took two galloping strides toward the stairs and leapt, clearing six or seven steps before landing a third of the way down. I grabbed Skipper around the waist and bounded toward the ground floor. When I reached the bottom, to my horror, I saw Anya's lifeless form sprawled on the marble floor with blood pooling by her head. My chest was on fire and my mind was churning. I ran to her and collapsed to my knees, sliding to a stop inches from her body. As I reached for her neck, praying I'd feel a pulse, I heard a sound that nearly stopped my heart.

In my panic to get to Anya, I'd forgotten about the dog who was now on full alert, barking ferociously, and charging toward me. Reflexively, I drew my pistol and pointed it in the general direction of the advancing canine. I yanked the trigger twice, but nothing happened. I'd foolishly wasted the last remaining rounds from my pistol on the dead gunman who'd shot Anya, and now I was going to pay for that mistake.

Skipper stepped between me and the charging animal. I couldn't fathom why she'd sacrifice herself to stop the dog. I reached up to grab her, hoping I could throw her out of the way before the dog's teeth arrived, but I missed by an inch.

She knelt between the advancing dog and Anya's body. "Harvey! Down!"

The dog put on his brakes and slid across the floor, coming to a stop in front of Skipper's knees. She took the dog's head in her hands. "It's okay, Harvey. It's okay."

The dog licked her hands and peeked around her, making sure I wasn't still a threat.

I dropped the empty magazine from my pistol and slammed a full one in its place. I placed two fingers on Anya's neck, but my heart was racing too fast to feel a pulse—if she still had one.

I couldn't let myself crash. I'd made a promise to Coach Woodley that I'd bring his daughter home. I'd been trained and honed into a weapon of war, and I couldn't turn my back on my word or my training. I hefted Anya's limp body onto my shoulder in a modified fireman's carry and yelled at Skipper. "Go! Out the front. My car's at the corner of the drive. It's a silver BMW. I'm right behind you!"

She jumped to her feet and ran for the door. Harvey bounded after her.

Hearing his feet hitting the floor behind her, she stopped. "No, Harvey. You have to stay, but I love you." She kissed the dog on the head and he sat, watching us race past him and out the front door.

I was thankful to see the soles of the fat guy's shoes still protruding from beneath the shrubs. I didn't want to have to deal with another gunman. I yelled to Skipper, "Open the back door!"

She yanked the door open and crawled inside. I laid Anya's body on the back seat, and Skipper pulled her inside the car. I slammed the door and ran to the driver's side.

Taking one last look toward the house, I saw two more men coming hard through the front door. I emptied my pistol in their direction and jumped into the car. Thankfully, Anya had left the keys where they belonged, and the car roared to life. Broken conch shells and sand flew into the air as we accelerated onto Fourteenth toward Meridian.

As I turned onto the MacArthur Causeway, I saw Skipper in the rearview mirror applying pressure to the exit wound on Anya's chest.

"She's got a pulse!" she yelled from the back seat.

I yanked my cell phone from my pocket and thumbed in the only number I could think of. Dominic Fontana answered on the second ring. He started into his long, drawn-out speech that he gave every time he answered the phone, but I cut him off.

"Dominic! It's Chase. Shut up and listen. I need your help. Anya's been shot, and we're coming across the MacArthur Causeway. She needs a doctor now!"

Dominic shifted from yacht broker to covert operative in an instant. "Stay on the Causeway 'til you cross Interstate Ninety-Five and take Twelfth Avenue Northeast. The VA hospital will be two blocks on the left. Don't take her to University. You'll see it as soon as you turn on Twelfth, but keep going to the VA. I'll let them know you're coming. What are you driving?"

"My silver BMW," I yelled into the phone.

Firmly, he said, "Listen to me, Chase. Do not stay with her. Someone will take her from your car and get her inside. As soon as she's out of your car, you have to disappear. She'll get the best care possible, and I'll call you as soon as I can get there to pave the way for you to come back. You don't want to try to answer their questions. Drop her and go. It doesn't matter where. Just go."

We left the Causeway onto mainland Miami and traffic picked up. There were cars everywhere, but I wasn't slowing down. I blew through the red lights at the interstate and started scanning for Twelfth Avenue. I spotted the exit and was thankful no one was in front of me. I glanced back to check on Anya. She didn't look good. There was blood dripping from her mouth and her blonde hair was now matted and crimson. Skipper had blood all over her hands and arms, but she was still holding pressure on the exit wound.

We made the turn onto Twelfth and traffic was standing still. I accelerated into the oncoming lane and roared through the first traffic light and past University Hospital. Accelerating through eighty miles per hour, I spotted the sign for the VA hospital and slammed on the brakes, sliding the car into the drive and under the canopy. Two orderlies with a gurney yanked open the back door and peered inside. They pulled Anya from the back seat and roughly laid her on the gurney. Seeing Skipper covered in Anya's blood, one of the orderlies asked, "Are you hurt?"

Skipper yelled, "No, I'm fine! Just take care of her."

I pressed the accelerator hard, slamming Skipper's door with the momentum as we roared back onto Twelfth and north toward the Julia Tuttle Causeway.

Skipper found a beach towel on the floor and started cleaning her hands and arms. I was driving more reasonably and things were starting to calm down, but I hated leaving Anya at the hospital. I needed to be with her, but I had to take Dominic's direction. He'd never led me astray.

When Skipper finished cleaning herself up, she said, "Chase, what's this all about? How did you find me?"

Noticing she was still wearing the bathrobe, I pointed to a bag on the floor. "There's some clothes in there that'll fit you. Put something on, and I'll try to explain."

Anya's clothes fit her pretty well. She climbed into the front seat, and I saw she still had a little blood on her hands and forearms. I tried not to look. She leaned across the console, placed her head on my shoulder, and sobbed.

I wrapped my arm around her. "It's okay," I said, trying to sound reassuring. "You're safe now, and I'm going to get you home. Your folks are worried sick about you."

She sat back up. "I can't go home, Chase. I can never go back there. My parents hate me, and I've made such a mess of everything. I can't go back."

I took her hand. "None of that matters right now. We'll figure it out. What's important is that you're safe, and I'm going to keep you safe."

Her face tightened, and she started punching me and screaming. "Where did you go, Chase? Why the hell did you run away?"

I let her punch me several times before grabbing her fist. "Stop it," I said. "There's a lot to explain, and it's going to be tough to understand, but you have to listen to me."

She yanked her fist from my grasp. "Okay, fine. Let's hear it."

I could hardly believe what my life had become since the last time I'd seen her. There was no way to make her understand or believe everything she was about to hear, but I had to try.

"When I got hurt, it was tough for me. I didn't want to see anybody who had anything to do with baseball. It was—"

"It was tough for me too, you asshole. You were like a big brother to me and you shut me out. You shut everybody out. It wasn't fair."

"I know," I said. "It wasn't fair, and I'm sorry. I'm really sorry. I shouldn't have done that to you. Of all people, not to you."

"You're right, you shouldn't have, but you did. Where have you been? Where did you go? And how the hell did you find me?"

"It's a really long story," I said, "and I'm going to tell you everything, I promise, but we have one more thing to do first."

I punched Clark's number into my phone. "Put a bullet in his head and I'll meet you out front in three minutes. We've got Skipper."

Clark said, "Roger," and hung up.

"Who was that?" she asked. "And put a bullet in whose head?"

"That was Clark, my partner, and the bullet's going in Giovani Minelli's head."

She scowled. "Put two bullets in his head . . . one for me."

Three minutes later, we pulled up in front of Paradise Productions and Clark walked out the front door as if he were a businessman on his way to lunch. Seeing Skipper in the front seat, he opened the back door and started to slide inside.

"Wait a minute," I said. "There's quite a bit of blood back there. Grab that bathrobe to sit on."

He pulled the robe over the blood and slid onto the seat. "Who's blood?"

My stomach churned. "Anya took a bullet in the back on our way out of the house. She's at the VA hospital on Twelfth. Dominic Fontana is smoothing that over. Do you know him?"

"Is she going to be all right?" he asked, showing sincere concern.

Skipper bowed her head and put her face in her hands.

Clark said, "That doesn't look good. What happened?"

Fighting off the nausea in the pit of my stomach, I said, "I've got a lot of tough questions to answer, and it's going to take me a while to get through all of them. First, Clark, this is Elizabeth Woodley. I call her Skipper. She's who we've been searching for."

"It's nice to see you safe and sound, Elizabeth. We've been worried about you."

* * *

We pulled into Pine Tree Park and found a remote parking spot.

"Skipper, I promise to get back to your questions in a second, but I have to fill Clark in on what happened."

"Okay." She wrung her hands and gazed out the window.

"We found the house, Clark. Anya told me not to go in alone, but I didn't listen. It didn't take me long to realize she was right . . . she's always right. They were gunned up pretty heavy in there. I found Skipper and got myself cornered and outnumbered. Thank God Anya showed up. We had to shoot our way out, and she took one in the shoulder blade and fell about ten feet onto a marble floor. We made it to the car and called Dominic. He sent us to the VA and told us to get lost until he could smooth things over. He's going to call as soon as the coast is clear. God, I hope he calls soon."

"I knew I should've gone with you," Clark said.

"No, it was my fault. I should've listened to Anya. I never should've gone in there alone. It was stupid, and I may have gotten her killed."

The three of us sat silently for several minutes.

"Skipper and I are going for a walk," I said. "We won't be gone long, but I have a lot of things to explain. If Dominic calls, we'll be headed back to the hospital, so stay close, okay?"

He pointed to a grove of pines. "I'll be right over there in the shade."

Skipper and I walked until we found a bench and sat together. I was trying to keep it together for Skipper's sake, but I was falling apart. The woman I loved was lying in a hospital a few blocks away fighting for her life, and I couldn't be beside her. Worse than that, my arrogance is what put her there.

Stilling myself, I put my arm around Skipper. "Are you okay?"

She shook her head. "No, I'm not okay, but I'm safe for the first time in a long time. Thanks to you."

I stared through the trees, gathering my nerve. "Like I told you before, it screwed me up pretty bad when I got hurt and couldn't play ball anymore."

She started to interrupt me again, but I took her hands in mine. "Just listen."

She sighed and squeezed my hands.

"I didn't deal well with seeing my dreams get flushed down the toilet after I got hurt, so I stayed away from everyone and everything related to baseball. I got recruited to work for the government, and I took them up on their offer. I ended up training for a couple years, and now I travel around and do things for them that no one knows about."

"So, you're some kind of secret agent, and they sent you to find me? That's stupid, Chase. You're making this up."

"No, they didn't send me to find you. I took Anya to see a ball game in Athens and had dinner with your mom and dad. Something was noticeably wrong, and we finally convinced them to tell us what it was. They have no idea what really happened to you. They still think you're running with the wrong people and probably messing with drugs."

She started crying. "That's how it all started. I hooked up with some people I thought were my friends and made a lot of terrible decisions. I got caught up in the whole thing and we ended up in the Keys. The people I thought were my friends bailed on me, and I was stuck down there with no money and no place to stay. That's when—"

I stopped her. "It's okay. None of that matters now. We started our search in Key West where we met a guy named Micky."

"If I ever see him again, I'll gouge his eyes out and cut off his—"

"Relax," I said. "You'll never see him again. I promise you that. No one will ever see him again."

She blew out a satisfied breath. "So, how did you find me here in Miami?"

"We simply followed the breadcrumbs," I said. "People like that aren't very good at covering their tracks. We hooked up with Clark along the way, and he helped us out. He's a former Green Beret and an all-around badass."

"No way," she said. "He's like my age."

I laughed for the first time in a while. "Yeah, he's actually thirty-four. I heard they called him Baby Face in the army."

She looked back toward the parking lot. "So, what's the deal with this Anya chick?"

"She's even harder to explain. We work together, but there's more to it than that. She's incredibly important to me. In fact, I'm in love with her. I'll tell you the rest later, but for now, we just have to keep praying she's going to be okay."

"This is a lot to take in," she said.

My phone chirped, and I grabbed it. "Yeah?"

"Chase, it's Dominic. Why don't you come on back to the VA hospital? I'll meet you in the front lobby."

"Is Anya okay?" I asked him.

He had already hung up.

"That was Dominic. We have to get back to the hospital. I'll tell you everything I can later."

We jogged back up the walking path and Clark met us beside the car.

"You sit up front, Clark," Skipper said. "I'll fit better in the back."

"I cleaned up a little while you were gone," he said. Clark had thoroughly scrubbed the back seat, and there was no evidence there'd been blood in the car.

I told him about the phone call and asked him again if he knew Dominic.

"Yeah," he said. "I know Dominic."

16

Broken

We parked and ran into the lobby of the VA hospital. Dominic was sitting in a chair away from everyone else. He rose when he saw us come through the door and seemed surprised when he saw Clark.

"It's good to see you again, Chase," said Dominic. "I didn't know you knew my son."

"Your son?" I glared at Clark. "He's your son?"

"He sure is," Dominic said proudly.

Clark said, "You asked if I knew him. You never asked if we were related."

"But your last name is Johnson."

"My mother's last name is Johnson and Dad wasn't around much when I was a kid."

Choosing not to take that any further, I asked Dominic, "Where's Anya. Can I see her?"

He put his hand on my shoulder. "Let's go for a walk, Chase."

I jerked away from him. "No! I want to see her. Where is she?"

"Chase, the wounds were too severe. I'm sorry, but she didn't survive. There was nothing anyone could do. She'd lost too much blood by the time you got her here."

I crumpled to the floor and held my face in my hands, gasping and desperate to catch my breath.

Skipper knelt beside me, but I shoved her away. "This is your fault! If we didn't have to come looking for you, she'd still be alive!"

Dominic put his hand on my shoulder. "Chase, you've got to—"

I slapped his hand away and leapt to my feet. "You don't get to tell me what I've got to do! None of you get to tell me shit!"

I grabbed a handle on one of the double doors leading beyond the lobby and into the depths of the hospital. The door was controlled by some mechanical lock and wouldn't budge when I pulled, so I thrust my forearm into the pane of security glass on the door and it rattled violently. I took a step backward and sent my right foot into the handle, shattering the lock and leaving both doors bouncing against the jamb. I yanked the doors open and ran through them, frantically scanning the hallway beyond.

The hospital was enormous. Believing I could find Anya was irrational, but that didn't slow me down. I jerked open doors and yelled at the top of my lungs for the woman I loved. I had to see her. I had to know she was still alive. I had to hear her tell me what she and the SVR knew about my family.

I'd made it to the second floor when a pair of rent-a-cop security guards showed up thinking they were going to stop my search for Anya.

"Sir, calm down," one of the overweight uniformed guards yelled. Calming down was not in my future, and taking me down was not in theirs. The larger of the two men grabbed my left wrist and tried to twist my arm behind my back. I let him turn my body, but I didn't let him stay on his feet. I continued the rotation and landed an elbow strike just beneath his third chin, sending him solidly to the white tiled floor.

His buddy, undeterred, decided to take his chances at apprehending me, and charged toward me with a Taser in his outstretched hand. I side-stepped the device and struck him in the wrist with a hammer fist, sending the Taser crashing to the floor. I used the guard's momentum to let him continue stumbling past me, and I clamped my arms around his neck and head.

"There's a twenty-five-year-old woman in this hospital with a gunshot wound through her right shoulder blade. You're going to tell me where she is or I'm going to snap your neck!"

The guard gagged and squirmed in my grip, but I wasn't going to let him go. I squeezed tighter until he grunted, "I . . . don't . . . know."

I shoved his head into the wall, leaving a stain of blood following his body to the floor. I didn't kill him, but he was out cold.

I ran back for the stairs, thinking if she was dead, she'd be in the morgue. Alarms were ringing and people appeared to be in panic. I plummeted down the stairs and forced my way through the doors into the morgue. Two men and a woman wearing white lab coats stood in shock when they saw me storm into the room. I delivered a palm strike to the larger of the two men, sending him to the floor, and I grabbed the other man by the throat.

"Twenty-five-year-old woman! Blonde hair! Gunshot to the back! Where is she?"

I saw the woman running for the telephone mounted on the wall at the end of the room, so I drew my pistol and put a bullet through the phone. I ordered, "Stop where you are!"

With eyes full of terror, the woman froze then fell to her knees. The man whose neck was clamped in my left hand shared the woman's look of fear and pointed toward a body covered by a white sheet. I shoved the man to the floor, holstered my pistol, and began scanning the gurneys for Anya's body. At the same time, four armed police officers—real officers this time—burst through the doors into the morgue.

I scanned the room for another exit and something seized my attention—a foot protruding from beneath a white sheet . . . on it, a tag tied to one of only four toes.

I grabbed a pair of gurneys holding two more bodies and shoved them into the center of the aisle. I sprinted toward an exit sign, leaving the cops stumbling over the gurneys and dead bodies. I made my way back up a set of stairs to the main floor of the hospital and ran through an emergency exit and out to the street.

My thoughts were scrambled. I continued running but had no idea where I was going. My life was crumbling at my feet, and I was an empty, broken man.

* * *

The next memory I have was a mouthful of sand and Clark rolling me over. I was lying under a dilapidated pier, covered in sand and reeking of Jack Daniels. My head pounded, and I felt like I'd been run over by a bus.

"Come on, Chase. Let's get you cleaned up. We've got to get you out of Miami."

Miami? It all came flooding back. *Anya's gone.*

Clark helped me to my feet. I'll never know how much of my pain was from a hangover and how much was from a heartache, but at that moment, there was no difference.

I showered in a rented motel room and threw on some clothes Clark had found for me. My head throbbed.

Clark forced two cups of coffee down my throat and shook me back to reality. "We've got to get moving. My dad is doing his best to deal with the fallout from your little episode yesterday, but we can't stay in Miami."

Through the fog in my head, I said, "Is Skipper okay?"

"She's fine," he said.

"I owe her an apology. I was an ass to her yesterday."

"You don't owe me an apology." Skipper was sitting in the corner of the room.

"Skipper, I'm really sorry. I didn't mean what I said. None of this is your fault."

She sat beside me on the edge of the bed. "Chase, stop it. I know you didn't mean it. I can't tell you how sorry I am about Anya."

She hugged me, and I tried to fight back the tears, but it was no use.

"We have to go," said Clark.

We left the grungy motel and headed south toward Key Largo and the Ocean Reef Club Airport. Hank wasn't there, but we found the King Air where he promised it would be. We left my car in the airport parking lot, covered it with its fitted cover, and Clark started the preflight inspection on the airplane.

I was in no shape to help, so I climbed aboard and strapped into one of the seats, pulled the shade down to keep the sun from sending my head over the edge, and sat silently, questioning everything.

Clark patted me on the shoulder on his way through the cabin and toward the cockpit. The engines spun up, and the air conditioner soon had the cabin nice and comfortable.

Skipper sat down across from me and put her hand on my knee. "I guess we're going back to Georgia, huh?"

"Yeah," I told her through squinted eyes. "We've got to get you home."

"I don't know if that's a good idea. Last time I talked to Mom and Dad, they were pretty mad at me. I don't think they ever want to see me again."

"You should've seen their faces when Anya and I told them we'd find you and bring you home. They were both in tears, Skipper. Trust me. They're going to welcome you with open arms."

Clark pulled off his headset and turned to the cabin. "Where are we going?"

"You're taking me back home to Athens," she said, hesitantly.

I tried to sleep on the flight, but I couldn't stop picturing Anya's face and replaying our last conversation.

She'd said, "This is terrible plan, Chase. You are walking into place, and you do not know how many men or where is girl."

Why didn't I listen to her? If I had, she'd still be alive, and I wouldn't be running from the Miami cops after shooting up the VA hospital.

Clark pulled me from my stupor when he leaned from the cockpit. "Hey, Elizabeth. Do you want to ride up here?"

"I'll stay back here with you if you want," she said to me.

"No, you go on up. I'm okay, and you'll like it up there."

She twisted into the cockpit and settled into the co-pilot's seat. I could see Clark showing her the controls and pointing out things on the ground, some five miles below. I finally fell asleep through the mass of thoughts churning in my mind.

I woke up when I felt the wheels touch down at the Athens Airport. My head was clearing, and I was beginning to feel almost human again. I peered into the cockpit to see Skipper with one hand on the yoke and the other on the throttles.

"You're a natural," I heard Clark say.

"Whatever," she said. "You did that."

"Well, I may have helped a little, but you did most of the work. Why don't you go wake up Chase and let him know we're down and safe?"

I stuck my head into the cockpit. "Don't tell me you let her fly."

"Did you see that?" Skipper said with wide eyes and a brilliant grin. "He let me fly. It's amazing, Chase! You'd love it!"

I tried to smile. "I'm sure I would."

Clark taxied toward the ramp. "Was that Dr. Richter's Mustang on the ramp in Key Largo?"

"It was," I replied.

He'd left the airplane there after flying it down to join Anya and me in our attempt to find and kill the last remaining Suslik. The gunfights and sinking boats that followed had left him stuck in Miami with a bullet in his shoulder.

"I think I'll stick the King Air in his hangar since it's empty," Clark said. "I'm sure the old man wouldn't mind."

We taxied to Dr. Richter's hangar, shut down the engines, and listened to them whistle to a stop. I opened the cabin door and stepped onto the tarmac, squinting against the sun and still trying to clear my head.

Skipper walked down the steps from the plane, shielding her eyes from the evening sun. Clark followed closely behind her and tossed me a small key ring. "Open up the hangar if you don't mind."

How did Clark get a hangar key? I don't have a hangar key.

I unlocked the hangar and pressed the button to start the big door rising on its motorized track. Dr. Richter's VW Microbus was parked beside the small tractor he used to tow his P-51 Mustang in and out of the hangar. I hopped in the Microbus and pulled it outside and around the King Air. Clark pulled the tractor out and attached the tow bar to the nosewheel of the big plane. I wasn't sure the King Air would fit, but Clark appeared to know what he was doing, so I stayed out of the way and watched. He pushed the airplane into the hangar with only inches to spare, and then parked the tractor beneath the left wing.

I stared at the brown couch where Dr. Richter had shown Anya the old pictures and letters from her mother. It had happened only a few days before, but it all seemed so long ago.

Clark hopped off the tractor. "Why don't you guys go have your reunion? I'm going to hang out here and get some sleep. I'm beat. I'll be here when you're ready to pick up your boat, Chase."

"You have a boat?" Skipper asked. "What kind of boat? Where is it?"

She had always been full of questions. It was nice to see that curious, mischievous girl I knew.

I'd almost forgotten about my boat at Jekyll Island, and I never called anyone to go pick it up. I hoped it was still tied up at the end of the dock.

"Yeah, I have a boat," I said. "It's a sailboat over at Jekyll Island. I'll have to go back and get it."

"Can you bring it here?" she asked. "We could go sailing down on Lake Oconee, and maybe Clark could come."

"Well, it's not really that kind of sailboat. It's fifty feet long and weighs about forty thousand pounds. It's not just my boat. It's also where I live."

"Oh, cool," she said. "Then maybe Clark and I could come see you on your boat."

"He's thirty-four," I reminded her.

She grinned. "Yeah, but he looks twenty-four."

"Come on. There's a couple of people who've been waiting a long time to see you again."

She twirled around on the ball of her foot and made a telephone sign with her right hand, sticking a thumb in her ear and her pinky finger near her lips. "Bye, Clark. Call me."

"Bye, Elizabeth. It was nice to meet you."

* * *

We drove for a few miles, and I noticed she was starting to fidget in her seat.

"Are you okay?" I asked.

"Yeah, I'm just nervous about going home. I don't know what it's going to be like."

"It's going to be like going home, Skipper. Your folks are going to cry and hug you, and it's going to be an emotional mess for a day or two. Then they'll want to ask you a lot of questions. It's going to be a big change for you . . . and for them. You left home an innocent little girl, and now you're coming back knowing a lot more about the world than you ever wanted to. But to them you're still that innocent little girl. They're not going to be ready to hear what you've been through, and you're not going to be ready to tell them. I'm not trying to tell you what to do, but I did spend a few years studying psychology."

She playfully shoved my shoulder. "Stop it, Chase. Tell me what you're thinking."

"It's okay to tell them you're not ready to talk about it. It's going to take some time for everyone, especially for you, to get used to being safe and sound at home. They're going to treat you like a little girl again and want to tuck you in and check on you during the middle of the night. Let them do it. They need that as much as you need the safety and security."

"Yeah, I guess you're right, but I'm still nervous."

"It's okay to be nervous," I said. "They'll be nervous, too."

"It's going to be tough for you, too, you know. I don't know if it's a good idea for you to go back to your boat all by yourself. I don't think you need to be alone right now."

"Some of us grieve better alone. I'm going to miss her and it's going to take a long time to get used to being without her, but I don't have a choice. I have to do it. I knew it could happen. It could just as easily have been me who took that bullet. Life sucks sometimes, kiddo, but like your friend Clark says, we've got to soldier on and embrace the suck."

We pulled into the driveway and she reached for my hand.

"It's going to be okay," I said.

"Please don't go," she pleaded. "I don't want to embrace the suck alone."

17
Dead to the World

We stepped from the Microbus and Skipper grabbed my hand. "Chase, if it's going to be as weird as you say, I want to tell you this now."

"What is it?"

"Thank you for saving my life," she said.

"I didn't save your life. I just got you out of a bad situation."

"Yes, you did. I had a handful of sleeping pills when you came into that bathroom. I wasn't going to live another day in that hell. You saved my life. Thank you."

Laura screamed from the porch. "Bobby! Bobby, get out here! Skipper's home!"

Skipper ran to her mother. Coach Woodley raced outside and joined his wife and daughter in a long-awaited and tearful hug.

I watched them from the yard, thinking no one would ever be that happy to see me. I was destined to be alone in a cold world of my making. The life I'd chosen, or perhaps the life that had chosen me, wasn't the kind of existence that led to moments like that. I might help create those moments for other people, but I'd never again know how they felt. I'd never again hold a woman in my arms and cry for her. I'd never again have anyone long to see me or hear my voice. I was alone, and I'd remain alone. My family was gone, Anya was dead, and my existence was practically invisible to the rest of the world. It had to be that way. When I would die in some miserable corner of the world at the hands of people who'd destroy life as Coach and Laura and Skipper knew it, I'd do so alone. No one would cry or mourn my passing. I'd be gone, and someone else like Clark would take my place. And it would continue. I was a tool in a very large box for the use of powerful men who I'd never see, and who lived in places I'd never go. When I'd end up lost or broken or no longer a tool they needed, I'd be replaced by a newer, sharper, equally dispensable tool.

My fate was sealed when I took their money, when they paid me to take the life of another and I did it. I became exactly what Anya said I was: a *nayemnik*, a mercenary. Now I'd become something far more sinister, something far viler. I'd become a man who would take the life of another, believing I had some superiority, some moral standing to declare another human being unfit to live, and to act as not only judge and jury, but also executioner. When I'd believed Micky had no value, I dispensed of his life in the blink of an eye. When I believed Giovani could deliver Skipper to me, I felt no remorse in destroying his hand and later ordering Clark to put a bullet in his head. I'd probably killed the woman I shoved through the glass of the shower, and most certainly killed the guards who were only doing a job for a price. I'd walked through those men as if their lives were meaningless. My carelessness and arrogance led me to belittle the woman who loved me and wanted to bear my children. I'd forced her into a battle that couldn't be won, a battle that was never hers to fight. Finding Skipper was my promise and my commitment, and I should've never asked Anya to wade into Hell to fight my war. I killed her with my arrogance and my stupidity. She was dead, and I was alone, and that's how it would always be.

Breaking my promise to Skipper, I climbed back into the Microbus and drove away, disappearing just like I'd done years before. If I'd stayed, it would've only been harder when I finally left. The leaving was inevitable and the pain unavoidable. Prolonging it by keeping my word would be crueler than walking away at that moment.

I drove back to the baseball field at the University of Georgia and squatted behind home plate one last time. I could feel the sweat and the weight of the helmet and mask and pads. I could smell the leather glove, and I could hear the roaring crowd. I remembered the feel and sound of a fastball landing in my glove at ninety miles per hour. I could taste the thrill of gunning down a runner sliding into second with a perfectly placed throw into the infielder's glove. I'd been one of the greatest collegiate catchers of all time. I would've been a major leaguer. I would've spent my entire life under the lights and the watchful eyes of cheering fans, but all of that went up in a cloud of dust on a hot June afternoon in Omaha, Nebraska when a baserunner came thundering down the baseline and collided with a twenty-one-year-old Chase Fulton guarding the plate.

When the dust had settled, my hand was so badly broken I'd never again throw a baseball, but I'd learn to hold a pistol and snuff out a man's life with the twitch of a finger. I'd learn to make a fist that could knock a man from his feet with a well-practiced punch. No, I'd never play ball in Turner Field, but I'd travel the world delivering those shots and punches that might've made it possible for the screaming fans to sleep at night, believing they were safe and sound, and that evil was held at bay by some force they'd never see. I was that force. Like Athena's battle shield, and like my boat lying on the bottom of the Atlantic Ocean, I was the aegis.

I rose from my crouch behind home plate and surveyed the field and then the empty stands. I saw the seat where Anya had spilled her chili dog all over herself a few days before. I'd never come back to that stadium. I'd never step foot on that field again. But I'd make sure I did everything in my power to keep that place free and safe for every boy like me who ever dreamed of hitting a game-winning home run, and dared to dream that he'd one day wear a Major League uniform.

I left the field and drove back to the airport where I parked outside the hangar door. I didn't want to go inside and risk waking Clark. He needed his sleep, and I needed to be alone, so I crawled into the back seat of the Microbus. My eyelids grew heavier with every breath. Alone, in the back of someone else's van, parked on the tarmac of an airport in a town that was once my home but could never be again, I drifted off to sleep.

I dreamed of the sea and sound of the waves lapping at the hull of my boat. Pelicans dived on baitfish, and seagulls squawked their shrill cries. I dreamed of my sister's laughter and my parents singing to us as children. I dreamed of the smell of Anya's hair and the taste of her lips.

* * *

I awoke to a pounding on the window, and as I reached for my pistol, I narrowed my eyes to see Clark peering through the window. I lifted the lock and opened the doors to the side of the bus.

"What are you doing out here?"

"Sleeping," I said. "At least that's what I was doing 'til you woke me up. Did you get some rest?"

"Yeah," he said. "I slept a few hours. I don't need much sleep, but you were dead to the world."

"That's a good way to put it," I said as I crawled from the back of the van.

"So, how'd it go with the girl's folks?"

"They were glad to see her."

"I'm sure they were. It's a hell of a thing what you did for them. You probably saved that girl's life, and you gave those people their daughter back, changing their lives forever. Don't ever take that kind of thing for granted. You made a real difference in their lives, and they'll never forget it. That's what makes what we do worth whatever it costs."

I was thankful for the sermon. "You're starting to sound like a wise old man, Baby Face. Now let's go to the Pancake Shack and get some real breakfast—none of that continental crap."

We ate more than either of us should have. Conversation was meaningless, and it was nice to pretend, if only for an hour, we were regular guys having a regular breakfast before we headed off to our regular jobs. Of course, regular would never be a word that could describe men like Clark and me.

On our way back to the airport, I said, "You know, Skipper has a major crush on you."

"No, it's not a crush. It's confusion. Come on, Chase, you're a psych major. You're supposed to know stuff like that. She's been stuck in a world where men want one thing and one thing only from her. When a guy's nice to her like I was, she doesn't know what to do with that, so her body responds with affection, and her brain turns that into infatuation. I'm the first guy who's been nice to her without trying to get her clothes off. Of course she's going to like me. It won't last long. She's young. Her body and mind will heal in time, and she'll figure out the world isn't completely filled with assholes . . . like you."

I slugged him. "Thanks for the psychology lesson, old man."

When we pulled up to the hangar, I was surprised to see Skipper sitting on the ground outside the door. Her knees were pulled up to her chest and her chin was resting on top of them. I shut down the van and ran and kneeled in front of her.

"Skipper, what are you doing here?"

She slapped my face. "You tried to do it again! You promised you'd stay, but you didn't. You tried to disappear again. Why do you keep doing that?"

I took her hands and helped her to her feet. "Let's go inside and talk."

I unlocked the door and flipped on the lights. It took a few minutes for the mercury vapor bulbs to warm up and fill the hangar with yellow light. I led her to the couch and had her sit down.

"It's difficult to explain, Skipper, but I don't belong here anymore. I made a promise to your father that I'd find you and bring you home, and that's what I did. When I watched you with your family, I knew I wasn't part of that family anymore. I don't belong there. I knew the longer I stayed, the harder it'd be to say goodbye, so I walked away. I thought it was the best thing for everyone."

"Not for me, it's not the best thing. I asked you to stay and you told me you would. I don't belong here anymore either. I'm not the same. I don't know what you've been through and what you've done, but I know how it feels to not belong. Like you, I'm not the person I was when I left here. I can't do it. I can't stay here. Take me with you. Please, take me to your boat and to wherever you live."

I stopped her. "Listen to me, Skipper. Your parents love you, and to heal, they need you with them. They've been hurting for a long time, hoping you'd come home and praying you'd be safe. It's been tough on them."

"I know, but I'm not ready to be back in that house. I'm not ready to be that little girl again. I don't think I'll ever be ready for that. It's not fair for them to ask that of me. And it's not fair for you to ask me to do that either."

I closed my eyes to gather my thoughts. What was I going to do? I couldn't take a nineteen-year-old girl into my world. What would I do with her when I got my next mission? What would I tell Coach and Laura?

I opened my eyes, and for the first time, I saw Skipper as a woman rather than a girl. She was troubled and alone and damaged, just like me.

I took a deep breath. "Okay. We'll go talk to your folks, and we'll tell them—not ask them—that you're coming with me for a little while. We'll make them understand you'll be perfectly safe and protected with me. We'll make it clear to them that you need time to heal and return to life as it used to be."

She smiled through her tears. "Thank you, Chase. You keep rescuing me, and someday I'll do the same for you."

Clark came through the door. "Hey, guys. I'm going to clean the plane up. She's getting a little grungy. Where are you two headed?"

Skipper smiled at him coyly. "Oh, hey Clark. We're headed to tell my parents that I'm going with Chase on his boat for a while. I'm not ready to be here yet. We'll be back in a little while."

Clark raised his eyebrows at me.

I spun the VW keys on my finger. "What can I do?"

* * *

We drove back to the house and pulled to a stop in the driveway.

"Are you sure this is what you want?" I asked. "They're not going to be happy, and this isn't going to be easy on them."

She exhaled and eyed the front door. "I know, but I can't stay here. I'll be safe with you, and they trust you."

We walked up the stairs, and Laura was tense when she opened the door. "Skipper, where did you go? We've been worried sick. Get in here."

Skipper set her jaw and gritted her teeth. I placed my hand on her back, encouraging her into the house.

Trying to defuse the already tense situation, I said, "Laura, Skipper's fine. She's been with me. Can we have a little talk? Is Coach here?"

Coach Woodley came through the French doors of his study and into the living room. I'd spent years in that house, and it almost felt like my own home.

Coach glared at Skipper. "There you are. You had us worried sick. You cannot be disappearing like that."

"Yes, I can, Daddy. I can go anywhere I want, whenever I want. I'm not a little kid anymore, and you can't expect me to pretend like nothing happened and that everything's okay. Nothing's okay. Tell them, Chase."

All eyes were on me.

"Okay, I think we should all take a breath," I said. "There's a lot of emotions flaring right now, and tensions are high. This is overwhelming for everyone."

"Look, Chase," Coach Woodley said, "don't come into my house and think you're going to lecture us about how to raise our daughter—"

I stopped him right there. "I'm not lecturing you, Coach, but you're not raising your daughter anymore. She's a grown woman now, and she's been through more than any of us can imagine. She's not ready to be your little girl again yet. She needs some time to adjust and heal."

Laura broke down in tears. "We can't lose you again, sweetie. You're our whole world."

Skipper took her mother's hands. "I know, Mom, and you and Daddy mean the world to me, too, but it's all too much right now. I can't tell you what I've been through yet. I'm not ready. It's going to take me some time."

I was proud of her. She was staying calm and standing her ground. The little girl we'd all known and loved was becoming a woman, but it wasn't easy for her parents to watch.

"Your daughter's safe now, and she's going to stay that way. She's going to come with me for a while and spend some time on the boat. I'll make sure she has a safe, comfortable place to live while she's putting the pieces back together. I wasn't just a ballplayer, Coach. I was a psychology major, too. I can help her work out what's going on in her head, and she—"

Coach stood and pointed his finger at me. "If you let anything happen to our little girl, so help me, Chase . . ."

I stood and pushed his finger back down to his side. "Coach, don't threaten me. You have no idea what I did to get your daughter back, and more than that, the woman I love gave her life saving your daughter. So you don't get to point your finger at me and make threats."

His eyes went wide and Laura stood with her mouth agape. She said, "No, Chase! Not Ana!"

"Her name was Anya. And she used to be a Russian intelligence officer. She was defecting to America, and she saved your daughter's life . . . and took a bullet in the back doing it."

"I'm so sorry, Chase," Laura said. "I had no idea. I'm so sorry."

Coach rubbed the back of his neck. "Chase, I . . . I don't know what to say. I'm sorry. I . . ."

"As I said, Coach, emotions are high all around. Skipper needs to decompress, and I don't think I should be alone. She'll be safe with me on the boat. I have plenty of room, and it'll be good for both of us."

Coach and Laura pulled their daughter in for a hug, and Skipper took my hand, pulling me into the circle.

"I'm going to pack a few things, okay?" Skipper climbed the stairs toward her old room.

"Tell us what happened down there, Chase," Coach said.

"I can't tell you everything, but what you need to know is that those so-called friendships she left here with didn't last long, and Skipper wound up in the hands of some pretty nasty people. I made sure many of them paid dearly for what they did to her, and they'll never hurt anyone again. Your daughter's safe now, and she's going to be fine. It's just going to take a little time."

"Thank you, Chase. We'll never be able to repay you."

"It's family, Coach."

Skipper rushed down the stairs with a bag thrown over her shoulder.

"Give us some time," I said. "The two of you will have to come spend a few days on the boat with us."

"You tell us when you're ready, sweetheart," Laura said to Skipper.

"I love you, Mom and Daddy. I'm going to be okay. I'll be with Chase. Just give me a little time, okay?"

18
My Hero

"Thank you. You were amazing back there," Skipper said when we pulled out of the driveway.

"No, you were the amazing one. I lost my temper, and I don't like doing that. You kept your head and never got heated. I was impressed . . . and proud of you."

"Well, whatever. Thanks anyway. You're my hero."

"I'm no hero," I said. "I'm just glad I found you. I've really missed you. We had a lot of fun together over the years."

"Yeah, we sure did. I'm really glad I found me, too."

We pulled up to the hangar, and Clark had the King Air sitting on the tarmac with the fuel truck alongside. I parked the car where Dr. Richter had always parked in the hangar.

"I told the gas guy you'd pay for the fuel," said Clark when we walked up to the plane.

"Of course you did." I handed the fuel man my credit card.

"I'll have to take it back up to the office to run the card. I'll bring it right back, okay?" he said.

Skipper tossed her bag into the airplane. "I need to go the restroom before we leave. Is it okay if I ride up there with the gas guy, and I'll bring your card back?"

"You don't have to ask permission to do stuff, Skipper. Just do it," I said.

She laughed and jumped in the front seat of the fuel truck.

"So, how'd it go with the parents this time?" Clark asked.

"About like I expected. They weren't particularly happy, but I think they understood. I think it'll be good for both Skipper and me to have a little time on the boat to decompress. She'll have some tough days ahead getting over all she's been through, and I don't expect it to be a cakewalk for me, either."

"I think you may be right," he said. "Now let's taxi up there and get her so she doesn't have to walk all the way back."

We climbed aboard and Clark pulled the door closed behind us. He plopped down in the first seat inside the cabin door. "You can fly this leg," he said. "I think I'll sit back here and enjoy doing nothing for a change."

I squirmed my six-foot-four-inch frame into the cockpit and adjusted the seat. I went through the startup procedure and watched the temperatures come up on both engines. With all the required checks done, I added enough power to get the big plane rolling, and then pulled the throttles back to idle. Approaching the terminal, I shut down the number one engine and feathered the prop so Skipper could climb aboard without getting blown around by the wind from the propeller and exhaust. Clark opened the door, and she skipped up the stairs into the cabin.

"I brought you a bottle of water," she said, handing one to Clark.

"Thank you. You can ride up front with Chase if you want. I'm gonna sit back and relax. Besides, he'll probably need your help. He's not as good at landing as you are."

She joined me in the cockpit and slid her headset on like an old pro. "So, you're a pilot, too?"

I fired up the number one engine as soon as I saw Clark close and lock the rear door. "Yes, I'm also a pilot."

She put on that crooked grin of hers. "You really are James Bond, and you really are my hero."

I made the radio calls and got taxi instructions to the runway. Shortly thereafter, we were cleared for takeoff and climbing to seventeen thousand five hundred feet for the short two hundred mile hop to Jekyll Island. I let Skipper do most of the flying with only a little help from me. I showed her how to use the autopilot, but she preferred flying by hand. Soon, the Atlantic Ocean came into view, and we could see the barrier islands off the coast. I showed her how to zoom in on the GPS screen and how to pick out airports on the ground. We pulled the power back and started our descent into Jekyll Island.

She screamed into the headset, "I see it! I see it! There's the airport!"

"You don't have to yell," I said. "I can hear you fine."

"I'm sorry. I got excited."

We set the power, flaps, and props for the approach and set up for runway one-eight. I made the radio calls and Skipper flew the airplane—with my assistance. When we were about five miles out, I said, "Gear down," and she reached for the landing gear lever. The three red lights came on, indicating the landing gear was in transit to the down position.

When the three lights turned green, she said, "Gear down and locked. Three green no red," just as Clark had taught her on the flight from Key Largo.

She positioned herself in the seat so she could clearly see the runway, and then placed one hand on the yoke and the other on the two throttle levers. She let us get a little too low and slow at one point, so I nudged the throttles up a hair and slightly pushed the nose over to get our airspeed back up.

"We're a little low and slow," I told her.

"If we're low, why did you push the yoke forward?"

"The yoke doesn't control our altitude—it controls our airspeed. The throttles control the altitude. It's a little complicated, but I'll show you next time we go flying."

It was obvious she wasn't grasping the concept, but she watched our speed increase and our descent rate decrease after the adjustments I'd made. We touched down a little harder than I liked, but we rolled out nicely without a bounce. All in all, it was a good landing.

Clark stuck his head in the cockpit. "That was Chase's landing, wasn't it? I told you he was going to need your help."

I shoved him back into the cabin. "If I can get rid of the bad habits you taught her yesterday, I think I can teach her to fly."

"Ha!" he said. "Elizabeth, you come spend a month with me, and I'll have you flying like an ace."

She twirled a strand of hair around her finger. "All you have to do is tell me when and where."

"He's thirty-four," I reminded her . . . again.

"We've been through this. He may be thirty-four, but he looks twenty-four, and he's so cute."

We went through the shutdown procedure together and soon had everything turned off and secured. By the time Skipper and I left the cockpit, Clark had our bags out of the plane and was tying the propellers. We locked the airplane and decided it would be a nice day for a walk rather than borrowing a golf cart or having someone from the Jekyll Island Club pick us up.

* * *

The island is beautiful every day of the year, but springtime on Jekyll Island is magnificent. Perhaps it wasn't the beauty of the island that brought me such peace. Perhaps it was the contrast to the concrete jungle where I'd hunted and killed, and where I'd watched the woman I loved give her life trying to save someone she'd never met. Perhaps I so hated the high-rise condos and filthy industry that had imprisoned Skipper that I would find any place beautiful and pure compared to that hell.

Skipper yanked me from my self-pity when she danced around, then took my hands in hers and skipped backward as we walked the tree-lined lane leading away from the airport.

"Hey, Chase. Thank you," she said.

"Thank me for what?"

"For letting me fly. And for bringing me here. And most of all, for coming back. I cried for a whole year after you left. Every night, I cried. I missed you so much."

Sincerity from a nineteen-year-old? Amazing.

"You're welcome."

She let go of my hands and grabbed Clark's. "And thank you, Clark, for helping Chase find me. You guys . . . and Anya . . . saved my life."

Hearing Anya's name felt like a stake being driven through my heart.

"You know, Chase tried to kick me off the team, but when I saw your picture, no way was I going pass up saving someone as cute as you."

She giggled and kissed him on the cheek. "Hey, where are we going?"

"I need to talk to the manager at the club and let him know I've come back for my boat. Also, I thought we might grab some lunch while we're there. They have an incredible dining room."

"When do we get to see your boat?" she asked.

"Right after lunch."

Jack Ford, the club manager, wasn't on the grounds, but he'd left explicit instructions to call him immediately when I or my representative showed up to get the boat.

I told the desk clerk I had Jack's number and I'd call him myself. That satisfied her, and like Skipper, she seemed to be drawn to Clark.

What is it about this guy that makes women melt at his feet?

I dialed Jack's number and listened to three rings before he picked up.

"Hello, Jack Ford here."

"Jack," I said. "Chase Fulton. I hope I haven't caught you at an inconvenient time."

"No, no, not at all. I'm so glad you called. Are you back on the island by chance?"

"I am. We just landed and are about to have lunch. I wanted to thank you for letting me keep the boat here. I'll be getting it out of your way soon."

"It's certainly not in our way, Chase. You're welcome to stay as long as you'd like. Although I do have an unexpected and perhaps bizarre request."

I was intrigued. "What is it, Jack?"

"Well," he said, "I have a couple staying with us who spotted your boat and asked if it was available for a day charter. They want to have a day on the water and were quite taken with your boat. Is that something you and Ana would consider while you're here?"

Hearing the alias Anya had been given hurt as bad as hearing her real name, but I kept my composure. "I've not really thought about that, Jack. Do they want me to take them sailing, or do they want to rent the boat without a captain?"

Jack said, "Oh, I'm sorry, Chase. I wasn't clear. They definitely want you to take them out for the day. Perhaps they'd enjoy a trip down to Cumberland Island and back. We can have the kitchen prepare a lunch for them, and of course, we'd compensate you for your time and for the use of your spectacular vessel."

"I don't know, Jack. I've had a tough few days. Let me give it some thought and I'll let you know in the morning. Is that all right?"

"Of course, that's fine. Enjoy your lunch. Have anything you'd like. It's on me. I'll call the dining room and let them know. Will it be just you and Ana?"

"No," I said. "Anya, I mean Ana, isn't with me this time. It's me and a couple of friends."

"Oh? Well, in that case, lunch for three. My treat. I'll talk with you in the morning. Goodbye."

I'd learned Clark wasn't the type to ask a lot of questions. He did a lot of observing, but not much talking. That was one of the things I liked about him. However, my conversation must have breached his limit for simply listening.

"I'm sorry to pry, but what was that all about?" He wrinkled his brow.

"I'm not sure. Jack Ford, the manager, told me a couple staying in the hotel wants to charter my boat for a day and have me take them sailing down to Cumberland Island. I don't know why, but it doesn't feel right. What do you think?"

"Is that typical in a place like this?" Clark asked.

"I don't know. I haven't spent much time in places like this, but it didn't seem to surprise Jack. It's not cheap to stay here, so I suspect the guests are accustomed to getting whatever they want."

"I don't know. It sounds pretty harmless. Maybe it's just some rich people doing rich people stuff," he said.

"Maybe you're right, but it feels funny to me."

The hostess seated us at a table next to a window with a view into Heaven. We admired the manicured gardens billowing with every imaginable flower. It was the best seat in the house. If Jack Ford treated all of his customers the way he treated me, they'd be life-long clients. A meal at the Jekyll Island Club, as I had come to understand and appreciate, was never merely a meal. It was a dining experience in a magical place where time stood still.

As we finished up, Skipper wiped her mouth with the corner of a white linen napkin. "So, can we go see the boat now?"

"Absolutely. It's a short walk across the street to the dock."

The waiter informed us that our lunch had been compliments of Mr. Ford. I thanked him and left him a more than generous tip.

We made our way to the dock and found the boat exactly where she'd been when I'd last seen her.

I motioned toward the big white catamaran. "There she is."

Skipper's eyes gleamed. "Is that really yours?"

"It really is," I said. "And now, at least for a while, it's your home, too."

She ran ahead and stood beside the boat, looking up at the rigging. She truly was a stunning boat. I was even having trouble believing she was mine.

"Can I get on?" she asked.

"Of course you can. I told you it's your home now. You don't have to ask to go in your own house."

She climbed onto the port side hull and then leapt down into the cockpit and stood behind the wheel. She must've been imagining what it would feel like to pilot such a boat. I'd soon make sure she knew how that felt.

She slid open the door to the main salon and peeked in. "Wow," she whispered.

I followed her inside as she explored the interior spaces.

"Where will I sleep?"

"You'll sleep in the port side forward cabin," I told her. "That's the left side of the boat and all the way at the front. My cabin is on the starboard side. We each have our own bathroom and personal space. I won't come on your side without your permission unless I have a good reason, like plugging a hole in the boat."

"It's your boat, Chase. You don't need my permission to go anywhere you want on your own boat."

"As I told you earlier, this is your home now. I'll respect your privacy and you'll respect mine. That's the only way two people can live together and not grow to hate each other—especially on a boat."

"Whatever you say, but it's still your boat."

When she was satisfied she'd seen every inch of the interior, she headed back out on deck and found the trampoline at the bow. "Is that a trampoline?"

"Well, yes it is, but not the jumping kind. It's for relaxing and watching the dolphins play beneath the boat."

That answer seemed to please her. We sat together on the trampoline and watched birds floating overhead and the occasional boat passing on the Intracoastal Waterway.

She bit at her lip. "I don't really know how to say this, but I need to talk to you about something."

I'd been dreading this conversation since learning what kind of life Skipper had been forced to live. I'd tried to mentally prepare myself for what was coming, and I'd practiced what I'd say when she finally got around to telling me how bad it was.

"It's okay, Skipper. You can tell me anything. I'll listen, and I promise to be nonjudgmental."

She appeared to be embarrassed. "I only have a couple changes of clothes and I don't have any money at all. I don't know what to do."

I was relieved. "There's no need to worry about that. I have some money, and there are plenty of great shops here on the island where you can find practically anything you want to wear. Life on the boat is pretty simple. We won't spend much time worrying about our wardrobe."

She smiled and closed her eyes, basking in the afternoon sun and enjoying the freedom of her new life. I wondered how the bratty little girl I'd known years before had become the bright, articulate young woman sitting before me. There had been such a tumultuous and unthinkable transition between those times of her life.

If her apparent strength was just an act, I'd see through it in a matter of days, but if she actually possessed such strength deep in her soul, if she were truly a survivor, she would be unstoppable.

I was thankful I had the skills to snatch her back from the brink of destruction in south Florida. But I feared that having her near me, entangled in the life I led and exposed to the dangers I faced, might deliver her back into the unthinkable jaws of peril she'd never see coming.

19

Freight Trains on Main Street

Skipper's breath become deep and steady as she drifted off to sleep on the trampoline. I crept away, hoping not to wake her. She'd been through more than most people could survive, and far more than anyone deserved. I didn't want to imagine the horrors she'd endured, the fears she'd known, and the loneliness she must've experienced. She deserved the sleep and peace I hoped I could help restore to her life.

While she slept, Clark and I had a cocktail on the stern deck and enjoyed the beautiful afternoon. I had a headful of questions for him but didn't know if it was against protocol to ask. I tried some verbal covert ops to avoid coming right out and asking him what I wanted to know.

"So, do you ever miss the army?" I asked.

"I miss the camaraderie and esprit de corps, but I like what I'm doing now."

"Okay," I said, "you're obviously not going to let me coerce it out of you, so how long have you been a civilian operator like me?"

He studied his half-empty glass. "I'm not like you. I'm nothing like you, in fact. You're a scalpel, a precise tool for slicing out cancer hiding behind healthy flesh. I'm a club—a splinter-filled wooden stick. I'm not cut out to be subtle. I kick down doors and knock heads together. I'm a knuckle dragger. Some of us sneak into Cuba and kill one man. Others, we drive a freight train down Main Street and kill everybody in sight. The world needs us both."

That was a nice speech, but he still hadn't answered my question.

I said, "You're more of a scalpel than you'll admit. You've heard me ask twice how long you've been doing this, and you've skillfully carved a path around an answer both times."

He laughed. "I arrived at The Ranch about three weeks before you left. I didn't have to be taught to shoot or fight, so my training was somewhat abbreviated. I've been off The Ranch and in the field less than a year."

"I guess your Special Forces background comes in handy," I said. "I'm envious of that experience and training. I've never been in the military. They plucked me right out of college. I think guys like you have a huge advantage over people like me. I think I could learn a lot from you."

He poured us each another drink, and said, "I've watched your tactics for a few days, and I can't think of a single thing I'd have done differently."

I thought back over what we'd done together and watched it play out like a movie reel in my head. "I probably shouldn't have killed Micky."

"Bullshit!" he said. "You did everything right that night. That thing you pulled with making Doc out to be the son of one of the Russian mafia kingpins was one of the most brilliant improvisations I've ever seen. That piece of crap deserved a pair of bullets in his head. He would've put two in your skull if he'd had the chance. You've got to get those thoughts out of your head, man. You were presented with a target, and you walked through that target. Don't look back. This is in your blood, dude. Don't start doubting yourself."

"How can you say I did everything right? I got Anya killed."

"Yeah, we lost an operator, and it sucks," he said, "but it won't be the last one. I promise you that. I also promise if you do this long enough, it'll be you in a body bag sooner or later. We don't live forever in this game. Anya, or Ana, whatever her name was, undeniably meant more to you than just a partner, and that makes it worse. But if you kick yourself in the ass every time somebody doesn't come back from an op, it won't take long 'til you lose your nerve and start second-guessing everything."

I closed my eyes. "Her name was Anastasia Burinkova. She wanted to be called Anya, and when she defected, her documents came with the name Ana Fulton. She was an SVR officer when I first met her, but she defected not long ago and helped me finish the Suslik job. I was in love with her. I know that's against all the rules, but rules don't stop some things."

With uncertainty in his eyes, he asked, "Are you telling me that you flipped a Russian agent and talked her into defecting?"

"No, that's not exactly what happened. I didn't really have much to do with it. We fell in love and it just happened, but it gets weirder than that. She was actually Dr. Richter's daughter from an affair with her mother who was KGB at the time. It's a long, convoluted story that's almost impossible to believe."

I took another drink and closed my eyes. "There's more, Clark."

He lifted his eyebrows.

"She told me that she and the SVR knew about my family."

"What? How could she know anything about your family?"

"I don't know, but she swore to me that she'd tell me everything as soon as Skipper was safe. I never gave her that chance. Now I'll never know what she would've told me, and there's nothing I'll ever want more than to know the truth of what happened to my family."

"I don't know, Chase. Something about that doesn't smell right to me. But I am really sorry you lost her. I know it sucks, and it's going to take a while to get through it."

"Thanks. You're right, it does suck, and I don't know if I'll ever get past it completely."

We sat in silence, and I believed we were both reliving the moments in our lives when we'd lost people we loved. Mine had been limited to my mother, father, and sister, and now Anya. I couldn't imagine how many times he must've watched his fellow soldiers fall beside him. I wondered if it would ever get easier to endure such tragedy.

"So," he said, "are you going to do the charter for the rich folks?"

"I don't know. I'm not a charter captain, and this isn't a commercial vessel. I'm not sure I want to get wrapped up in that kind of thing."

"What kind of thing?" he asked. "It's you taking a couple of rich people sailing as a favor to the guy who let you keep your boat here, rent free, and who bought us a pretty terrific lunch."

"I guess you're right. What's the harm? I'll call him in the morning and let him know I'll do it. I hate to ask you, but maybe you could hang out with Skipper for the day while I take them out."

"I'd love to," he said, "but I have to get back to work. I have a mission, so I'm blowing town in the morning. If I were you, I'd put her in a cute little sundress and have her serving cocktails and hors d'oeuvres. She might even get a nice tip at the end of the day."

"A mission?" I asked.

"Yeah, I've been tasked to go back to the Middle East and kick in some doors. The intel pukes have been picking up chatter about some Arabs planning some sort of big attack on the U.S. later this year. I'm not privy to the intel. I just go where I'm told to go and shoot who I'm told to shoot."

He obviously wasn't going to volunteer any details.

"Keep your head down and your powder dry," I said.

"You know I will, brother."

When the sun began to set, I thought Skipper might want to watch it, so I woke her up and invited her to join us.

She stretched. "How long have I been asleep?"

"A few hours," I said. "You needed the rest. We're watching the sunset and thought you might like to join us."

"Yeah, I'd like that."

We sat on the cushions and stared off into the western sky, watching the orange orb disappear behind the mangroves and sawgrass. The sky bloomed with vivid and breathtaking reds, purples, and oranges. I wished Anya could've seen it.

"Elizabeth, what's your favorite food?" Clark said, out of the blue.

"Pizza!"

"Great! Mine, too. I know a great pizza place not far away. How about you and I go grab a pizza while Chase gets ready for the charter tomorrow?"

"Wait, what charter?" she asked.

"That's a great idea," I said, "I have plenty to do on the boat. Bring me back a slice."

"Will do." Clark grabbed Skipper's hand and headed off down the dock.

I didn't know what the pizza date was all about, but I was looking forward to spending a little time alone and gathering my thoughts. There was nothing I could do to make the boat more charter-ready, so I had a couple of hours to relax and reflect.

I remembered the first time I visited that island and met the characters who talked me into becoming what I am. I'd smoked my first cigar and drank my first glass of anything that cost more than four bucks.

I strolled to the hotel and found the old marble-top table where Dr. Richter, Ace, Beater, Tuner, and I had sat that day. I ordered up a twenty-year-old scotch and the best cigar they had in the humidor. Watching the ice melt in my scotch and the plume of white smoke encircle my head, memories of that day, and every day since, engulfed me and made me glad I'd become part of something meaningful.

I doubted I'd ever become a historical figure like the four men I was remembering. Tuner developed the science of acoustic signature detection. Ace had been one of the great fighter pilots. Beater had interrogated more prisoners than anyone in history and taught those skills to hordes of future interrogators. And Dr. "Rocket" Richter had been instrumental alongside Chuck Yeager in breaking the sound barrier in manned flight. So far, I'd thrown away a promising professional baseball career by being arrogant and believing I could block home plate and overcome the inertia of a charging baserunner. I'd chopped up a Russian assassin and helped kill and send his brother to the bottom of the Atlantic Ocean from my beloved sailboat *Aegis*. I'd found and rescued a nineteen-year-old girl from the hands of pimps and pornographers in south Florida and managed to get the woman I loved killed in that operation.

I doubted any of my accomplishments would become influential world history. Maybe I'd make a difference at some point along the way. Perhaps patience would pave my way into immortality like my recruiters. If I couldn't play ball, at least I could drink old scotch, smoke great cigars, and perhaps save the world one mission at a time. My concerns and doubts about my potential impact on history would turn out to be the ignorance of innocence. In the years to come, I would have history fall into my lap on far too many occasions to count, and I'd be saddled with the awesome responsibility of ridding humanity of evils before they were allowed to surface. I'd never asked for that responsibility, but I would never turn my back on it, or the people who depended on me, and I'd keep them safe in their comfortable world of oblivion.

20
Just Chase

When I returned to the boat after my scotch- and cigar-infused stroll down memory lane, I found Skipper sound asleep in her cabin. I'd broken my promise to not invade her privacy in the portside hull, but felt justified in doing so to make sure she was safe and secure. I also found a small cardboard box with two slices of pizza in the refrigerator. On the inside of the lid, I read "I'll be your wingman anytime." I appreciated the sentiment and Clark's obvious homage to *Top Gun*.

My bed smelled like Anya, and I hoped it always would. I was lonely with my eyes open and haunted with them closed. I lay on my back and practiced the meditation techniques I'd been taught at The Ranch in the event I ever became a prisoner. Measured deep breaths punctuated with focused thoughts on specific moments in time when I felt safe, content, and fulfilled. The moments in my life which met that criteria were limited to two. The first was at home with my mother, father, and sister, and the second was when I was holding Anya in my arms and listening to her sleep. Focusing on those two episodes did nothing except remind me of what I'd lost and warn me against loving anyone ever again.

I finally drifted off to restless sleep sometime around midnight and awoke with the sun. Dawn had long been a personal and private time for me when I would pray and think about my responsibilities to myself, those around me, and God. A few days before,

Anya reminded me of what she perceived as my faith and belief in a God she didn't know. What I'd been taught about the hell awaiting the souls who died not knowing Him terrified me. Anya died while saving Skipper's life. That alone had to have some value in the here-after. If it didn't, what else could have any value?

My morning prayers rarely included requests for anything for myself. I'd never felt worthy to ask for anything from other humans, and certainly not from God Himself. I always opened my prayers with appreciation and closed with apologies. For the first time, I was having trouble finding reasons to say thank you. Doubt and questions had always been part of my belief. Perhaps faith can't exist without doubt, just as light can't exist without darkness. I'd never have the big answers, but I'd never be without big questions.

Coffee made everything better, as it almost always does. I sat on the stern deck and watched a snowy egret catch minnows in the shallows behind the dock. I envied the egret's simple life until I watched her fly away in fear when a water snake swam a little too close. I guess we all have our threats. It would be nice if all of them were so easily identified as the snake to the egret.

I was pouring my second cup of coffee when Skipper came stumbling up the stairs.

"Good morning, sunshine," I said. "Would you like some coffee?"

"That'd be great," she said.

I poured her a cup and we headed back up on deck. She wiped the sleep from her eyes and reluctantly came to life. I never remembered her being a morning person.

"What are you doing up so early?"

"I smelled the coffee and heard you moving around," she said. "Besides, I slept all afternoon and went to bed around ten last night."

"I'm glad you're catching up on your sleep. How was your date?"

She kicked at my leg. "It wasn't a date. It was just pizza. He's a super nice guy, and he's really worried about you."

"Worried about me?"

"Yeah, he's worried that you're going to keep beating yourself up over stuff that isn't your fault, but I told him I'd take care of you."

"I know you will," I said. "So, I'm going to need your help. We're going to do a day charter for a couple who's staying at the hotel where we had lunch yesterday. I owe the manager a favor. I need you to play hostess for the day, serve drinks, and wait on them. They'll probably tip pretty nicely if you treat them well and do a good job. Are you interested?"

"Sure," she said. "It actually sounds kinda fun."

I called Jack and told him I'd be glad to do the charter for him after all he'd done for me. He asked if a thousand bucks would be enough.

"No way, Jack. I don't want the money. You've been too accommodating already. You rolled out the red carpet and let me keep my boat here. I can't accept any payment. If you're going to bill your guests, give your desk clerks and kitchen staff a bonus with the money. When do your guests want to go sailing?"

"Chase, the Jekyll Island Club has a long and storied history with your . . . company. You and your partners are always welcome here, and the hotel will always be at your beck and call. Never thank us for our accommodations. After all, over the years, your partners have rendered services for the club that were priceless. We consider you part of our family."

I thanked him and asked again, "Do you know when your guests would like to go sailing?"

"I'll have to check with them," he said, "but I would think today would be a perfect day if you're available."

"In that case," I said, "I'll await your confirmation call, but today's fine with me. We're ready when they are. I'll need some provisions from your bar and kitchen, though."

"The couple—Michael and Sara Anderson—is at breakfast now. I'll make contact with them and let you know. I'll have the kitchen and bar managers make a delivery to your boat as soon as we confirm."

"Thanks, Jack. I really appreciate everything."

I hung up and yelled for Skipper. When she showed up on deck, she was wearing a towel wrapped around her with wet hair dripping down her back.

"We'll probably be doing the charter today, and there are some clothes in my cabin you can wear. You'll find a couple dresses in the hanging locker and plenty of shorts and things in the dresser. You'll probably want to wear a sundress for the charter. I plan to wear pants and a button-down. We'll look professional, even if we have no idea what we're doing."

She grinned. "I was just coming up to tell you I had nothing to wear for a fancy charter."

"Anya was a little bigger than you, but her things should fit you fine until we can do some shopping."

She left to try on clothes, and my phone trilled.

"This is Chase."

"Mr. Fulton," came a pleasant voice. "I'm Barnard, the bar manager at the club. Mr. Ford asked me to provision your boat for an all-day charter for the Andersons. I'll have one of my bartenders deliver what you'll need for the charter, and I am also to stock your boat after the charter with whatever you'd like. Of course, we'll be sending a case of very nice scotch, but if you'll put together a list, I'll see that you have whatever you'd like."

"Thank you, Barnard. That's very kind of you and Mr. Ford. I assume this means our charter is on for today?"

"Yes, sir," he said, "Mr. Ford said ten o'clock this morning. Goodbye, Mr. Fulton."

I passed the word to Skipper as she climbed from the starboard hull into the main salon wearing the sundress we'd bought for Anya less than a week earlier. She was beautiful in the dress and sounded sincerely excited about the charter.

I stowed everything onboard that looked personal in nature and tried to make the boat appear as much like a charter boat as possible. I laid out a pair of life jackets and a couple bottles of sunscreen. I had Skipper round up a couple of blankets in case the Andersons were to get chilly after sundown. I planned to show them a full day of cruising the barrier islands. I was starting to enjoy the idea of the charter, thinking it might be good for my spirits.

The bartender and kitchen deliveryman arrived on the dock with dollies loaded with provisions. I invited them aboard, and we started a bucket brigade until we had the provisions stowed away and easily accessible.

When we finished, I wished both men a good day.

"I'm supposed to sail with you," the bartender said. "Mrs. Anderson likes a Vodka gimlet, and Mr. Anderson is a White Russian man. I make their drinks for them. Also, I'll prepare lunch for your crew and guests."

"That's fine with me," I said. "We appreciate the help. Are you okay in the galley if the sea gets a little rough? Some people get sick when they're stuck inside in rolling seas."

"I'll be fine," the man said. "I was a bartender and chef on a private yacht for six years. I think I can make it one more day, but thank you for the concern."

"In that case, make yourself at home. I'm Chase. I'll be the skipper, and Elizabeth here will be our hostess and server. She'll be available to help you with anything you need."

"I'm Vinny," he said as he shook my hand. "It's a pleasure to meet you, Captain Chase."

"Just Chase," I said.

Vinny shuffled his feet.

"Is everything all right?" I asked him.

He glanced away as if he were trying to decide if he should tell me what was on his mind. I was intrigued.

He eyeballed Skipper then wiped his hands on his apron. "Uh, Chase, I try not to stick my nose where it doesn't belong, but I'd really like to talk with you if you don't mind."

"Of course," I said. "Let's go inside."

"Well, I'm going to take a little walk up to the club," Skipper said. "I think I may have left something in the restaurant."

I liked her skills of perception. She'd developed an ability to read people's intentions and body language. That was a skill that would serve her well, regardless of what she did for the rest of her life.

Vinny and I walked into the main salon, and I closed the door behind us.

"Have a seat," I said. "What's on your mind?"

I could see the hesitance still on his face.

"Captain Chase," he began.

"Just Chase," I reminded him. "Look, something is clearly bothering you, and I see it's important enough that you want to talk to me about it. I'm listening, and no matter what you tell me, I'll keep it between us—if that's what you're concerned about."

He licked his lips and appeared to gather his courage. "It's not so much that I want you to keep it between us, and it might not be anything at all. I just overheard the Andersons talking about you yesterday, and I thought maybe you should know."

Vinny was starting to sweat.

"Would you like a drink, Vinny?"

"Oh, no sir. I couldn't. I'm on duty."

"Yeah, you're sort of on duty, but it's sea duty today, and everyone knows all good seamen get a daily ration of grog."

His shoulders relaxed and he even smiled. "Thanks, Chase. I could go for some water if you wouldn't mind. Oh, but I can get it! You're the captain. I'm just the bartender."

I pulled two bottles of water from the cooler and handed him one. "Okay, so let's hear what the Andersons were saying about me."

He opened his bottle and drank half of its contents. The tension in his face said his nervousness was returning.

"Bartenders hear lots of stuff, and it's kinda like our code that we don't talk about what we hear. You know, like a doctor–patient thing." He finished what was left of his water. "So, I was setting up their nightcaps . . . they're kinda picky about their cocktails . . . and anyway, I don't think they knew I could hear them."

My impatience was swelling, but I stayed relaxed and let him go at his own pace.

"I try to be invisible when I'm serving, and I think maybe I was a little too invisible because they were talking like nobody was around."

I nodded and leaned in to indicate that he had my full attention.

"Do you know anybody named Captain Norikova?" he asked.

"Captain Norikova? Uh, no, I've never heard that name."

"Yeah . . . are you sure?"

"I'm sure I'd remember a guy named Norikova," I said.

"I don't think it's a guy. Mrs. Anderson said she saw Captain Norikova on your boat . . . and she thinks you killed her.'"

"What? Are you sure that's what you heard?"

"Yeah, I'm sure. And I'm not trying to get involved in anything. I don't know you and I don't know the Andersons. I just thought maybe I should talk to somebody about this. I wanted to talk to Mr. Ford, but I don't know . . . it just didn't seem right."

"Listen to me, Vinny. This is obviously a big misunderstanding. I don't know anyone named Captain Norikova, and I've certainly never killed anyone by that name. If you don't feel comfortable doing the charter, I'll tell Mr. Ford you aren't feeling well, and I'm sure he can find someone else to fill in."

Vinny shook his head. "Oh, no. I feel fine about the charter with you. I just didn't feel good knowing something like this and not telling anyone. It sounded pretty serious to me. I'm really glad I told you, Captain Chase."

"Just Chase," I said.

21
Exchanging Glasses

The Andersons arrived at precisely ten a.m., and unlike what I would expect of most wealthy people, they actually asked permission to come on the boat.

"Please come aboard. I'm Chase Fulton. I'll be your captain for the day. This is Vinny and Elizabeth. Vinny will ensure that you have your Vodka gimlet and White Russian exactly as you like, and Elizabeth will make sure the glasses arrive in your hands before you ask. If there's anything we can do to make your day more enjoyable, or if there's anything in particular you'd like to see, let us know. We're at your service."

They looked nice enough, but they didn't strike me as being wealthy like I'd assumed. Skipper showed them the boat and helped them get comfortable on the trampoline while I fired up the diesels and checked the gauges. Everything was working as it had been designed to work. I cast off the lines, and we headed out to the channel and into the great expanse of the North Atlantic. I was happy to see a wind out of the southwest. That would mean the seas would be relatively flat and we wouldn't get tossed about.

The morning breeze was freshening and already blowing around ten knots. I turned south and had the sails set and trimmed in less than two minutes, and I listened as the diesels fell silent. There aren't many sounds in the world sweeter than a sailboat slicing through the water and the wind whistling in the rigging.

Skipper proved to be a perfect hostess and server. Before their glasses were empty, she was standing beside them with a fresh cocktail. She served a beautiful tray of cheeses, fruit, and crackers that Vinny had prepared in the galley.

About an hour into the cruise, Mrs. Anderson came aft and asked to use the restroom. I hadn't thought about them needing to use the head. I'd left my towel on the deck and shaving kit spread over the countertop in the starboard head. I glanced at Skipper.

In another display of her impressive skillset, she read my mind and mouthed, "It's clean."

"The restroom is in the left side hull. Turn left in the main salon and go down the stairs. The bathroom will be on your right," I said.

"Thank you, Captain."

I was headed for Cumberland Island, thinking the Andersons might enjoy seeing the beautiful barrier island from the ocean side. About six minutes after Mrs. Anderson had gone into the main salon, I saw her return as if she'd been in the starboard hull instead of the port side as I had told her. When she returned to the deck, she wore a look of dissatisfaction.

"Is everything all right, Mrs. Anderson?" I asked.

"Fine. Do you live on this boat alone, Captain Chase?"

Her question seemed inappropriate and a little odd.

"Well, yes ma'am, I do, but Elizabeth is temporarily living aboard as my guest. Why do you ask?"

"Oh, I see. I thought I saw you aboard with a young lady a few nights ago. She was blonde, tall, and slightly heavier than Elizabeth, but maybe I'm mistaken."

The conversation with Vinny bounced around inside my skull like a rubber ball, and I tried to deflect her statement. "No ma'am, it must've been Elizabeth. I've not had anyone else aboard."

Had she seen Anya and mistaken her for someone named Captain Norikova?

I didn't like the feeling I was getting in the pit of my stomach, and there was definitely more to the Andersons than met the eye. The look on her face told me she was unconvinced.

As soon as Mrs. Anderson was back on the trampoline, I motioned for Skipper to come to the helm. "If either of them asks how long you've been on the boat, tell them a couple of weeks. Mrs. Anderson was asking questions about Anya, and I'm not sure what to make of it yet."

"Okay. Is anything wrong?"

"I'm not sure yet. Maybe I'm just being paranoid, but there's something not quite right about those two."

Skipper kept serving drinks, and I noticed Mr. Anderson checking his watch every three minutes, and then looking up into the cloudless sky each time.

I called for Skipper to come to the helm again. "Stand here at the wheel and look like you're driving. The autopilot is on, so you don't have to do much other than look diligent. I'm going up to talk with our guests."

"Why are you being so paranoid?"

"I'm sure everything's fine," I said, trying to reassure her. "I just want to talk with them and see what time they want to have lunch."

I could tell she was skeptical, but she did as I asked. Walking to the bow, I pulled on the shrouds and inspected the rigging as I went.

I knelt on the deck behind the trampoline. "I hope the two of you are enjoying your day with us."

They both smiled, and Michael said, "It's a beautiful day and a gorgeous boat. Thank you for having us aboard, Captain."

"Please call me Chase. I thought we might tuck into a beautiful little anchorage behind Cumberland Island called Brickhill River. The scenery is breathtaking, and it'd be a wonderful place to have lunch. Vinny's preparing a fantastic meal for you."

"That sounds wonderful," Sara said. "Doesn't it, Michael?"

"It certainly does," he said. "What did you say the name of the anchorage is?"

"It's Brickhill River, a quaint little inlet off the Intracoastal Waterway. There's plenty of privacy, and we'll be out of the wind, so it should be a perfect spot for lunch. Please continue to make yourselves comfortable, and if there's anything you want or need, let Elizabeth or me know."

"Thank you," they said.

I headed back to the helm and thanked Skipper for playing along. I glanced back to the bow to see Michael on his cell phone and checking his watch and the sky again.

Skipper glanced conspiratorially at the Andersons. "So, James Bond, what did you find out?"

"Get out of here. Go help Vinny or do hostess stuff."

She winked as she danced away. I hoped I was being unnecessarily concerned, but I felt like I had every reason to question who and what the Andersons were.

Just as Michael had said, it was a beautiful day and a magnificent boat. I was sailing and nobody was shooting at me. That added up to a pretty good day in my book.

About an hour later, I dodged the shoals and breakers at the northern end of Cumberland Island, and I made my way into the delta formed by the Satilla and Cumberland rivers. Turning back southward into the Cumberland, I found the wind had fallen off to less than six knots. It wasn't going to be possible to sail down the river as I had hoped, so I started the engines and furled the big genoa up front. I left the mainsail aloft for the sake of appearances.

I motored down the Cumberland River until I came to Terrapin Cove, a larger anchorage about two and a half miles north of Brickhill River, and dropped my anchor in eleven feet of water.

Vinny had set a beautiful table on deck with flowers, china, cloth napkins, and elegant silverware. I headed to the bow to attach the snubber, a large piece of hard rubber designed to act as a shock absorber between the anchor chain and the boat.

As I passed the Andersons, I said, "Vinny has your lunch prepared and he's set a beautiful table for you in the back."

They rose and headed aft, but I was surprised to see Michael walking down the portside while Sara took the starboard.

When we made it to the stern, Michael said, "I'd like to wash up before lunch if you wouldn't mind. Where would I find the men's room?"

I pointed into the interior of the boat. "Make your way through there, turn left and down the stairs. The head is on the right."

He went into the interior, and I slid the door open so I could see and hear if he was pilfering around inside my boat. Shortly after, he returned to the deck with his hands still wet, so perhaps he really was just washing up for lunch. I needed to relax. The Andersons were nice people, and I was trying to turn them into something sinister.

Vinny served them salads and then poured a taste of pinot grigio into Michael's glass. Vinny stepped back while the man sniffed and tasted the wine. Following a silent nod of approval, Vinny poured two glasses and walked away. Skipper watched with obvious interest as Vinny worked.

The main course came out as soon as Skipper cleared the salad plates and replaced the wine glasses. Vinny presented a bottle of chardonnay and Michael inspected the label. After examining the bottle, Michael slid his fresh glass to the edge of the table and Vinny poured another taste. Michael swirled the glass and held it up, staring intently into the wine. He stuck his nose in the glass and inhaled deeply before tasting it and declaring it perfect. Vinny smiled, poured, bowed, and backed away.

I was watching the show from the navigation table inside the main salon. Vinny's performance was impressive, and Skipper seemed to be learning a new collection of skills from the seasoned bartender and chef. I watched the Andersons carefully and noticed Michael scanning the marshy shoreline every few minutes.

I called Vinny over. "What are you serving for dessert?"

"I'm doing a nice cheesecake with fresh mango and diced pineapple with a mint garnish."

"Sounds fantastic," I said. "What wine will you serve with it?"

"Definitely a sauvignon blanc," he said, as if I was supposed to know which wine paired with cheesecake.

"Can you do me a favor? Just for fun?" I asked.

"I guess so," he said. "What is it?"

"I want you to pour out the bottle of sauvignon blanc and refill it with a pinot noir. Serve it in champagne flutes. No, wait. On second thought, have Elizabeth do it. That way if it goes south, you can claim she's learning, and you can make it right."

"Why would I do that?"

"It's just a hunch," I said. "I don't think these people know as much about being rich as they're pretending to know. I'd like to have a little fun and see if my hunch is correct."

"Okay, but if this screws up my tip—"

I put my hand on his arm. "If it screws up your tip, I promise I'll make it up to you."

He shrugged. "Okay. You're the captain."

He went to work emptying the white wine into a carafe and re-filling the empty bottle with a beautiful red pinot noir. He pressed the cork back into the bottle until it was flush with the lip. He briefed Skipper on the plan and then sent her to refill their glasses with the chardonnay. I liked Vinny's tactics. It appeared he wanted the Andersons to see Elizabeth at the table before pulling the red-for-white prank during dessert.

As the couple was finishing the main course, I walked onto the deck and stood with my hands crossed behind my back. "I hope you're enjoying your lunch. Vinny is quite the chef and sommelier. Wouldn't you agree?"

Sara smiled. "Everything is marvelous. We couldn't be happier." She had no discernable accent and spoke almost flawlessly.

"I hope you're finding Jekyll Island to your liking," I said. "Where do you call home?"

Michael and Sara locked eyes before he said, "We're from the Midwest originally, but we live in New England now. We travel a good bit and always enjoy coming to the South—when it isn't too hot, of course."

He was devoid of accent as well, and his answer to my question couldn't have been more vague.

"Well then," I said, "it looks like it's time for dessert, and has Vinny got a treat for you."

I stepped aside as Skipper cleared the table and replaced the silverware. She stood tall, thin champagne flutes in front of each of them. She stepped aside and allowed Vinny to present the dessert plates with the creamy white cheesecake. They sighed in admiration of the beautiful dessert, and Vinny took a small bow. Skipper returned to the table and held out the sauvignon blanc bottle for Michael to review.

He glanced at the label for less than a second before looking up at her with a furrowed brow. "You're pouring a sauvignon blanc and you set up champagne flutes."

I moved to intervene, but Vinny beat me to it. "I'm so sorry," he said. "Please forgive me. It's my fault. I had originally planned a champagne with dessert, but I reconsidered and thought you'd prefer the sauvignon blanc."

Michael said, "No apology necessary, and champagne actually sounds good with the cheesecake. Let's see what you had in mind."

Okay. Wrong again. He knows his wine. Maybe he is a rich guy after all.

Vinny returned with a chilled bottle of Marc Hebrart Rosé Brut and offered it for Michael's inspection.

He checked the label and offered his flute. Vinny poured a taste.

"Keep pouring, chef," Michael said. "Everything you've served has been perfect. There's no reason to taste test a bottle that good."

"Yes, sir. Enjoy," he said, then he headed straight for me. "Well, I guess that's not what you expected."

"No, not exactly," I said, "but thanks for playing along."

Maybe I was wrong about the Andersons. I'd spent too much time learning to mistrust everyone around me. It was time to chill out and play boat captain.

"We have a decision to make," I said.

Michael and Sara perked up.

"I've checked the conditions outside the islands, and the wind has picked up to twenty knots. That means we can do one of two things. One, we can take a leisurely sail back up the Intracoastal Waterway. It'll be nice and calm with ten knots or so on our starboard stern quarter. We can watch the birds and probably see quite a few cruisers headed both ways. The second option is we could head back out, away from the protection of the barrier islands. We'll hoist every sail we can find and see how much fun we can have on a big catamaran in twenty knots of wind. I know what I'd pick, but this is your day. So, what'll it be?"

"Let's have some fun!" Sara said.

"Perfect. I'll tell Vinny to batten down the hatches."

I started the diesels, removed the snubber, and idled forward, bringing the big anchor back aboard. We motored out of the Cumberland River and into the channel leading us out into the mighty North Atlantic. When we came out of the lee of Cumberland Island, I unfurled and trimmed the headsail, and eased the mainsheet to rig the boat for sailing on a beam reach. She accelerated beautifully. The wind had taken over, and there was no need for the noise of the engines.

The further we sailed from the barrier islands, the harder the wind blew, until it was blowing a sustained twenty-six knots. I had a little too much sail up for that much wind, so I turned the boat into the wind, brought the mainsail down, and stowed it in its cover. Back on course, the boat felt like a new Ferrari. She heeled about five or six degrees and bit into the waves. My former boat, *Aegis*, would've been heeling thirty degrees, and everything that wasn't tied down would be crashing all over the cabin. The tendency of the catamaran to sail flat was one of the things that made her so comfortable.

After setting the autopilot to hold our course, I turned to the Andersons. "If you want to go back up front, it'll be a lot of fun, but you're going to get wet. I have some bathing suits downstairs if you want them. I recommend the upper deck above our heads. It'll be a great ride, and you'll stay dry."

Sara wasted no time. "I wanna drive!"

Michael shrugged. "The lady wants to drive."

"Then drive she shall," I said.

I showed Sara to the wheel and told her there was nothing to hit, so she should have some fun. She turned the boat about twenty degrees to the south, and I directed Michael in trimming the sail for the new course.

I explained, "The closer to the wind Sara steers, the tighter we have to keep the headsail. When she turns away from the wind, we have to ease the sheet and let the sail out."

"The sheet?" he asked.

"I'm sorry. I forgot to tell you that sailing has its own language. A sheet is a line used to trim a sail. This is the genoa sheet," I said, holding the red and white line in my hand. "The genoa is the big sail upfront. It's all the sail we need in this much wind. In fact, if the wind picks up much more, we won't need all of the genoa."

The boat picked up speed and started cutting through the waves. When we'd hit a wave just right, the hull would send a wall of water up and over the bow and crashing onto the cabin top ahead of us.

The boat started losing speed and the genoa flapped in the wind.

"What happened?" yelled Sara.

I laughed. "You turned into the wind—we can't sail that way. This is called 'being in irons' because we can't go anywhere. Turn the wheel all the way to the left, and wait for the bow to fall off and fill the sail again."

She did as I said, but it wasn't happening.

"Now, turn the wheel all the way to the right and be patient," I said. "We're too far into the wind to turn left, so we'll have to let her come all the way back around."

The bow fell off to the right, and the boat came lazily around, making a giant circle in the water.

Sara giggled. "Oops. I'll try not to do that again."

"Don't worry about it," I said. "Everyone does that at first. You're doing fine."

When she had the boat headed in the right direction, we started picking up speed again. The boat was heavy, but she accelerated impressively. When we stopped picking up speed and settled back into the groove, I glanced at the GPS and saw we were making twelve knots. I couldn't believe a sailboat could make twelve knots upwind. I was becoming more impressed with my new boat by the minute.

Sara made the boat dance and skip across the waves. "Michael, you've got to try this! It's amazing!"

I pointed to the helm. "Michael, if you can get her away from there, it's all yours."

I watched and listened as Sara told Michael what to expect and how to steer. I was impressed with his ability to let her go on without interruption.

Sara finally surrendered and jumped into my arms, hugging me. "That was great! Thank you, Chase. Now show me how to sheet the sail or whatever."

We went through the same instructions I'd given Michael, and she caught on quickly. Soon, she and Michael were working together like a well-oiled machine. It was fun to see them enjoy themselves.

They took turns piloting the boat and trimming the sails for the rest of the afternoon. As evening approached, I told them we needed to get back to Jekyll Island. The channel and inlet could be tricky in the dark.

Turning downwind, we eased the genoa sheet, converting the huge sail from a lifting wing into a kite, and suddenly everything was calm and placid. We were running before the wind and making twelve knots, but it felt like we were sitting still. The boat was well-behaved, and I couldn't have been happier with her.

We made it back to the dock just as the sun was making another spectacular exit. I recommended having a seat up top and enjoying another cocktail as the sun sank into the western horizon. It was the perfect punctuation to a fantastic day at sea.

* * *

Three young men slipped out of a white service van sitting in the parking area. Two had dollies laden with cases of liquor and wine, and the third man had a rolling garbage can. I hopped from the boat and stopped the men who were eager to get their jobs done and go home.

I said, "Hey, can you guys wait a few minutes until our guests disembark? I don't want them to get in your way, or vice-versa. They'll be leaving in just a few minutes."

The men groaned and grumbled. I returned to my boat to help the Andersons ashore.

They finished their cocktails and made their way down from the upper deck. They ignored me and headed straight for Skipper and Vinny, where they thanked them, shook their hands, and pressed a thick fold of cash in each of their palms.

The Andersons approached me. "Chase, we had an amazing time today. Thank you for everything. Your boat is beautiful. Your crew is amazing. The food was spectacular. And, you, our new friend, are a great captain."

He stuck out his hand, and I could see several one hundred-dollar bills folded in his palm. "I'm not a shaker," I said. "I'm a germaphobe." I closed my fist and offered him my knuckles for a fist bump.

He turned away from me and whispered to Sara before she jumped into my arms again. I thought I felt her touch my butt, but I didn't react.

"Chase, this was the most amazing day. I wish we could do it again, but we're leaving tomorrow. Thanks for everything," she said.

They left the boat, and my crew emerged from the main salon.

Skipper held out a wad of cash. "Can you believe they gave me a four-hundred-dollar tip? We've gotta do more of these charters."

Vinny counted off seven hundred-dollar bills and slipped them into his apron. "Thank you, Chase. I enjoyed the day on your boat, and Elizabeth is fantastic. If she ever needs a job, have her look me up."

I thanked him for the great work and for the previous night's conversation about overhearing the Andersons.

He said, "My guys in the van are going to stock your bar and carry away the trash. Do you mind if they come aboard?"

"Of course not," I said. "Anyone bearing free liquor is always welcome on my boat."

The men went about provisioning and cleaning the galley. Vinny gave them explicit instructions and jogged up the dock toward the hotel. His guys were finished in less than five minutes, and the interior of the boat looked brand-new.

When the men were gone, Skipper came out of the main salon with a scotch on the rocks for me.

"Thank you, but you aren't the hostess anymore. You don't have to serve me."

"You've worked hard today," she said. "You deserve a drink."

"You did a great job today. I couldn't have asked for more from you."

I left the deck to change clothes and make sure everything was still where it had been before our adventure at sea. When I removed my pants to slip on shorts, I felt a lump in the back pocket. I reached in and pulled out ten hundred-dollar bills.

So that's what Sara was doing when I thought she was grabbing my butt.

I carried the cash back out on deck and handed it to Skipper. "Here's a little jump-start for your new wardrobe."

She stared at the bills and grabbed me, pulling me into a long, intense hug. "Thank you, Chase. You're the best!"

"Don't get used to fourteen-hundred-dollar days on the boat. I don't anticipate doing any more charters."

22
Someone's Watching

Vinny had secretly made us a little dinner and dessert care package and left it on the boat. After Skipper and I devoured our meal, she got up from the table and danced into the main salon. I liked how she never seemed to walk anywhere. She was either skipping or dancing. I think that spoke volumes about the happy child who still lived inside her, despite the horrors she'd endured.

She returned with the half-full bottle of champagne and two flutes. "Do you think it'd be okay if I had a glass of champagne?"

I took the bottle from her hand and poured two flutes of the bubbling amber champagne.

"Thank you for not treating me like a kid."

"Thank you for working so hard today. You did a great job. Even Vinny said so."

"It was fun," she said. "I learned a lot. It was hard work part of the time, but I liked it. What were you doing when you had me take the wrong glasses to the table? I mean, I didn't even know there were different kinds of glasses for different kinds of wine."

I scoffed at my previous behavior. "I'm just paranoid. The work I do makes me not trust people. The whole thing about a couple wanting to go sailing, specifically on my boat, made me a little wary. Also, Sara said she saw a woman on the boat with me and she described Anya to a T. I was doing a little test to see if they were really a rich couple or just people pretending to be what they aren't. I figured they wouldn't know champagne from Chablis if they were pretending, but they knew their stuff. I was just being cautious."

I suggested we hit the sack.

"You can sleep in as long as you'd like tomorrow," I told her. "We don't have anything to do except take you shopping. I guess you're getting tired of wearing Anya's clothes."

"No, I actually kind of like her stuff. She has good taste. After all, she picked you."

"She had good taste," I corrected her, "but not in picking me. Picking me got her killed."

"I'm sorry. I didn't mean to . . . ."

"It's okay," I said. "It's going to take a while for me to get over her and what happened."

She wrapped her arms around me and laid her head on my shoulder. "I know. I'm so sorry for everything."

"It's not your fault. Bad things happen sometimes, but I promise not to let anything happen to you."

She kissed me on the cheek. "Good night. I'll see you in the morning. And I'm holding you to that shopping trip you promised."

I rubbed the top of her head, messing up her hair. "Good night, Skipper. I'll see you in the morning."

"Are you ever going to stop calling me Skipper?"

"Probably not," I said.

* * *

Sleep came, and I awoke with the sun as usual. I made coffee and hosed off the deck and hulls to get rid of the saltwater spray from the previous day's adventure.

I'd hadn't seen the underside of my new home, so I pulled a set of scuba gear from a locker and slid into the water. I was impressed with the underwater lines and surprised how shallow the draft was. I swam between the hulls and rubbed at a couple of smudge spots that came off easily. Just before I reached the bow, I saw a small black disk beneath and behind the trampoline. I kicked upward, trying to reach it, but it was too far out of the water for me to touch. I made a mental note of its position and climbed out of the water. I rinsed off myself and my dive gear with the hose on the dock, and shook like a dog shedding water before climbing back on board. I lay down on the trampoline and tried to push my hand between the mat and the lacing holding it in place, but my hand was too big.

"What are you doing?" Skipper was standing by the mast with a cup of coffee in her hands.

Frustrated, I said, "There's something stuck on the hull of the boat, but my hand's too big to get it."

She set her mug on the deck and slid down the front of the cabin top. "Maybe my hand will fit."

"Good idea." I pointed to the object. "See if you can reach it. I don't know what it is, but if you can get it off, I'd like to see it."

With ease, she stuck her hand through the lacing. "I can feel it, but it's stuck on there pretty good."

"Keep trying, but I have an idea." I walked to the back of the boat and lowered the dinghy into the water. I fired up the outboard engine and motored around to the bow. I cut the engine and pulled myself beneath the trampoline, hand-over-hand, until I was directly beneath the object. Skipper was still twisting and pulling, but whatever it was wasn't going to come off the hull easily.

When she pulled her hands away, I saw it—a satellite tracker. I motored back around to the stern and lifted the dinghy back onto its davits.

Skipper met me in the cockpit. "Did you get it off?"

"No, I'm going to leave it for now."

"What is it?" she asked.

"It's a satellite tracker," I said. "It sends a signal to a specific satellite, and anyone who has access to the data from that satellite will always know where this boat is."

"Well, isn't that a good thing? If you ever get in trouble, someone will know where you are."

"Like most tools, it has its positive side when used for good, but when the wrong people are looking, I don't always want them to know where I am."

"Do you think the Andersons put it there?"

"I don't know yet, but if they did, it had to be Sara. Michael's hands would've been too big."

I called Jack Ford.

"Good morning, Jack. Chase Fulton here. I have a couple favors to ask."

Jack spoke in his usual friendly tone. "Of course, Chase. Anything you need. Just name it."

"First, I wonder if you could get me that little red Porsche I had last week. And second, I need to come talk with you about Sara and Michael Anderson."

"The answer is of course, yes, to both. I'll have Stephanie arrange for the car, and I'll be in my office all morning. Come by at your leisure."

Before Skipper and I left the boat, I was careful to lock every hatch, and I activated the boarding detection system, a handy little gadget that would let me know if anyone had been aboard in my absence.

"Where are we going, Chase?" Skipper asked.

"We're going up to the hotel to pick up our rental car, and I need to talk with the manager for a few minutes."

We climbed the steps to the lobby of the hotel.

"Go in and order us some breakfast, and I'll be in to meet you in a few minutes," I said. "I'd love an omelet and coffee."

"Sure. I'll see if we can get our favorite table."

* * *

Stephanie was at the front desk. "Good morning, Mr. Fulton. Mr. Ford is expecting you. Go right on in."

"Thank you, and good morning to you, too, Stephanie."

Jack rose to greet me, and I took a seat in front of his massive desk.

"It's good to see you, Chase. I heard the charter went splendidly well."

"We had a nice time, and Vinny was incredible. You're lucky to have him."

"We certainly are," he said. "He's been with us for almost fifteen years. He started as a dishwasher and will probably be executive chef one day. He's dedicated and hardworking. I could use a dozen more exactly like him."

"I'm sure you could," I said. "Listen, Jack. Some things came up with the Andersons that rang a little bell in my head. If you don't mind, I'd like to ask you a few questions about them."

"Sure, fire away. I'll tell you all I can."

"Great. First, how often do they stay with you?"

He cocked his head. "This was their first time on the property. They came in the day after you arrived without a reservation and booked a room for ten days, but they checked out this morning."

"I may be pushing my luck here, but can you tell me what address they listed as their home address, and how they paid for the room?"

He pressed a button on his phone. "Stephanie, bring me the Andersons file, please."

In seconds, she appeared in the doorway with the file in her hand. She offered it to Jack, but he pointed to me. "Give it to Chase. Thank you, Stephanie."

I opened the file and thumbed through the contents. It indicated they'd paid with cash and listed a post office box in Wilmington, Delaware as their home address. No phone numbers were listed.

Jack gave me plenty of time to go over the file before he asked, "What's this all about? What has you concerned?"

"I don't know, Jack. I just felt uneasy with them, and this file is so vague. They could be anyone from anywhere."

He squirmed in his seat. "Forgive me for asking, but is everything okay with Ana? I haven't seen her since you came back, and now you have a new young lady with you."

"Oh, yes, Jack. Everything's fine. Ana was called away for work, and I brought an old friend's daughter to help get the boat back to the Keys. Thanks for the information—and for the concern."

He didn't look satisfied with my answer, but I wasn't going to give him the chance to probe further. I stood, placed the file on his desk, and offered my hand. He opened his mouth to speak, but I cut him off.

"I greatly appreciate your hospitality, Jack. I think we'll be leaving tomorrow. It looks like we have a pretty good weather window for our trip back down south. Thank you for everything."

"You're quite welcome, Chase. We're always at your service."

I met Skipper in the dining room at what had become our favorite table overlooking the garden. The waiter was delivering our plates as I arrived.

We enjoyed our breakfast and watched several birds playing outside the window. When we'd finished, I signed our bill and the hostess handed me the same key fob from the previous week. I thanked her, and we headed out the doors and down the steps.

"Hey, you have a driver's license, right?" I asked.

"Sure I do," she said.

I tossed her the keys and pointed toward the bright red convertible Porsche sitting by the curb. "Good, then you can drive."

"Are you serious? That's our rental car?"

"Yep, it sure is. Now let's get to that shopping trip I promised you."

I slid into the passenger's seat, and she slipped into the driver's seat and buckled her seat belt. The car roared to life at the touch of a button, and she pulled away from the curb.

We stopped at the same shops Anya and I had been. I tried not to let the memory put a damper on my mood, but I'm sure Skipper could tell I wasn't myself. Shopping with Skipper was nothing like shopping with Anya. Where Anya had been efficient and decisive, Skipper was agonizingly slow to pick out anything and insisted on my approval for everything she tried on.

I took her by the shoulders. "Pick what you want. It doesn't matter what it costs. You're going to need clothes if you're going to be living on the boat for a while."

"But I only have fourteen hundred. You said I'll have to make it last since we won't be doing any more charters."

"I may have misspoken. Keep your money. The shopping trip is on me. You've earned it."

"Seriously?"

"Yes, seriously."

She squealed. "Thank you, Chase! You're the best."

I gave my credit card to the clerk and pointed toward Skipper. "Put whatever she wants on this. I'll be sitting over there."

The clerk took a good look at me and then Skipper who was no-ticeably younger than I was. "Of course, sir. Some gentlemen like to impose a limit on what their lady friends spend. Shall I limit what she buys?"

I decided to have a little fun with the clerk who disapproved of what she thought was going on between me and Skipper.

"I'll tell you what," I said. "If it's more than a hundred bucks, let me know. I may need to split it up onto another card or two."

I let her stew for a minute.

"On second thought, don't worry about the total. I assure you my lady friend, as you so eloquently called her, is worth whatever she costs."

With that, I retired to a comfortable overstuffed chair near the dressing rooms that had, undoubtedly, been placed there for gen-tlemen waiting for their lady friends to finish shopping.

Our shopping trip turned into stops at nine more shops. While I was waiting for Skipper, I called Dominic to ask if he'd placed the satellite tracking device on the hull of my boat. He assured me the boat had no tracking devices aboard except the EPIRB, the emer-gency position-indicating radio beacon, which would notify the Coast Guard if the boat were to sink.

I made a mental note to point that device out to Skipper.

"Why do you ask about a tracking device?"

"I found one on the hull, behind and beneath the trampoline," I said.

"If it was beneath the trampoline, it's unlikely that it would work very well without a clear view of the sky, and unless it's hardwired to a power source, it can't remain active very long."

I thanked him and told him about Skipper being aboard. "We're going to head south in the morning. I plan to make St. Augustine tomorrow afternoon. What's the likelihood of me getting a new assignment anytime soon?"

"I don't know. That's not my area," he said, "but I'll put out some feelers and see what I can find out. Do you need a little time to catch your breath and gather your wits?"

"Yeah, about fifty years should do it."

He sighed. "I understand. Check in with me when you make St. Augustine, and I'll let you know what I find out about upcoming assignments."

We hung up as Skipper walked up, looking battle weary from over-shopping.

We found a great burger joint and talked about how things used to be. I told her about my plan to leave Jekyll Island the next morning and head south, probably to St. Augustine, and then further south in the coming days. I told her I'd like to get to the Virgin Islands if the weather would cooperate.

She seemed excited about her first real trip aboard the boat. "Can you teach me to sail?"

I agreed to turn her into a sailor, and we decided an early night was in order so we could get underway when the sun came up. It was a perfect ending to a very long day. I had no way to know the days to come wouldn't end so peacefully for either of us.

23

Lessons

As usual, I woke as soon as the first rays of the sun came through my portlight. I was surprised to smell coffee brewing in the galley, and when I climbed the stairs into the main salon, there were two mugs sitting beside the pot, but there was no sign of Skipper. Perhaps she'd started the coffee and gone back to bed. I was certainly capable of getting us underway without her help, but I was thankful for the coffee.

When I walked out on deck, I saw her dragging the heavy hose from the diesel pump down the dock and toward the boat.

"Oh, good. You're up," she said. "I thought we should take on fuel and water before we left this morning, so I got the gas guy to turn the pump on for me."

I set my mug down and reached over the lifeline for the pump nozzle. She hefted it up, and I started filling our tanks.

"Hand up that water hose, and I'll top off the fresh water tanks while we're here," I said.

She did as I'd asked, and the tanks were soon overflowing. The boat had an automatic water maker, but I wasn't sure how much water it produced per day. It appeared to be keeping up with our water usage quite nicely, but there was no excuse not to fill the holding tanks.

"We need to turn our car back in."

Skipper leapt to her feet. "I'll do it! Where are the keys?"

I pulled the fob from my pocket and tossed it to her. "Park it out front at the hotel and leave the keys with the clerk at the front desk. Oh, and if Jack Ford's in his office, have the clerk give me a call, and I'll run up and say goodbye."

"Okay," she said, "I'll be right back."

I'd asked Vinny to have one of his guys provision the boat for us while we were out shopping the day before, and once again, he exceeded my expectations. We had everything we needed for at least two weeks at sea, but it wasn't my plan to do any overnight trips. I needed Skipper to learn enough about the boat so she could stand watch while I slept a few hours during the day. It'd be a while before she was ready.

I heard the Porsche accelerate out of the marina parking lot as if Anya were at the wheel. It made me smile. Twenty minutes later, Skipper was on the dock, singing and dancing her way back to the boat. When I saw her coming, I fired up the engines and checked for oil pressure and raw water flow for the cooling systems. Everything was in order, so I had Skipper cast off the dock lines before she climbed aboard.

"Mr. Ford wasn't there yet. Stephanie said he'd be in around nine."

I'd motored away, and we were well clear of the dock. "Here, take the wheel," I said. "You have to start learning sometime, so how about now?"

She grabbed the wheel with both hands and stood on her tip-toes, looking out over the bow.

"Point us toward the center of the bridge. It's sixty-five feet at the highest point and our mast is sixty-two feet above the waterline. I'm going to bring in the fenders."

I went to work hauling in the big rubber fenders we'd hung over the side to protect our hull from the dock. Skipper did exceptionally well handling the boat beneath the bridge and down the Intracoastal Waterway. I explained the importance of the buoys and how to read the GPS chart plotter.

It didn't take long for us to make our way out of the mouth of St. Andrew Sound and into the North Atlantic. I feared we'd have a headwind all the way to St. Augustine, but I was pleased to see the wind shifting out of the west, making a fast, comfortable sail to the south. It was less than sixty-five miles to the St. Augustine inlet, so we would be there in time for dinner.

Just after lunch, Skipper stood at the helm, and I was nodding off in the cockpit.

"Chase! What's that?"

I awoke and jumped to my feet. I saw the conning tower of a navy submarine heading west in front of us.

"That's a submarine," I said. "He's headed into the Mayport Naval Station." I pointed into the southern end of the mouth of the St. John's River. There were several naval vessels tied up in the basin.

"That's so cool. Are we going to be in his way?"

"No, he's moving a lot faster than us. He'll pass in front of us, but just to be safe, let's turn a little to the east so he'll know we see him."

We made our turn and Skipper retrimmed the sails for the new course without any direction from me. Perhaps we'd be making overnight passages sooner than I expected.

"That reminds me," I said. "I want to show you something."

I pointed out the fluorescent green device resting in its holster on the bulkhead. "This is the EPIRB. If we were to sink, this would float free of its little holster and send out a rescue signal to the Coast Guard."

She studied the device. "Do we have to be sinking for it to work?"

"No, we don't have to be sinking for it to work. If you hold the red button down for five seconds, it'll activate. We'd only do that if we were on fire or damaged in a storm. There's no way to know ev-erything that could go wrong, but I think you get the picture."

We made the turn into the St. Augustine Inlet, and I stepped to the wheel.

She pushed me away. "Let me do it. If I screw it up, you can take over before I kill us."

I liked her confidence and newfound love of seamanship. She did everything I would've done, and she even spotted and avoided the sandbar south of the Usina Bridge. Even with our shallow draft, we could've found ourselves aground if we hadn't stayed in the channel.

We dropped anchor in the Matanzas River north of the Bridge of Lions in Old St. Augustine. As the sun was setting, we turned on the anchor light and hoisted a pair of chemlights, one blue and one orange, up the pennant halyard so we could identify our boat in the dark.

We took the dinghy ashore and had dinner at a Cuban restaurant where a salsa band was playing to a hoard of dancers, twisting and gyrating to the irresistible rhythm.

"Come on, Chase. Dance with me," Skipper said.

"I don't know how to dance."

I guess she didn't hear me. She pulled me from my chair and onto the dance floor, which was little more than an empty area surrounded by tables pushed out of the way.

She yelled over the music and grabbed my hands. "It's easy! Just feel the rhythm and let your body do what feels good."

It was awkward at first, but Skipper was amazing. She pushed and pulled, coiling our arms together in what felt like crazy tangles, but soon unwound us in time with the music. Her feet were a blur, and her hair flew around her head like a tornado. I soon caught on and started to feel the music instead of simply hearing it. My feet seemed to know what to do even though my brain did not. I'd never considered myself a dancer, but I was having fun.

The song ended and another began. We bumped into a couple dancing beside us on the crowded floor. The man was tall, thin, and Latin. He was the epitome of the exotic Latin lover most women dream of, and she was his perfect partner. Her dark skin, long black hair, and curvy physique gave her an exotic look that was impossible to ignore. They were obviously experienced salsa dancers.

He turned to Skipper, offering his hand, and she danced away with him, surely relieved to have found a better dance partner. The woman smiled and put her hands on my shoulders.

"Relax," she said. "Salsa is about being sexy and loose. Let your body think about making love with me, all sweaty and hot. Now let's dance."

She didn't move like Skipper. Everything about her was exotic and erotic. The way she urged me to move with her was intoxicating. I don't know if we danced for two minutes or two hours, but I was exhausted and drenched in sweat when Skipper took my hand again. Our partners danced away together as if their night had just begun.

"I have to get a drink and sit down," I said. "I'm exhausted. Who knew salsa dancing was so much work?"

We found a table and motioned for a waitress. Skipper leaned into me. "Can I have a daiquiri?"

I held up two fingers. "Two waters and two daiquiris, please."

The waitress assessed Skipper, who was glistening with sweat and had her hair pulled back into a ponytail.

She returned a couple minutes later and placed the drinks on our table. "Both of the daiquiris are for you, right, sir?"

I handed her a twenty. "Of course."

By the end of the night, I was doing pretty well. I'd never be a Latin lover, but I was no longer embarrassing myself. When we'd danced until we couldn't dance another step, Skipper laced her sweaty arm through mine, and we headed back through the old city. Judging by the empty streets, it must've been after two a.m.

We hopped back into our dinghy and motored out toward the boat.

"Hey, the boat's pointed in the other direction from when we anchored," Skipper said.

"That happens when the tide turns. That's why we only anchor from the bow and give plenty of room for other boats around us to swing."

I could tell she was tucking away another tidbit of nautical knowledge. We climbed out of the dinghy, reattached it to the davits, and hoisted it out of the water.

I noticed the end of a line dangling from the cabin top near the door to the main salon. I didn't remember the line being there when we left the boat, but I dismissed it. Skipper had probably tossed the line onto the cabin top instead of coiling it. I was being overly paranoid again, but I wasn't going to let my paranoia ruin what had been a great day, and an even better night for us. We were doing a good job of keeping each other's spirits up and remembering to live instead of merely existing.

"This was the best day of my life, Chase, and it's all because of you. Thank you for everything."

"It's been a pretty great day, and you're an amazing dancer."

She gave me a playful shove. "You're the dancer. You looked great out there, all sexy and hot. You're a natural. Even the Brazilian hottie was checking you out." She kissed me on the cheek. "Good night, Chase. I'm taking a shower and crashing. Do we have to get up early?"

"I'm doing the same. Sleep as late as you want. We have nowhere to be tomorrow."

She frolicked down the stairs into her hull, and I limped down into mine. I was going to be sore by morning.

* * *

I was asleep minutes after my head hit the pillow. I dreamed of dancing with Anya like I'd danced with the dark-haired beauty earlier that night. I could hear Anya's laugh and smell her hair. I could feel her on top of me and remembered how she moved when she surrendered to her desires and—

A sharp pain in my neck jolted me awake. I swatted at the stinging, and my hand struck flesh and bone. I struggled to see who or what had stung me, but my cabin was dark and my vision wasn't clear. I grasped at the flesh I'd hit. It felt like a woman's wrist, but my strength was fading, and the little vision I had was becoming blurred and tunneled. I was losing strength, and as my vision faded to utter darkness, I thought I caught a glimpse of a hypodermic needle. I tried to yell out to warn Skipper, but the words dissolved in my throat.

24
Interrogation

When I came to, Skipper and I were tied back-to-back. Our arms were pulled backward and our hands were tied across each other's stomachs. Several wraps of line were around our necks, holding the backs of our heads together. My legs were secured together above the knee and at the ankle. I wasn't going anywhere. Skipper was breathing behind me, but she was unconscious. I tried to gather my wits and assess our situation, but I was still groggy from whatever I'd been injected with. The boat was moving, and I could hear a diesel engine.

Skipper began to wake and pulled at our bindings.

"Skipper, listen to me. We've been drugged and abducted. Try to wake up and listen to me."

Her voice trembled with terror. "Chase, what's happening? What do we do?"

My mind and vision were clearing, and I recognized that we were in the workshop on my boat.

I tried to sound calm. "I don't know who did this to us, but they're pros. They injected us with a drug to knock us out, and whoever tied us up knew exactly what he was doing. Are your legs tied together?"

"Yeah," she said, still trembling. "They're tied at my knees and ankles. What do we do?"

"Try to stay calm." My brain spooled into action, trying to devise a plan. "They don't want us dead or they would've killed us in our sleep. They know enough about us to know we're dangerous. You don't tie someone up this well unless you're afraid of him. They probably know how long the drugs last and will be checking on us at any minute. The good news is they probably won't separate us. They've gone to too much trouble tying us together. The bad news is they're probably going to interrogate us. We—or more likely, I—know something they need to know. At least one of our captors will be aggressive—that's how it works. So don't resist. Every question they ask, tell the truth. They'll probably threaten to hurt one or both of us. They'll probably threaten you to get me to talk. I'm going to be defiant or I'm going to lie, but I won't risk letting them hurt you."

"I'm scared," she whimpered.

"I know. It's okay to be scared. Just tell them whatever they want to know, and don't worry about what they do or threaten to do to me. Sooner or later, they'll make a mistake, and we'll capitalize on it."

"I'll try," she said.

"The next few hours are going to suck, but I'm going to get us out of this. Embrace the suck for a little while. It'll be over soon."

Her trembling body pulsed through my own.

I inspected the workshop to locate anything we could get our hands on to cut ourselves free, but everything was on or above the workbench. There was no way we could stand up, and even if we could, we wouldn't be able to walk.

Footsteps drummed on the cabin sole outside the door. The latch on the door clicked, and the door swung open. The face peering through the doorway was Sara Anderson, Michael's wife.

"Oh goody," she said, "you're awake. Are you comfortable? Can we get you anything? Perhaps a pinot noir in a champagne flute?"

Shit. I knew there was something about those two. I should've listened to my gut.

"Michael! Our guests are awake!"

Skipper's back was to the cabin door. "Is that the woman from the charter?"

"Yeah," I said. "I don't know what's going on yet."

I heard the engines slow to idle and Michael coming down the stairs. He pushed his way through the cabin door and placed his booted foot on my left kneecap.

I took a deep breath and tried to prepare myself for the imminent pain that would come as soon as he put his weight on my knee.

Sara knelt beside me. Her breath floated across my neck as she whispered, "Where's Anya?"

I'd prepared myself for as many questions as I could dream up, but not that one. Who were these people and what was their connection to Anya?

Even though I knew the pain was coming, I furrowed my brow, feigning confusion. "Who?"

Michael's weight came down hard on my knee, and I bellowed in agony as I felt my kneecap grind into the joint.

Skipper screamed, "Stop It! Stop It! Don't hurt him!"

Sara rolled a dish towel into a gag, stuffed it into Skipper's mouth, and taped it in place. I could feel Skipper breathing in shallow gasps of air, so she could still breathe through her nose. After all the horrors she'd endured, it sickened me to know she'd been plunged back into the depths of Hell because of me. Even if I died doing it, I would ensure Skipper survived the ordeal, no matter what the cost.

"I guess you didn't hear my question over all the screaming, so let's start over," Sara said. "Where is Anastasia Burinkova? She's not reported in to Colonel Tornovich for several days. What have you done with her?"

Michael lifted a pair of pliers from the workbench and held them in front of my face. I was about to have a little dental work done.

I opened my mouth. "Would you mind starting with the molar on the bottom right? I think it has a cavity anyway." I spat in his face.

Instead of probing into my mouth with the pliers, Michael was a little more creative. Without wiping my spit from his cheek, he jammed the jaws of the pliers up my nose and locked down on my septum. The blinding pain lit a fire that surged through my face and body. My impulse to writhe only deepened the torture, so I sat still, praying I'd pass out. I'd been hurt in a lot of ways by a lot of people in the previous few years of my life, but I'd never known physical pain like that.

He plunged the pliers deeper into my nose, and his knuckle pressed against my lip. I bit down on his knuckle with every ounce of strength I could muster, and I tasted blood, but I didn't know if it was from his finger or my nose. I didn't care. I kept biting, unwilling to surrender. When he could no longer withstand the pain, he opened his hand and dropped the pliers right into Skipper's hands, which were still tied together at my stomach. I refused to release his finger from my teeth, knowing that was my only means of attack. I let go only when I saw a large black object rushing toward my head.

* * *

When I regained consciousness, Skipper was working violently at the bindings on her wrists, using the pliers she'd caught to grind away at the ropes.

A self-assessment determined how much more torture I could survive—I knew more was coming. I only hoped I'd be able keep Skipper alive. My head ached as if I'd been hit by a truck, and my face was on fire. I could taste the blood dripping from my nose. I tried to flex my knee, and it moved without unbearable pain so it probably wasn't broken. Michael must've hit me with the fiberglass emergency tiller lying on the cabin sole. It had a nasty blood stain on the fat end. If Skipper could manage to cut through her bindings before Michael and Sara came back, and if my knee would support my weight, I'd have a fighting chance against the two of them when I got my hands on that emergency tiller.

"Skipper, I'm okay. Keep working on those ropes."

The engines were back up at cruising RPM, so I assumed Michael and Sara were taking us to rendezvous with another team.

Did Sara say Anya hadn't reported to Colonel Tornovich? Why would she report to him?

It hit me like a freight train. Anya was still working for the Russians. She'd been reporting every move we made back to Colonel Victor Tornovich, her SVR handler. I'd been sucked into a gorgeous, blonde honey trap, and Anya had played me like a Stradivarius. The Russians had perfected the honey trap, in which an irresistible operative would seduce both the body and mind of an American, leaving him to feel, hear, and believe only what the seductress wanted. All her talk of honeymoons and babies in the future was line for line, right out of a script. The SVR now knew everything Anya knew about me. I'd willingly given her the keys to the castle, and she'd passed them right along to Tornovich. How could I have been so naïve and stupid? How could Anya have been so convincing when she lay in my arms and told me she loved me? I'd been played. I felt like I'd been gut-punched by a demon, and I could taste the bitter bile worming up my throat.

As the rage in me boiled, I felt Skipper's hand break free. She untangled her arms from mine and pulled the tape and gag from her mouth. Blood dripped from her fingers where the handles of the pliers had torn into her skin as she twisted and ground against the ropes. "Are you all right, Chase?"

We didn't have time to talk about how not all right I was.

"Reach up with your right hand. There's a knife on the corner of the workbench. Cut my hands free and give me the knife."

I knew she was capable of cutting us free, but I wanted the knife in my hand if Michael or Sara came back through the door. I cut the ropes binding our necks and abdomens. When we were free from each other, I sliced my leg ropes and turned to do the same for her. She'd found a box cutter from the workbench and cut the ropes from her legs before I got to her.

"Do you have any guns on the boat?" she asked.

"I do, but not on this side. I'd have to cross the main salon to get to it."

"When this is over," she said, "I really want one on my side of the boat."

I didn't know what happened inside her head in the preceding few minutes, but she'd gone from terrified, crying little girl, to badass in a flash.

Our situation had improved, but we were still on a boat with two Russian operatives who were highly skilled in the art of torture and interrogation. I was certain they were armed, so taking back our boat wasn't going to be a cakewalk. We needed to know Michael and Sara's location, and how well-armed they were. I feared we might learn the latter an instant too late.

25
I Missed!

There was going be a fight. There was no chance Michael and Sara would give up the boat without fighting for their lives, so Skipper and I had to embrace the same mentality. I searched the workshop for anything we could use to help even the playing field, or at least tilt it in our favor.

I found a flare gun and six flares, and I handed them to Skipper. "This has to be a last-resort weapon. If we fire these and they stay on the boat, we'll have a big fire to deal with, and there's almost nothing worse than a fire on a boat."

"How about two assholes with guns and a knot-tying fetish?" she said.

"Okay, maybe that's worse."

I kept searching for anything we could use as a weapon—and I found it. It was a forty-eight-inch speargun designed for shooting fish under water. I'd never fired a speargun out of the water, so I didn't know if the shaft would fly straight and have enough energy to stop a human, but I guessed we'd find out.

Skipper tucked the flare gun into the waistband of her pants. I handed her the speargun and showed her how to load the shaft by attaching the elastic bands and pressing the tip into the cabin sole until it locked in place.

"You need to be very close to Michael when you pull the trigger. With three bands, the shaft will probably keep sinking until it comes out his back or it hits a bone. Either way, he's going to be hurt. Try to shoot him in the center of his chest."

"Why do I have to shoot him? Why don't you do it?" she asked.

"I'm the one he's going to be watching when we go up on deck," I said. "I'm the one he's afraid of. He thinks you're just a hostess, and he'll never be expecting you to have a weapon. But don't get nervous and shoot me."

"What about the woman? Why aren't you worried about her?"

"I am worried about her, but I'm stronger than she is, and I don't think she had a gun. At least she didn't have one when she was kneeling beside me. Michael's stronger and probably better armed. If we can eliminate him, our chances of coming out of this alive go way up."

I picked up the emergency tiller from the deck and realized how much it felt like a baseball bat. I'd swung a few baseball bats and hit more than my share of homeruns in my days on the field. My confidence level was increasing.

"Chase, when this is over . . . are you going to explain what's really going on?"

I slid my hand around the back of her neck and pulled her to me. "I promise I'll tell you everything as soon as those two assholes are off our boat."

The sound of the engines quieted and the boat slowed.

"They're coming back," I said. "We have to change our plan."

"I'm listening," she said.

"Instead of taking the fight to them, we need to ambush them. I don't know which one will come through that door first, but we'll have to act quickly. Stand with your back against the workbench and have the speargun aimed at the door. As soon as it cracks open, I'm going to yank it the rest of the way. I'll be staying low, so you'll have plenty of room to shoot over me. If it's Michael, shoot him in the middle of his chest the instant you see him. Do you understand?"

"Yeah, okay, but what if it's her?"

"If it's her, I'll grab her and force her to the ground. You get her mouth taped as fast as you can, and we'll tie her up, but we have to keep her from screaming. It's crucial that you get her mouth taped as soon as possible."

"Why not kill her?" she asked.

"I'll explain that later, but for now, stick to the plan, okay?"

"Okay. Let's do this."

She took her position in front of the workbench and raised the speargun level at what would be Michael's chest.

I heard footsteps outside the door, but they didn't sound heavy enough to be Michael's. I'd much rather have seen Skipper put a steel shaft through the man's chest than wrestle with Sara, but we had to take advantage of every opportunity as it came. I knelt by the door, ready to pull it open as soon as it cleared the jamb. The footsteps came nearer, but I still couldn't tell who they belonged to. The metallic click of the door latch released above my head, and I glanced at Skipper, who was laser-focused on the door.

The boat turned to the right, and a slapping sounded against the hull.

"Sara!" Michael yelled. "Get back up here. There's something wrong with one of the engines."

The door latch closed, and I heard Sara run back up the stairs.

"What's happening?" Skipper whispered.

"I'm not sure, but I think we may have picked up a piece of rope or fishing net on the starboard propeller."

"Is that bad?"

"Not for us," I said. "In fact, it's great. It'll get their attention focused on the problem and away from us. We'll have an opportunity to surprise them."

The engines shut down, so I listened for movement on deck. Michael's heavy footfalls echoed through the main salon and down into the opposite hull. He must've been going to check on the starboard engine. Our opportunity had come.

"We're going up," I said. "You're going to stand in the galley and shoot him when he comes back up the stairs. I'm going onto the deck to subdue the woman. No matter what you hear outside, do not leave the galley. Put that shaft through his chest, then yell as loud as you can that you've done it. Do you understand?"

"Yeah, I've got it. Shoot him in the chest and yell for you."

We opened the door and peeked into the companionway. We didn't see a soul. Creeping from the workshop, we climbed the stairs to the main salon. I was in front with the emergency tiller and Skipper was on my heels with her speargun cocked and locked.

"Remember, no matter what you hear outside, your job is to shoot Michael in his chest."

"I got it," she whispered.

She broke off to my right, and I watched her take up a position in the galley. Moving carefully toward the door to the deck, I glanced over my shoulder to make sure Skipper was in the correct spot. She was braced against the counter with the speargun pointed straight at the starboard side stairs.

When I reached the door, I quick-peeked to see if I could see Sara. She was leaning over the starboard aft rail looking down into the water. Perfect. I could be on her in less than four strides and either have her subdued or knocked into the water in seconds. I raised the emergency tiller in my left hand and sprang through the door.

The instant I reached her, Skipper screamed, "Chase! I missed!"

I swung the tiller at Sara's head as if I were unloading on a hanging curveball, but she'd also heard Skipper's scream and turned reflexively. She had just enough time to see the tiller racing through the air at her head. I felt the fiberglass tiller strike hard. I'd been swinging at her head, but she'd raised her arm to deflect the blow, and it redirected into her rib cage. I heard bone crack, and she dropped to the deck. I turned to see Michael swing the long speargun and connect with Skipper's left jaw. She went down like a felled tree and Michael threw the empty speargun to the deck beside her.

He started through the door and straight for me as his right hand went for his belt. He was reaching for a gun, but we'd only be a few feet apart by the time he drew his weapon. I closed the distance between us and swung the tiller as hard as I could, aiming for his gun hand. He turned to take the blow in his gut rather than on the bones of his right arm. It would still hurt, but not as bad as I'd hoped. When the contact came, it sent him stumbling backward, but I hadn't made contact with any ribs. We were about to be in good old-fashioned fisticuffs.

He took a hard swing at me with a left hook, but I'd been expecting that, so I rolled to my left and let the punch fly harmlessly past my head. The momentum he'd built during the punch carried his body into the oversized cushion on the portside settee. He reached for his gun again, and I caught a glimpse of the black metal of the automatic as it came from his belt and started upward. At that range, if he'd gotten off a shot, it would've been impossible for him to miss me. I uncoiled, and in a desperate attempt to stay alive, I swung the tiller. Its fat end connected with the automatic. The collision sent the weapon sailing through the air and into the dinghy hanging on davits at the stern.

I'd begun to level the playing field, but there were still two of them and only one of me. Sara was injured, but not unconscious.

Unfortunately, I hadn't made contact with Michael's hand when I'd swung at the gun. I'd hit the gun cleanly and left him unhurt. He leaned forward from the cushion and lunged at me with his arms outstretched. He'd decided to turn our fight into a wrestling match. I wasn't interested in going to the deck with him and preferred to stay on my feet, but so far, nothing was going the way I wanted.

When his shoulder hit my chest, it forced me against the steering wheel. The blow folded me backward across the wheel and left me temporarily shocked. I gathered my wits, and in rapid succession, threw three sharp elbow shots into the back of his neck. He keeled over as the blows took effect and sent him to his knees.

I turned to see Sara climbing back to her feet and reaching for her waistline. I didn't want to deal with another gun, but what I wanted didn't seem to matter. I'd dropped the emergency tiller when Michael forced me against the wheel. I hoped he'd stay down long enough for me to deal with Sara.

To my initial relief, I watched the shiny blade of a five-inch double-sided dagger leave the sheath on Sara's hip. I could deal with a knife. She came at me swinging left and right in strong, short chops. She'd evidently been to the same knife-fighting school as Anya. I knew she'd soon plant her left foot and lunge for my abdomen. As soon as that happened, I spun to my left and stepped sharply forward and right. The thrust came, but I'd anticipated it. I grabbed her wrist as she sent the knife toward me, and I twisted it up and over her head. As she fell forward, I forced her arm in the opposite direction. She screamed as her arm inverted at the elbow and the knife fell to the deck.

I didn't want to kill her. If I could keep Sara alive, she had potential to be a great source of intelligence and a nice bargaining chip for international relations, but she seemed determined that only one of us survive. She grabbed at her broken right arm and bellowed. I wrapped my right arm beneath her chin and locked it in place with my left. I had her in a sleeper hold. She would fight, but without her right arm, she had no hope of getting me off her. Her face turned red, then finally pale, as the lack of oxygen to her brain turned her legs to mud. I let her fall, and I picked up her knife.

Michael was back on his feet and charging again. I didn't have time to get the knife positioned to inflict any damage before he plowed into me. This time, there was no wheel behind me to stop our momentum, and I tumbled over the rail into the water. He tried to push me free of his grasp before I went over, but I'd held on and carried him overboard with me. We hit the water, tangled together, but I kicked free and put some distance between us. I'd believed I'd gained at least a slight advantage—I was comfortable in the water and still had the knife.

Like a fish, he faded away beneath the surface, eliminating my advantage, and I lost sight of him. I kicked for the stern of the boat —the only possible place to get back on board. The ladder at the stern was my only exit from the fight.

Just as I thought I'd made the ladder, he grabbed my right ankle. I kicked at his hand with my left foot, but he captured both of my legs. I took a breath and bent at the waist, thrusting the knife in front of me as I doubled over, hoping to get at least a glancing blow, but we were in his element. He moved like a barracuda and dodged my jabs. He threw my feet upward and sent his knee crashing into my gut, forcing the air from my lungs. Fighting in the water was definitely his strong suit.

I kicked as hard as I could with both feet, hoping to make contact and give myself a chance to get another breath. It half worked. I didn't make contact, but when he dodged my kicks, it gave me a few feet of separation and a chance to stick my head above water long enough to refill my lungs.

I was getting my ass kicked and running out of ideas and stamina at the same time. Not wanting to fight anymore, I chose flight and turned to swim for the starboard side of the boat. If I could outswim him around the bow and back to the stern, I could get back on the boat and get my hands on the pistol I'd knocked into the dinghy. I dug my hands into the water and kicked with all the energy left in my body. I was stroking for the stern, but ten feet before I reached the ladder, it felt like I'd been snared by a sea monster.

The harder I fought, the more bound I became. Then, it hit me. I was caught in the same net that had stopped the starboard engine. Fighting against the net would be in vain. I tried to remain calm and come up with a plan to get back to the surface, but my lungs were burning and I'd lost the ability to form a rational thought. My fate had been sealed when I went overboard, and I was going to drown. I was at peace. I relaxed and stared toward the surface. I would see Anya again.

In the tranquility and disorientation of the moment, I felt a splash in the water behind me and soon felt two strong arms around my waist. Michael had come to finish me off and watch me die, but he wasn't pulling me deeper—he was pushing me up.

When we broke the surface, I filled my lungs with air and my heart with the will to continue the fight. I kicked at him like a mule. I had to get him away from me. Realizing I was never going to overpower him in the water, I reached for his eyes. If I couldn't drown him, maybe I could blind him. Instead of the soft flesh of his face, my thumbs found something solid and slick. I shook the water from my eyes and saw the man I was fighting was wearing an orange hood, a diver's mask, and a snorkel. Just past him was an orange and white U.S. Coast Guard patrol boat with a young, uniformed man training the deck-mounted fifty caliber automatic rifle on my boat. The man I was fighting wasn't Michael Anderson, he was a Coast Guard rescue swimmer saving my life.

Standing on the ladder of my boat was Michael with his hands on top of his head and his fingers interlaced. In a show of surrender, I stuck my hands into the air. I didn't need the Coast Guard thinking I was the bad guy.

I caught my breath and yelled, "My name is Chase Fulton. This is my boat. There's a nineteen-year-old woman in the main salon with a head wound. She's with me. That man and the woman with him are pirates."

I coughed out a mouthful of salt water and tried to apologize to the rescue swimmer for fighting him.

He spit out his snorkel. "Ah, it's all right, Mr. Fulton. You didn't hurt me, and we already know who you are. You and Ms. Woodley are safe now. The Coast Guard's got this."

How does he know who we are?

Two armed, uniformed men stepped from the patrol boat and onto my catamaran. They handcuffed Michael. Seeing Sara's damaged arm, they showed a little sympathy and chose not to cuff her. One man stood with his sidearm drawn, undoubtedly in case Sara decided to get frisky. The rescue swimmer hefted me toward the ladder of my boat, and I crawled out of the water and sprawled out on the deck.

Skipper was sitting in the doorway of the main salon with the flare gun in one hand and the EPIRB in the other, her thumb still pressed solidly on the red button. One of the Coast Guardsmen gently removed the flare gun from her hand and knelt to examine the wound on her face. He shined a small penlight into her eyes and took her pulse.

26
Small World

I climbed into the cockpit and reached for Skipper's hand. Hiding the physical and emotional pain behind a forced smile, she let me help her to her feet and onto the settee.

She grimaced. "Oh, Chase. Your nose looks terrible. It must be killing you."

I touched my face. It was painful, but I was more concerned about Skipper. I studied the wound on her face inflicted by the butt of the speargun. It wasn't cut, but it was going to be a nasty bruise, and she'd need some X-rays. "You saved our lives with the EPIRB," I said.

She blinked her eyes through the pain. "We weren't on fire, but we've definitely been through a storm."

"One hell of a storm," I agreed.

"I'm so sorry for missing him with the speargun. I don't know what I did wrong. It was like the spear went crazy when I pulled the trigger."

I stroked her hair. "It's not your fault. Everything worked out fine in the end."

"I was so scared, Chase. I'm ashamed of how scared I was."

"Shh, there's no reason to be ashamed. Anyone would've been scared, but you had the sense to keep fighting and finding a way. If you hadn't activated the EPIRB, we'd probably both be dead."

"Please tell me it's really over and it won't ever happen again."

"I wish I could," I said, "but I can't make that promise. It's the nature of the work I do. I never could've predicted this, so I can't say for sure it won't happen again."

Another uniformed, older man stepped from the patrol boat onto my deck. "Mr. Fulton, I'm Lieutenant Rutherford, the commander of the patrol boat."

I started to stand, but Skipper held on to me with a death grip.

Lieutenant Rutherford noticed Skipper's hold on me. "Keep your seat, Mr. Fulton."

"Is he with you?" I asked, pointing toward a black boat racing toward us with blue flashing lights.

Rutherford glanced toward the oncoming boat. "That'd be the FBI. They're not really with me or anybody else. They tend to do their own thing. They'll be taking these two into custody, and my men and I will get you and your boat back into St. Augustine safely."

The FBI pulled up and tied off to our port side. Two men in black-soled boots stepped aboard and produced a pair of credentials.

"You know, guys," I said, "it's polite to ask permission from the skipper of a boat before you jump aboard—especially with black soles."

One of the FBI agents said, "We don't need permission to come aboard."

Lieutenant Rutherford cleared his throat. "Actually, without a warrant, you do need the captain's permission. The Coast Guard is the only entity who's exempt from that pesky little rule."

The man ignored Rutherford. "I'll be taking my prisoners now."

Rutherford cleared his throat again. "They're my prisoners until I release them to you, Agent. Neither has been Mirandized or questioned. The woman has a broken right arm that needs medical attention, and the gentleman isn't hurt, but he's a little feisty. They're all yours now. Try not to wreck your pretty little boat on the way back to dry land. Oh, and one more thing. Dry land is that way."

Handcuffed and dripping wet, Michael glared at me as if he were making plans to rip my heart out. "Where is Anya?"

Skipper leapt from the settee with remarkable speed and slapped him violently. "Anya is dead, asshole, and you should be, too!"

The two agents grabbed Michael's arm and dragged him aboard the sleek FBI boat where they shackled him to a D-ring on the deck. They were a little more careful with Sara, but not much. She got the same shackling treatment, but they were again kind enough not to cuff her broken arm.

Michael, shackled to the FBI boat, never took his eyes from mine. He said, "You know, Chase, you're harder to kill than your father was."

I exploded from my seat, evading Rutherford as he tried to grab me, and I leapt over the gunwale of the FBI boat, landing at Michael's feet. He ducked his head and instinctively raised his shoulders in a vain attempt to protect himself from my attack. My first punch landed with a crack just in front of his left ear, whipping his head to his right as my left uppercut landed beneath his chin. Blood and spittle flew from his mouth as the force of my punch rendered him unconscious. As I repositioned my feet and prepared to deliver the next blow that would shatter his neck, an agent and Lieutenant Rutherford plowed into me simultaneously, sending me to the deck beneath their weight. I fought against them, determined to finish the man who said he killed my father ten years before. I thrashed like a fish on the deck and did everything in my power to break free, but it was no use. The two men had me pinned.

"Calm down, Mr. Fulton," said Rutherford.

"I'll calm down when I rip his heart out for killing my family. Now, get off me," I said, still twisting and writhing in their grasp.

"You know we can't do that," said the agent. "We'll find out everything he's ever done and he'll pay for everything, but you have to leave that to us. Now, let's get you back on your boat."

The two men began frog-marching me back toward my boat. I feigned a fall and planted my left knee on Sara's broken wrist. She wailed in agony and shoved at me with her free arm.

I jerked away from Rutherford and the agent and positioned my face inches from hers. "I'll find you, and I'll kill you both. No matter what rock you crawl under, I'll be there. You're going to pay . . . with your lives."

The agent grabbed each of my arms and a Coast Guardsman placed me in a powerful headlock that left me completely under their control. With blinding speed, they hurled me across the gunwale and back onto the deck of my boat. I came to rest facedown with Rutherford's boot planted on my spine and the two FBI agents, guns raised, making sure I wasn't getting within ten feet of their prisoners.

"Stay down, Chase," came Rutherford's calm words. "Just stay down. I know what you're thinking, but not here. Not now. You'll get your chance."

I grunted my submission, but not my agreement.

The FBI boat disappeared as quickly as it had arrived, but Michael and Sara Anderson, or whatever their real names were, hadn't seen the last of me.

Lieutenant Rutherford removed his boot from my back, allowing me to sit up. He sat on the bench seat. "As I told you before, we'll be making sure you get back to St. Augustine safely this afternoon. Is your boat still seaworthy?"

I tried to calm myself, but my head was pounding and I could taste my lust to end Michael Anderson. I exhaled, trying to focus on my immediate situation. Accepting that my revenge would have to wait, I said, "Except for the net wrapped in the starboard propeller and an EPIRB that's still going off, I think the boat's fine."

"Rutherford deactivated the EPIRB. My swimmer will have your fouled prop clear any minute."

"Thanks," I said, "I appreciate you having him take care of that."

"Oh, I didn't have him do it," said Rutherford, "he just does stuff like that. I can't keep him out of the water. When he saw you flailing around down there, he was in the water and on his way to you before I could get the boat stopped."

"Well, then, I suppose I owe him a bottle of whatever he drinks."

Rutherford laughed. "I suppose you probably do."

The swimmer emerged from the water with a huge section of commercial fishing net in his arms. He dumped it aboard the patrol boat, along with his mask, fins, and snorkel, then climbed aboard my boat.

The orange-clad swimmer stuck out his wet hand. "Mr. Fulton, I'm Petty Officer Third Class Tony Johnson. I think you know my brother, Clark."

So that's how the Coast Guard knows who we are.

I stood up to greet him. "It's nice to meet you, Tony. I guess it's a small world."

"No, sir," he said. "The world ain't small. It's just the part of the world you and my brother live in that's small."

I had to agree with him on that one. "So, Tony, what do you drink?"

"Well," he said, "Clark and me grew up in Tennessee, a long way from the ocean, so I'm kinda partial to Jack Daniels."

"Follow me," I said, leading him into the main salon. I handed him a bottle of Gentleman Jack. "Thanks again, Tony. If you hadn't come along, my day would've ended quite differently. You saved our lives."

He stared at the bottle and then at his lieutenant. "Savin' lives is what we do, Mr. Fulton, but the old man ain't gonna let me take this on his patrol boat."

I patted him on the back, ushering him out of the salon. "I have a feeling your lieutenant might look the other way just this once."

"Get on the boat, Tony," Rutherford said. "And for God's sake, stow that contraband somewhere I don't have to see it."

Tony gave him something resembling a salute, then he said, "Hey, Chase, did you know there's a speargun shaft stuck in your overhead in the cabin?"

I pointed my thumb at Skipper. "Yeah, she's trying out new decorating ideas. It's part of the décor."

He and Skipper locked eyes.

"You're cuter than your brother, Petty Officer Third Class Tony Johnson."

Tony winked at her. "Yes, ma'am, I know." He leapt onto the deck of the patrol boat, whiskey bottle in hand.

"Commanding that boat full of misfits is like trying to herd cats," Rutherford said, "but I sure am thankful for that herd."

"Not as thankful as we are," Skipper and I said.

I scanned the water and didn't see a speck of land or another boat in any direction. "Where are we, Lieutenant?"

Rutherford glared at me as if I'd ask him the meaning of life.

Skipper cleared up the confusion. "We've been downstairs tied up for a while, so we're a little disoriented."

"Oh, that makes sense. We're twenty-five miles east of Matanzas Inlet at Red Snapper Sink. Have you heard of it?"

"I've heard of Matanzas Inlet, but not Red Snapper Sink."

"It's a hole in the ocean that's charted at seventy-three fathoms, but nobody knows for sure how deep it really is."

"How deep is seventy-three fathoms?" Skipper asked.

I tried multiplying six feet times seventy-three in my head, but Rutherford beat me to it.

"It's four hundred thirty-eight feet, but like I said, nobody knows for sure how deep it really is. I've thought about sending Tony down in there to see if he can find the bottom." Rutherford yelled toward the patrol boat. "What do you think of that idea, Tony?"

Tony popped his head up. "What's that, Skipper?"

Rutherford and Skipper yelled back, "Nothing, Tony!"

"So, my guess is those two planned to get what they wanted from you, have their pickup boat rendezvous with them, and send you and your boat to the bottom of Red Snapper Sink. There's no telling how many boats are at the bottom of that hole."

I considered what he'd said. "I guess that was a pretty good plan 'til you showed up."

"Yeah," he said. "We tend to mess up good plans like that from time to time."

I walked to the helm and started both engines. Like always, I watched for oil pressure and raw water flow. "If you don't mind," I said, "I'd like to make sure my starboard sail drive is still working before you guys take off."

"Sure. We'll stay as long as you need us. We'll even follow you back ashore if you want."

I put the right transmission in gear and we started a gentle turn to the left without the port side transmission engaged. I then pulled the starboard transmission into reverse and gave it a little throttle. It shifted smoothly and turned the boat to starboard.

"I think we're going to be fine, Lieutenant. We'll sail back to St. Augustine and get Skipper's jaw checked out."

"Are you sure there's nothing else we can do for you?" he asked.

"Oh, I almost forgot. There's a gun in the bilge of my tender." I pointed to the dinghy hanging from the stern davits. "I knocked it from Michael's hand with my emergency tiller, and it landed in the dinghy. I guess we should've sent that with the FBI guys."

Rutherford walked to the stern of the boat and peered into the dinghy, the gun clearly visible. "Hmm, you must be mistaken. I don't see any gun."

I nodded knowingly. "Oh, well, I could have sworn it was in there. There is one more thing I'd love Tony to take care of while you're here."

"Name it," he said.

"There's a satellite tracker on the underside of my hull, behind the trampoline. Do you think we could twist his arm and get him back in the water to pry that thing off?"

Rutherford turned to give the order and we saw Tony diving off the stern of the patrol boat with a pouch of tools in his hand. The three of us walked to the bow and peered through the trampoline. Tony kicked up and out of the water until he could grab the back edge of the trampoline with one hand and work at prying the tracker off with the other. He worked at the task for several minutes before finally pulling it free and slipping it through the gap and onto the trampoline.

"Thanks, Tony," Skipper said.

He winked again while still hanging by one hand beneath the trampoline. "You're welcome, ma'am. Did I hear the lieutenant say you were headed back to St. Augustine?"

In spite of the pain she must have felt in her jaw, she grinned. "Yeah, we're going back to St. Augustine. Why?"

"Well," he said, "seeing as how you've had a rough day and all, I figure you'll need a day or two to rest before I take you out dancing."

27

It's Classified

Rutherford powered away, but he didn't head back for St. Augustine as I'd expected. Instead, he brought the big boat up on plane and headed east, into the deep of the North Atlantic.

"Rutherford left you a little gift in the dinghy," I said to Skipper. "Why don't you stow it away somewhere safe on your side of the boat?"

Skipper approached the lifeboat and looked inside. The nine-millimeter pistol I'd knocked from Michael's hand was lying in the bottom of the small boat on a coil of line. She reached in, took hold of the pistol, and smiled.

"Didn't you say you wanted one on your side of the boat when all this was over?" I asked.

She scoffed. "If you'd have thought about this a day earlier, we wouldn't have had such a terrible day."

"Yeah," I said, "but you also wouldn't have met Tony."

She bumped hips with me then carried her new pistol down to her cabin.

I turned the boat into the wind and set the sails. In less than five minutes, we were headed back for St. Augustine Inlet to find Skipper a doctor.

When I shut the engines down, I heard a thundering sound coming from dead ahead, so I stepped from beneath the hardtop and scanned the horizon. I saw an orange and white Coast Guard helicopter coming straight at us at top speed. It flew directly over us, seemingly only a few feet above our mast.

"What was that?" Skipper asked.

"It was a Coast Guard helicopter going somewhere, fast. It was probably backup for the crew who rescued us. They must be running a little behind."

I was pleased to see Skipper holding two paper plates with sandwiches and chips. With all of the day's excitement, I hadn't realized how hungry I was.

"Thank you," I said. "I'm famished."

"What would you like to drink?"

"Do you know how to make lemonade?"

She chuckled. "Yes, of course I do. Everyone knows how to make lemonade."

The last time I had lemonade was the day Anya vanished from the boat near Virgin Gorda. I wondered how long I'd be tying simple things like lemonade to my memory of Anya.

"I should've offered the Coast Guard guys something to eat," said Skipper, showing her genetic Southern hospitality.

There's a phenomenon that occurs in people who've endured extreme prolonged stress. It manifests itself in one of three ways. Many times, the victims find themselves physically and mentally exhausted, incapable of staying awake, and will often sleep for twelve or more hours. In about equal numbers, some victims will suffer an extreme psychological breakdown and cry uncontrollably for hours. The third manifestation of this phenomenon is what happened to me. I found Skipper's declaration that she should've fed the Coast Guardsmen to be hilarious, and I burst into raucous laughter. I laughed for ten minutes as Skipper stared at me, most likely questioning my sanity.

"What is so funny?" she asked a dozen times before I could get myself under control.

I regained my composure. "It's been a pretty crappy day. Are you sure you're all right, Skipper?"

"I'm fine," she said, "but I'm worried about you. I've never seen you laugh like that. Are you sure you're all right?"

"Yes, I'm sure. It's just the way the brain deals with stress."

"Maybe your brain deals with it that way, but mine never has. Don't ever do that again, okay? It freaked me out."

"We were attacked, knocked out, tied up, tortured, beaten up, and almost killed, but me laughing is what freaked you out? Maybe *I'm* not the one you should be worried about."

She wadded up her paper towel and threw it at me. I flattened my hand into a paddle and swatted at the paper ball, knocking it back over her head and into the wind where it hovered for an instant before flying back toward me like a boomerang.

"See? Even Mother Nature's throwing things at you."

"Yeah," I said, "and both of you throw like a girl."

* * *

An alarm sounded from the chart plotter.

"What's that?" Skipper asked.

I walked to the helm and saw the conflict alert on the screen. Our radar had picked up a boat approaching from astern at nearly fifty knots. I grabbed the binoculars from their nest and spun to identify our unexpected visitor.

"What's happening, Chase?" she demanded.

"I'm not sure." I scanned the eastern horizon for the oncoming aggressor. "That alarm was the conflict alert. It predicts when another boat might get too close to us. It's telling me there's a boat approaching from behind that could collide with us if he doesn't turn."

"Well, do something! Don't just stand there. Shouldn't you be turning to get out of his way?"

"No," I said, "that's not how it works. We're required to maintain our course and speed, and the captain of the boat that's overtaking us is required to change course. It's regulation."

She stood and joined me in the search for the oncoming boat. "Who cares about the regulations if he's going to hit us? Shouldn't we be turning?"

"We'll change course or speed if a collision appears imminent. Right now, whoever they are, they're still five miles away. It'll take them over six minutes to catch us, so we still have plenty of time. I just don't like anyone sneaking up on me."

"It doesn't sound to me like they're sneaking."

I ignored the comment and kept scanning. I rechecked the radar and found the boat had closed the gap to less than four miles and made no course change.

I handed the binoculars to Skipper. "Keep looking out there. You should see them any minute."

"Where are you going?" she asked as I sprinted to my cabin.

I pulled my pistol from a small compartment near the head of my bed and pulled back the slide enough to see a round chambered. I returned back to the deck where Skipper was frozen in place and focused on a single point on the horizon.

"Do you see anything?" I asked.

"Yeah, but I can't tell what it is. How far are we from land?"

I checked the chart plotter again. The boat was less than two miles behind us.

"We're still over two hours from shore, and we can't outrun a sea turtle, let alone a boat that can do fifty knots," I said.

She handed me the binoculars, and I followed what had been her line of sight until I saw the white bow wave of a good-sized boat coming at us like a rocket.

"Go below and get your pistol. Get back out here as fast as you can."

I'd expected her to question my instructions, but she didn't.

She left and returned, pistol in hand. "Tell me what to do, Chase."

I could tell she was scared.

"We're not going to do anything until we know for sure that boat's coming for us. It could be some joyriders coming back from The Bahamas. There's no way to know. We're going to be patient and wait. If we have to defend ourselves and the boat, I want you to shoot for center mass on one man at a time. Don't just point and shoot. Make every shot count."

"I'm better with a real gun than with that speargun."

The billowing white bow wave in front of the boat had become visible with the unaided eye. I watched again through the binoculars and then exhaled a long sigh of relief. "It's Lieutenant Rutherford on the patrol boat."

Skipper let her head fall backward. "Oh my God! Is it always going to be like this? Are we going to grab guns and binoculars every time a boat gets near us?"

Her question was valid, but she wasn't saying what she really meant.

Rutherford pulled abeam our boat and blew his horn, slowing to match our speed. The patrol boat's loud speaker crackled and Rutherford's voice boomed over the speaker, "Heave to. We're coming alongside."

"What's that mean? What's going on?" Skipper asked.

"*Heaving to* means stopping the boat without bringing the sails down. We'll turn the boat until the sails work against each other to stop the boat. That's what he wants us to do."

We performed the maneuver and brought the big catamaran to a stop. Seconds later, the patrol boat came alongside our rail, and her engines fell to idle.

Rutherford leaned over the rail. "Did you see the helicopter?"

"We did," I said.

"That was the HITRON bird out of Cecil Field. We intercepted the rendezvous boat that was going to pick up your unwanted guests after they'd sent you to the bottom of Red Snapper Sink," he said.

"What's a HITRON bird?" asked Skipper.

Rutherford said, "It stands for Helicopter Interdiction Squadron. It's the helicopter equivalent of my patrol boat. They're heavily armed and fast. We have snipers onboard the choppers who can take out an engine on a go-fast drug-running boat at a hundred miles an hour. Whoever those guys were, they were well organized and put up a pretty good fight when we showed up." Rutherford scraped his boot along the top of the gunwale. "Are you going to tell me what this is all about? Tony's father, Dominic, called us this morning and asked us to keep an eye out for you. All he could tell us was that you were supposed to be in St. Augustine the night before and you hadn't checked in. He wouldn't tell us much more, but we know what kind of work Dominic does, so I suppose you're in the same business. We knew there had to be more to the story, but it wouldn't have done any good to ask any more questions. Dominic wouldn't have told us a thing."

"I wish I could tell you more," I said, "but it's classified. I'm sure they'll send somebody down from some high place to debrief me on every detail of what happened. When that happens, I could ask them to read you in if you have sufficient clearance, but I'm just a small fish in a big pond. I don't make policy decisions. I just do what I'm told . . . most of the time."

He handed me his card. "I have a clearance, but probably not a need-to-know, so I doubt they'll read me in. But I'd appreciate you asking when they show up. It's nice to understand what's going on sometimes, but not always."

I took his card and promised to make the request.

He pointed to Skipper. "How about putting that gun away when any other law enforcement boats want to stop you for a chat?"

She didn't miss a beat. "We didn't know you were a law enforcement boat when you came sneaking up on us. We were getting ready to repel boarders if you guys had been pirates."

"You'll want to hang on to that one, Chase. She's a firecracker."

"What did you do with the people aboard the rendezvous boat?" I asked. "Are they in custody?"

"Like I said, they put up a pretty good fight when we got there to intercept them. Between our fifty cal on the bow and the HITRON bird, there wasn't much left to take into custody when the smoke cleared."

"That's too bad," I said. "It would've been nice to interrogate them."

He shrugged. "They didn't give us much choice. When somebody shoots at us, we shoot back—but with bigger bullets. It's what we do. You two be careful getting back into St. Augustine. If you need anything, give us a call. We're always listening."

The patrol boat turned and roared away back toward St. Augustine, and we brought our boat out of the heave-to condition and got her sailing again.

Skipper wasted no time. "Okay, I don't care about clearances or what's classified or whatever. It's time for you to tell me the truth about what's going on. Let's have it, Chase. Start talking."

She wasn't going to let me get away with hiding behind the classified fence. I had to come clean. I set the autopilot and settled in for a long talk.

28
Earl from the End

"This isn't easy to explain," I began, "and it is classified. I'm not allowed to tell you any of this, but you deserve the truth after what you've been through today. What I told you before wasn't a lie, it just wasn't the whole truth. I do work for the government, but not directly. I'm a type of independent contractor. They call on me to do things they can't use conventional government employees to do. I'm trained to sneak in and out of places undetected and to do nasty things while I'm there."

"What kinds of things?"

"Sometimes it's as simple as taking pictures or gathering information, but other times, it can get a little sticky," I said.

She put her hands on her hips. "Come on, Chase. I'm not a little kid anymore. What kind of sticky things?"

"Sometimes it becomes necessary for me to kill someone. I didn't like it when I did it in the past, and I'm not looking forward to doing it next time, but it's part of my job, and I do it because I believe in democracy and keeping the world as free as possible. Sometimes people like me have to do some bad things to protect the good guys—people like you and your family."

She sat silently.

I needed to gauge her reaction and tolerance for additional information, so I said, "There's more . . . a lot more. Do you want to hear it?"

With confidence, she said, "Yes."

"The Russian intelligence service is called the *Sluzhba Vneshney Razvedki*, or SVR for short. It's a lot like the American CIA. You've probably heard of the KGB."

"Yeah, I've heard of that."

"The SVR is essentially the old KGB with a new name. Anyway, Anya was an SVR officer. They sent her to find me and interrogate me after I'd done a job down in Cuba last year. To make a long story short, she found me, but instead of interrogating me, we fell in love, or at least I thought that's what happened. As it turned out, I was very wrong about that. It appears she was acting the whole time to get inside our service and report back to the Russians on everything I was doing."

Without a word, Skipper stood and walked into the main salon, leaving me alone on the deck. She returned with a tray containing two cups filled with ice, a bottle of rum, and a pitcher of lemonade. She poured two shots of rum topped with the lemonade.

"This is all getting a little tough to believe," she said. "It sounds like a movie . . . not real life."

"I wish it were a movie, but, unfortunately, it's my real life, and now it's part of your life, too. I've dragged you into my world, and I'm eternally sorry for doing that."

"You didn't drag me anywhere," she said. "I wanted to come. In fact, I don't think I gave you a choice in the matter. Who knew this was going to happen?"

"I'm still sorry for putting you in the middle of this mess."

"Chase," she said, "it's not your fault. Now keep talking. I want to know how Michael and Sara fit into all of this."

I took a sip of the concoction she poured. "I don't really know what was going on with the Andersons, but I'm sure that isn't their real name. I do have a theory, though. Over the years, especially during the Cold War, the Russians placed individuals and couples in the United States as deep cover assets. These people blended in perfectly with American society. They had normal jobs and children and seemed like run-of-the-mill Americans, but they were actually spies for the KGB originally, and later, the SVR. The CIA called these people i*llegals*. They were very hard to sniff out and rarely got caught. In fact, we have no idea how many illegals the Soviets placed in the States during the Cold War. We believe the practice of placing them has died down, but we can't know for sure. I believe Michael and Sara were a team of illegals who were sent to find out what happened to Anya when she didn't check in with Moscow on time."

I took another drink, hoping Skipper would have a question or two. I needed any excuse to distract me from what I had to say next.

"So, it hurts to admit it, but here's what I believe. I believe Anya was playing me all along and planned to keep on playing me as long as I'd let her. She said she wanted to get married and maybe even have kids one day. Can you imagine that? Can you imagine living like that?"

"Maybe you're wrong. Maybe she really did love you, and maybe she did want to marry you and have your babies. Maybe that was her way out of Russia."

"If that was true, then why would she have been reporting back to Tornovich?"

"Who's Tornovich?"

"I'm sorry. I forget you don't know all of this. Tornovich is a Russian SVR colonel who Anya worked for. According to what Michael and Sara said, Anya hadn't reported in to Tornovich for several days. That would mean she'd been reporting in prior to getting shot in Miami. If she was truly in love with me, and if she was really going to defect, she wouldn't be reporting." The longer I talked, the more my anger festered. The thought of being used and played like that was more than I could stand. I had to stop. I had to catch my breath and calm down.

"Chase, are you all right? Your face is bright red."

"I'm fine. It just infuriates me to believe Anya could've been that deceptive and manipulative, but worse than that, I can't believe I fell for it."

Skipper slid toward me on the settee and put her arms around me. I was in no mood for affection, but I wasn't going to push her away again. I'd done enough of that already, so I wrapped my arms around her and held her as my breathing and heart rate returned to normal.

"You don't have to tell me anymore, Chase. I get the picture. I don't like seeing you so upset."

I touched her face and she flinched in pain. The wound was swelling and turning red.

"Let's get you to a hospital and have a doctor look at your face."

She looked down at my swollen and bruised knee. "I'll only go to the doctor if you go, too. Your knee looks bad, and your nose looks even worse."

"It's a deal."

* * *

We reached the St. Augustine Inlet. Skipper wanted to handle the boat, and because I enjoyed seeing her fall in love with it, I surrendered the boat to her.

"Are we going to the same anchorage beside the Bridge of Lions?"

"No," I said, "let's go to the city marina below the bridge. We can plug into shore power there and have a mechanic come take a look at our starboard sail drive to make sure the fishing net didn't do any real damage."

"How will we get under that bridge? It's not even twenty feet high."

"I'll show you," I told her.

We were about a quarter mile north of the bridge when I picked up the VHF handset, switched to channel nine, and pushed the button.

"Bridge of Lions, this is the sailing vessel *Aegis II* requesting you open the bridge for southbound traffic."

"Open the bridge?" Skipper said in disbelief.

The bridge tender answered my call. "Sailing vessel *Aegis II*, we'll have it open for you shortly."

Skipper watched as the center of the ornate Bridge of Lions began to tilt upward.

She gasped. "It's a drawbridge. That's so cool!"

"Yes," I said. "It's very cool."

After we'd made it past the bridge, I called the city marina on the VHF and asked if they had a slip available for a week. Skipper maneuvered the boat into our designated slip number as if she'd been doing it her whole life, and I had us tied up in no time.

Marinas are interesting places full of fascinating and bizarre people. The St. Augustine City Marina was no exception. Within thirty minutes of arriving, a dozen people stopped by our boat to welcome us and get a look at the new catamaran in town. We weren't the biggest boat in the marina, but we were a sailboat. A fifty-foot catamaran gets a lot of attention almost anywhere. Several people offered us a cocktail and invited us to come visit with them on their boats. The community mentality of a marina is unlike that of any other group of people.

Many of the older ladies who stopped by for a visit commented on what a cute couple Skipper and I made. We didn't bother correcting them. They were going to believe whatever they wanted no matter what we said. All of the younger guys who came by, as well as many of the older ones, gazed a little too long at Skipper to suit me. It wasn't jealousy. I felt responsible for her and didn't want to see her become an object to anyone—especially not a boat bum like me. Besides, Petty Officer Third Class Tony might not be as forgiving as some if he caught those guys ogling the current object of his affection.

With so many cruisers and live-aboard owners in the marina, I took advantage of the opportunity to ask for the name of a good mechanic and fiberglass repair specialist. Everyone I asked said, "Earl at the end is the best around." With a bevy of recommendations like that, how could I go to anyone other than Earl at the end?

"I'm going to meet Earl. Do you want to come?"

Skipper wrinkled her nose. "No, I think I'll just hang out here."

Protective big brother mode kicked in. "Okay, but don't wander off."

She stuck out her tongue. "Oh, I won't. Besides, Earl from the end might be super cute, so maybe I want to be here when you bring him back."

I strolled down the dock, admiring the boats and greeting the owners as I went. When I made it to the end of the dock, I saw a thirty-something-year-old guy in cutoff shorts and a John Deere hat sitting on a Mainship 34, his feet on the rail and a Corona dangling from his fingertips.

"Are you Earl?" I asked.

The man squinted into the sun. "Nah."

I waited a beat. "Do you know where I can find Earl?"

He poured the last few inches of his Corona down his throat. "What do you want with Earl?"

I wasn't sure I had any reason to tell him why I needed a mechanic, but I was intrigued, so I played with him a little. "I've got this tooth way back here," I said, pulling the corner of my mouth back and pointing to my molar. "It's been giving me a fit and the folks down the dock said Earl could fix anything. So, here I am."

He pointed his empty beer bottle at me. "You know something, man . . . you're funny." He tossed his empty into a bucket on the deck and yelled, "Hey, momma! There's some guy up here to see you. He says he's got a bad tooth and needs you to pull it."

Mother? Skipper's going to be sorely disappointed.

The man pulled two more Coronas from the cooler, opened both of them, and handed one to me. "Here," he said, "this'll have to do for anesthetic."

I raised my bottle, offering a toast, and took a long swallow. An older woman with spiked gray hair and reading glasses perched on her nose came through the sliding door of the boat and onto the stern deck.

She stuck out a greasy hand. "Hey, I'm Earline, but everybody calls me Earl. Come on aboard, and I'll take a look at that tooth of yours."

I stammered, "Uh, it's not really a problem with my tooth. I need someone to look at my sail drive."

She slapped her son on the shoulder and cackled like a drunken mother hen. "I'm just messin' with you. I ain't no dentist, but I'd probably make a good one. Don't you think?"

"Yes," I said, "I think you'd make a fine dentist."

"What's wrong with your sail drive?" she asked as she opened a beer of her own.

"Nothing, I hope, but I picked up a chunk of fishing net about thirty miles offshore this morning, and I just want to have somebody look at it to make sure I didn't do any real damage."

She stared down the dock. "You're in the cat?"

"Yes, ma'am," I said. "We just pulled in a few minutes ago and several people told me you're the best mechanic around."

She scratched her face with her filthy hand. "Yeah, they're right about that."

I waited several uncomfortable seconds for her to say something else, but she sat down and started drinking her beer.

"So, when do you think you might have time to take a look it?" I asked.

"I ain't cheap."

The conversation was getting weirder by the minute.

"That's okay. I don't mind paying for a good mechanic."

"It's twelve bucks plus four beers an hour unless it goes over three hours, and then it's just ten bucks an hour 'cause after twelve beers, I ain't near as good a mechanic as I was three hours ago when I's sober."

I couldn't tell if she was serious. I said, "I'll make it twenty bucks and a six-pack an hour, but no money or beer until you're finished."

"Finished with what?"

I yanked the corner of my mouth back again. "Pulling this tooth. What else?"

She grabbed a toolbox and followed me back to the boat. When we arrived at the cat, I laughed to myself when I saw Skipper had changed clothes and brushed her hair. I had a suspicion Earl wasn't her type.

"Skipper," I said, "this is Earl. She's going to take a look at our sail drive."

"Hey, Skipper," said the spikey-haired woman. "I bet you thought you were gonna be the prettiest thing ever on this boat . . . 'til I showed up. Sorry to bust your bubble, beauty queen."

Skipper stared at me, and all I could do was shrug.

Earl asked, "So which motor is it, the front or back?"

I liked Earl. She went into the boat, and I heard her whistling a song I'd never heard.

"What the hell was that?" Skipper asked.

"That's Earl at the end," I said, as if that answered anything.

After just over an hour of working in the engine rooms, Earl appeared on deck. "Have you got a plastic baggie?"

"I'll check," Skipper said.

She came back with a one-gallon bag and handed it to Earl, who turned on a small flashlight and dropped it into the bag. She wrapped the top edge of the baggie around her wrinkled mouth. Like she'd been smoking for decades, she struggled to inhale all the air from the bag before she sealed it shut. She pulled off her shoes, pants, and shirt, and stood there in her bra and panties—all sixty years and two hundred pounds of her. She pointed her finger at me. "Don't you be getting no ideas. You could never handle this much woman with that bad tooth of yours."

Skipper's entire body quivered as she tried to suppress her inevitable laugher. I couldn't wait to see what Earl was going to do for her next trick. Whatever it was, it would've been a bargain at twice the price.

She picked up her bagged flashlight and walked right off the back of my boat and into the water. Skipper couldn't hold in her laughter.

I stood there in awe, shaking my head. "It's Earl from the end."

Earl emerged from the water with a spiny lobster in one hand and her flashlight in the other. She laid both on the table. "That'll be thirty bucks and eight beers. I went over an hour, but not much, and you said twenty bucks and a six-pack an hour."

I retrieved a fifty-dollar bill and two six-packs from the boat and handed them to her. She tucked the fifty into her soaking wet bra and scooped up her belongings. "I ain't got no change, and your motors and sail drives are fine."

Without drying off or getting dressed, she strolled back toward her boat, leaving a trail of greasy saltwater in her wake.

About fifty feet from our boat, she turned back and yelled, "Thanks, hon! You were great! I ain't had me a man that good in thirty years." She blew me a kiss and walked away.

"Is she for real?" Skipper said.

I held my chin up high. "She ain't had her a man this good in thirty years."

29
The Pain

The following morning, we found a maxillofacial surgeon who could work Skipper in. Her jaw wasn't as swollen as we thought, but her pain was pretty bad. When the nurse finally called for her, Skipper insisted I go with her. I reluctantly agreed.

They took some X-rays and checked her vitals, and then placed us in a small exam room. The doctor introduced himself as Doctor Lane and washed his hands at the small sink in the corner of the room. Wasting no time, he got right into it. He had Skipper open her mouth as wide as she could and then wiggle her jaw left and right. That made Skipper yell out in pain. The surgeon grunted and kept prodding and squeezing her face. Without saying a word, he stuck an X-ray film onto the wall-mounted light box and studied it.

He grunted. "How'd this happen?"

Skipper blurted out, "Two maniac Russians snuck on our boat, knocked us out, and tied us up, but we got free. Then, I tried to shoot one of them with a speargun, but I missed, and he took the gun from me and hit me in the face with it."

I had hoped she'd lie about how she received her injury, but seeing the look on the doctor's face made the truth a lot more fun.

He looked at me quizzically.

"Hey, I didn't see it," I said. "I was busy trying to knock the other Russian off the boat."

"Yeah, that's right. He was!" Skipper said.

The doctor grumbled something under his breath. "I see. Well, your jaw bone isn't broken. It's just deeply bruised, and your teeth seem to be fine. But there is the matter of assault. I'm required to notify the police of these sorts of things. I'm sure you understand. Are you sure you want to tell the police the same story you just told me?"

"The police know all about it," Skipper said. "The Coast Guard and the FBI arrested the Russians and took them away right after it happened. Oh, and Chase broke the woman's arm. So, yeah, I'm sticking with my story. It's the truth."

"The FBI? I've heard a lot of tales over the years, but this one takes the cake. I'm going to prescribe an anti-inflammatory and some pain medication. Don't take them with alcohol or other drugs, and don't do anything to aggravate the injury. The bruising will last a week or so, and the swelling should be gone in a couple of days."

"Hey, doc," I said, "where's the best local place to eat?"

He squinted at me. "Let me take a look at that nose. Did the Russians do that, too?"

He shined his light up my nose, and I flinched as he probed around.

"Well, that'll heal too, but it's going to hurt for a while. Keep some ointment on it, and try to keep your hands off of it for a few days." He pocketed his light. "Oh, and Cap's on the Water is everyone's favorite local restaurant."

* * *

We were both pleased to hear that her injury was only a bruise and not a break. I paid for the exam, and we left the building.

"Wait a minute." Skipper grabbed my arm. "You promised to get your knee checked out."

"It's fine," I said. "It barely hurts today."

She yanked me around and led me back into the physician's building. She scanned the information board and found an orthopedic surgeon on the fourth floor. She pushed the elevator button and waited for the doors to open. When they finally did, she walked into the elevator and stuck her palm in the center of my chest, stopping me from following her. "If it's not hurting, then you can take the stairs. I'll meet you on the fourth floor."

"Point taken," I said.

The lady at the window said there had been a cancelation and she could take me back right away. Just like they'd done for Skipper, the X-ray technician took several shots of my knee. The orthopedic surgeon took my breath away. She was tall, blonde, and stunning . . . just like Anya. I expected an Eastern European accent, but when she spoke, it was obvious she was all-American.

"I'm Katherine Everett," she said.

"Chase Fulton." I stood to shake her hand.

"Sit!" she ordered. "You're hurt."

I obediently followed her order.

"And you must be Mrs. Fulton."

Skipper pointed to her bruised and swollen jaw. "Do you think I'd marry a man who'd do this to me?"

The doctor glared at me with disdain and jammed the X-rays into the clip of the light box.

"I'm just kidding," said Skipper. "He didn't do this to me, and he's not my husband . . . yet."

The doctor chuckled. "I think I like you, future Mrs. Fulton. Now let's take a look at that knee of yours, alleged fiancée beater."

She studied the X-rays for several minutes then began to poke and prod at my knee. "How did you hurt it?"

I pointed at Skipper. "She stepped on it."

The doctor gave Skipper a high five. "Good for you, girl. That'll teach him to put his hands on you again. Okay, seriously," she said, "what really happened to this knee?"

"Seriously," I said, "someone stepped on it. But it was someone much bigger than her."

"I see. Well, it's in pretty bad shape. Are you a long-distance runner or hiker or anything like that?"

I laughed. "No, ma'am, but I was a baseball catcher for a decade."

"Ah, that explains it. It isn't broken. It's just sprained. I'm going to give you a neoprene brace to wear for a couple of weeks and some anti-inflammatory medication. Be gentle with it, and take the meds until you run out, even after it stops hurting. Alternate heat and ice several times a day, and stay off of it as much as possible. You"—she shook her reflex hammer at me—"keep your hands off that girl's face, or next time she'll do more than just step on your knee . . . and I'll help her."

"Thank you, doctor, and I promise to be well-behaved from now on."

"I doubt that," she said as she began to leave the room.

"Doctor, wait!" said Skipper. "What's your favorite local place to eat?"

"Cap's on the Water, of course."

We left the physician's building and found a pharmacy where we got our prescriptions filled and picked up a heating pad and a few necessities for the boat.

"So, Cap's on the Water for lunch?"

"I'll hail a cab," she said.

When we pulled into the parking lot at Cap's, I wasn't so sure about our doctors' recommendation. The place looked like a hodge-podge of weathered waterfront buildings shoved together on the banks of the Tolomato River.

The cabbie handed us his card. "You guys picked a great place. Call this number when you're ready, and I'll pick you up."

The old adage about never judging a book by its cover was appropriate for Cap's. Everything we put in our mouths was magnificent, and the waitress was friendly and spot-on with every recommendation. Cap's was everything the good doctors had claimed.

The six-mile cab trip back to the boat took just over twenty minutes. We were looking forward to a leisurely afternoon aboard the boat, nursing our wounds, and doing nothing. What we discovered at my boat would not only shatter our plans for a quiet afternoon, but would also change my life forever.

30
Honey Trap

Near the stern of my boat, and in a collection of secondhand lawn chairs, sat Dr. Richter, Dominic Fontana, Clark Johnson, and two men in suits who I'd never seen. I tried to conceive the odd collection of men, but my imagination wasn't creative enough.

"What's all this about?" I asked as we approached the boat.

Each man wore a somber expression, and they rose in unison. I didn't like the look of that, and I didn't like how it made me feel.

"Take your shoes off before you get on my boat, and thank you for not boarding without asking," I said, trying to sound confident.

Inside, I was trembling with anxiety over what was about to happen. I'd killed several people while on an unauthorized operation to get Skipper out of the hands of the cretins who had made her their personal slave. I didn't know who the suits were, but I believed I was on the verge of paying for my sins.

"Skipper, you might want to go check out the sights," I said. "You probably don't want to be a part of whatever this is."

"She should stay," said one of the suits.

I saw the fear in her eyes. "Everything's going to be fine, Skipper. Just tell the truth. No matter what they ask you, just tell the truth."

We boarded my boat and I offered drinks, though everyone declined. One of the suits took Skipper to the portside hull.

"I'll be going with them," Clark said. "I'll look after her, Chase. It'll all be over in a few minutes, and everything will be just fine."

I studied Dr. "Rocket" Richter, my mentor, and the closest thing I'd ever have to a father after losing my own, but I couldn't find loss or sorrow in his sunken eyes. What I saw was anger. They were the eyes of a man who'd been wronged. Had I been the cause of that anger and betrayal? Was he disappointed with me for what I'd done to find Skipper? Knowing that I'd led his beloved daughter into a gunfight that took her life had to be torturing him.

I embraced him. "Dr. Richter, I'm so sorry. I can't tell you how—"

"It's not what you think, son. It's worse. Just follow the advice you gave the girl. Let's go inside and talk."

I was introduced to Agent Garret Knox of the CIA. He was the remaining suit. I assumed the other man with Skipper and Clark was also CIA, but I didn't ask.

Agent Knox questioned me about every detail of my relationship with Anya. I'd take the advice I gave Skipper and I'd tell the truth, but I didn't believe everything would be fine that day—or ever again.

When I'd truthfully answered every question he'd asked, I felt as if I'd been dragged through the desert by my heels.

"Excuse me for a moment," I said. "I need some water. Can I get anyone else anything?"

No one spoke.

I pulled two bottles of water from the icebox and started down the stairs into Skipper's side of the boat.

"You can't go down there!" Agent Knox called out.

I ignored him and continued through the door into Skipper's cabin. She was sitting on the bed with tearstains on her face.

The other agent stood up. "You can't come in here!"

I pushed him aside and handed the bottle of water to Skipper. "Are you okay?"

The agent grabbed my arm and repeated, "You can't be in here. I'm conducting a—"

I hooked my right heel behind his left knee and shoved him backward onto the settee. "You listen to me," I said. "This is my boat, and I go where I want, when I want, aboard my boat. Neither you nor anyone else will give orders on my boat. You will treat this lady with respect, and you will use some manners, or you and your cheap suit will find yourselves overboard. Is that understood?"

His nostrils flared as he pushed himself back to a standing position and clenched his fists, but I wasn't afraid of him or anyone else.

I drove my finger into his chest. "Respect! Do you understand?"

* * *

I walked back to the main salon.

"She wasn't my daughter, Chase." Dr. Richter's words were molten lava crashing into me.

"What are you talking about?"

"We ran the DNA. She's not my daughter. She's also not Katerina Burinkova's daughter."

What he said sent my mind into a spiraling plummet toward disbelief and heartbreak. No matter how hard I tried, I couldn't meld his words into my reality.

I stammered, "But the pictures . . . and letters . . . her eyes."

"She was the best infiltration agent we've ever seen," said Agent Knox. "It's almost impossible to explain, and we don't have all of the answers yet, but here's what we know so far."

I held up my hand. "Just give me a minute, here. I need a few seconds to get my head straight."

I pulled four tumblers and a bottle of eighteen-year-old Laphroaig from the locker. I poured three fingers into each glass and set them on the table. Mine disappeared in one swallow and I poured another. There was no reason to recork the bottle—both it and I were going to be empty vessels by the time we finished the coming conversation.

Agent Knox ignored the scotch and started talking. "Do you know what illegals are, Chase?"

I nodded slowly. "Yeah, they're Russians living in the States as Americans, blending in with society, and are almost impossible to detect."

"That's right," Knox said. "That's exactly what Sara and Michael Anderson were. Thanks to you, once we had them in custody, they cut a deal to save their lives. With the results of their interrogation and a number of other sources, we were able to determine what happened. The woman you knew as Anastasia Burinkova was an SVR captain who would have made colonel if she had succeeded in her mission. We believe her real name was Ekaterina Norikova, but we're still not certain. What we do know is that she worked for Colonel Victor Tornovich, who, until he lost his best officer, was in line to receive his first general's star and probably a director's position in the Kremlin. Captain Norikova, or Anya, was dispatched by Tornovich to find you, seduce you, and convince you to take her to America. How the Russians knew who and what you were was a mystery to us until we discovered that Jarrod Thompson, the man you knew as Dutch, was a mole who'd been selling intelligence to the Russians for nearly a decade . . . right under our noses."

I held up one finger, trying not to erupt. I drew in what I had intended to be a calming breath. "So, you're telling me that Anya, or Captain Norikova, was . . ." My mind played countless scenes forward and backward, freeze-frame, and in slow motion. I'd lost my train of thought. "But she killed Dmitri Barkov because he killed her mother."

The three men shook their heads no.

"What? Damn it! Talk to me!"

"She killed Barkov because Victor Tornovich ordered her to kill him. Barkov had become a thorn in the side of the regime in Moscow, so he had to be killed. How better to do that than as a dramatic punctuation to an undercover infiltration? Tornovich is a tactical genius. He's known Richter for decades. They were spooks on opposite sides of the Iron Curtain during the Cold War. He knew about Richter's history with Katerina Burinkova and with Barkov."

I stopped him with a wave of my hand. "Hang on just a minute. I'm going to need another drink. I'm afraid I'm having a little trouble keeping up."

Agent Knox ignored my need for a break. "They hatched a diabolical but brilliant plan to weave an intricate web of lies filled with just enough forty-year-old truth to make everyone involved lap it up like a thirsty dog. They knew Richter would believe anything if he could be convinced Norikova was his daughter. And Chase, they knew you well enough to know that getting Anya close to Richter would only solidify your relationship with her."

Dr. Richter drained his tumbler and poured himself another. I sat in silence, rage boiling in my chest.

Knox continued, "You're not the first, nor will you be the last American operative to fall into a Russian honey trap. There's no one on Earth better at that than the Russians."

"But we were in love," I growled through clenched teeth.

"No, Chase," said Knox. "*You* were in love. She was acting, simply doing her job . . . the job Tornovich trained and ordered her to do. Nothing more. As terrible as it is to hear, it's the God's honest truth."

I threw my tumbler of scotch across the salon and watched it explode against the navigation station. I picked up the bottle by its neck and Dr. Richter placed his hand over mine, easing the bottle back onto the table.

"Chase, you're not the only one," said Dr. Richter. "Under Tornovich's orders, she deceived Dutch, Clark, Dmitri Barkov, and me. Tornovich's planning and Norikova's execution were flawless. She played each of us to perfection."

"That's where you're wrong, Coach!" My newborn hatred for Victor Tornovich exploded into indescribable fury, and I could barely breathe. I stormed from the main salon and onto the aft deck, sweat and scotch dripping from my face, looking for something to destroy, something to shred into oblivion with my own hands. My rage exploded in uncontrollable waves. The salon door closed behind me, and I felt a hand on my shoulder. I turned around, ready to rip the throat out of whoever dared touch me. I froze when I saw Dr. Richter standing there.

"Chase, Tornovich did this to all of us, but especially to you and me. With Anya—or Norikova—dead, and Michael and Sara in custody, Tornovich's infiltration scheme has come to a screeching halt. There's nothing more we can do." His face sagged and he hung his head.

Seeing Dr. Richter surrender hurt me almost as badly as Anya's betrayal and Tornovich's treachery.

"Yeah, I know that bastard Tornovich fooled all of us, but here's the difference between me and everyone else she fooled."

I gripped the shoulders of the man who loved me like a son, and who I respected more than anyone. A sudden, searing plan thundered within me, and I looked through Dr. Richter's haunted eyes and into the depths of his soul.

"I'm going to make him regret ever drawing a breath on this Earth. I'll find him. I'll pull him out of the Kremlin and put him on his knees. And I'll laugh while he begs for his life at my feet . . . right before I tear him into pieces that not even God could recognize."

About the Author

Cap Daniels

Cap Daniels is a former sailing charter captain, scuba and sailing instructor, pilot, Air Force combat veteran, and civil servant of the U.S. Department of Defense. Raised far from the ocean in rural East Tennessee, his early infatuation with salt water was sparked by the fascinating, and sometimes true, sea stories told by his father, a retired Navy Chief Petty Officer. Those stories of adventure on the high seas sent Cap in search of adventure of his own, which eventually landed him on Florida's Gulf Coast where he spends as much time as possible on, in, and under the waters of the Emerald Coast.

With a headful of larger-than-life characters and their thrilling exploits, Cap pours his love of adventure and passion for the ocean onto the pages of The Chase Fulton Novels series.

Visit www.CapDaniels.com to join the mailing list to receive newsletter and release updates.

Connect with Cap Daniels

Facebook: www.Facebook.com/WriterCapDaniels
Instagram: https://www.instagram.com/authorcapdaniels/
BookBub: https://www.bookbub.com/profile/cap-daniels

Made in the USA
Coppell, TX
13 February 2024

28977683R00150